DEAD OF
Winter Break

KELLY BRAKENHOFF

Dead of Winter Break

A Cassandra Sato Mystery

Copyright 2020 by Kelly Brakenhoff

All rights reserved. This book or any portion thereof may not be reproduced or used in any manner whatsoever without the express written permission of the publisher, except for the use of brief quotations in an article or book review.

This is a work of fiction. Any references to historical events, real people, or real places are used fictitiously. Other names, characters, places, and events are the products of the author's imagination or used in a fictitious manner, and any resemblance to actual persons, living or dead, or actual events and locales is entirely coincidental.

Cover Design and Artwork by Melissa Williams Design
University building © MSSA, Shutterstock; Dog © a7880ss, Adobe Stock; Trees © Ardea-studio

Interior Formatting by Melissa Williams Design

Author Photo by Susan Noel

Editing by Steve Parolini

Published by Emerald Prairie Press

kellybrakenhoff.com

DEAD OF
Winter Break

KELLY BRAKENHOFF

Emerald Prairie
PRESS

OTHER BOOKS BY KELLY BRAKENHOFF

Cassandra Sato Mysteries
Dead End (Short Story)
Death by Dissertation
Dead Week

Duke the Deaf Dog ASL Series
Never Mind
Farts Make Noise

For my Read It or Not book club friends:

Gail Johs, Donna Barnes, Jean Hinton, Chris Timm,
Linda Hohbein, Ronna Meyer, Teresa Hardy, Lisa Sullivan
and Jodi McGill. Cheers to 20 years of reading and wine!

Chapter One

December in Nebraska was best left to poets droning on about the dubious merits of frosty icicles and face-freezing temperatures. Inside the stuffy Performing Arts Center, Cassandra Sato felt sweat rivulets slide down her back under her academic regalia. Easing the light blue velvet sash a few inches away from her throat, she crossed her ankles and inhaled deeply to slow her heartbeat.

Moments earlier, while the Fall Commencement speaker—an economist who had graduated in the 1950s—launched the concluding salvo in his uninspiring remarks, Cassandra had glanced across the stage at Board of Directors Chairman Alan Hershey, Master of Ceremonies and owner of an age-defying head of hair that never fell out of place. Hershey had raised two fingers of his right hand and dipped his chin in a subtle greeting to someone in the audience.

Cassandra had followed his gaze to the parents and guests in the lower level seating that curved behind the Morton College graduates. The center's Gothic interior resembled an old European chapel. Except instead of a central altar, a stage was flanked by two levels of box seats.

Decorative carvings on the pillars and ceiling continued the impression of an old, stately theatre.

She smiled at the families wearing their finest clothes, pride in their new graduates obvious as they snapped photos of every aspect of the auspicious day. She loved commencements. Poignant endings and eager degree candidates brimming with promise for the future made her heart swell.

Cassandra had met a small number of parents in her four-plus months as Vice President for Student Affairs. As her eyes slid down a row about halfway up the section where Hershey had nodded, she hadn't expected to recognize any of the faces.

Which was why her heart had lurched so suddenly.

With narrowed eyes, she confirmed the tall, thin, gray-haired man with the unruly eyebrows was indeed her former boss. Why was Dr. Gary Nielson sitting in the commencement audience instead of floating in a fishing trawler off the Florida coast wearing the goofy hat he'd posed in for the postcard Cassandra had received less than two weeks ago?

She racked her brain for a good reason why Nielson would end his sunny retirement trip so abruptly and return to wintry Carson, Nebraska. The skin on his face was several shades darker than the pale complexions he and his wife had sported in early November upon departing to begin their new life. His unexpected exit had thrown Cassandra's office into a bit of chaos while the administrative departments divided up his duties and the board of directors hired an interim president.

That had not worked out as anyone had hoped. Now they were back to a vacancy, with Chairman Hershey making important decisions while pursuing a suitable replacement.

Just minutes before spotting Nielson, Cassandra had daydreamed of the time when she would become president of a university and it would be her duty—no, her *deepest pleasure*—to impart her own wisdom while standing before a crowd of beaming graduates and well-wishers.

The rest of the ceremony had passed in a distracted rush of excited motion and frustration while Cassandra waited to corner Chairman Hershey. The ending bars of Pomp and Circumstance echoed in the main hall while the stage party and graduates marched out to the lobby.

Unzipping her black outer gown, Cassandra left her floppy velvet tam in place so she wouldn't mess up her hair. "Mr. Hershey, a moment—"

"Dr. Sato!" Hershey was only a few inches taller than her in heeled knee-high boots. "Glad I caught you before the reception. Dr. Nielson has changed his mind and will be reinstated as president for the spring term, giving us ample time to search for a permanent replacement."

Six weeks of retirement under his belt and Nielson had changed his mind. Who does that? Disappointment pinched a nerve in her temple. "Reinstated? He just left in November—"

"You well know the past two months have been controversial," Hershey nodded. "Donors have complained. Parents have encouraged their children to transfer. Dr. Nielson was kind enough to oblige us on short notice."

One student's death, another violently attacked, campus protests, and media controversy had made for an exhausting first semester. All Cassandra wanted for the next four weeks of Winter Break was to watch mindless TV, wash every surface of her house, and write a telecommunications grant proposal.

Nielson's reappearance seemed too coincidental. "But sir—"

Hershey's hair-sprayed head leaned closer to her ear. "Personally, I wish you had the age and experience to apply for the president's job," he said. Parents and audience members streamed into the lobby to meet up with their graduates. "Although I feel obligated to mention that it's doubtful you'll be seriously considered for the job here, no matter how mature or experienced you become. You, um... well, you don't fit the Morton presidential mold..."

Without a trace of malice in his voice or expression, Hershey had just dismissed her aspirations as easily as one casts off a pair of shoes because she wasn't the right style or color. Cassandra squinted and squeezed the heavy cardboard program in her hand until it bent in half. *How dare he?*

Cassandra's face reddened and she'd just opened her mouth to reply when she felt a strong hand grip her elbow and an arm settle on her waist. She was steered away from Hershey and hustled off to the alcove leading to the women's bathroom.

Cassandra yanked her arm away. Shaking out her poufy green striped velvet sleeves, she directed the indignation she'd felt toward Hershey at her friend Meg O'Brien instead. "Why are you pushing me?"

Meg held both her palms up in mock surrender, flipped her wavy red hair over one shoulder, and glared back at Cassandra using a stink eye so authentically Hawaiian that Mama Sato would have been proud. "Is *that* how you thank me, wahine?" Meg's index finger came up between them and hovered just inches from Cassandra's chin. "I saved you from making a scene in front of all those people."

If Meg ever used that look on her ten-year-old son, Tony, he'd probably turn to ash. Cassandra batted Meg's finger away. Her face was inches from Meg's, and she stage whispered, "I wasn't making a scene! That patriarchal good ol' boy just assured me I'd never get the president's job here."

"I overheard that part," said Meg.

Cassandra backed away from her best friend and opened the bathroom door. They stepped around the corner into the lounge and huddled together on a chaise, out of range of others using the restroom stalls and sinks. "Does he think I'm too female or too Asian to fit the Morton presidential mold?"

Meg had worked at the commencement in her role as Morton's ASL Interpreter Coordinator. A cantaloupe-sized baby bump protruded from her black sweater dress. Black tights and black boots made her outfit funeral-ready, but that was her standard uniform for stage events. "Mr. Country Club Helmet Head wasn't trying to piss you off. He thought he was giving you friendly advice. Hershey likes you, Cass, although he's oblivious to how backward he sounds. Didn't you tell me after the fiasco with Dr. Winters that you won't be applying for the vacant president's job?"

The ladies lounge door banged open and Cinda Weller zeroed in on Cassandra and Meg in the corner. "I'm not wearing your ridiculously heavy outfit, but I'm still dying in this overheated mausoleum." Cinda fanned herself with a souvenir program while her bouncy, blonde hair wilted into frizz. Morton's Counseling and Career Services Director was practically defined by her dry humor and oddball Southern sayings. Several years younger than Cassandra and the mom of two young sons, she'd quickly become Cassandra's friend.

Cassandra adjusted her robes. "I love the costumes only slightly more than I love commencements. I only get to wear mine twice per year."

At the same time Cassandra and Cinda said, "It's old school." One of them meant it as a compliment, the other did not.

Cinda wore navy slacks with a Morton blue blazer and minimal makeup. She shook her head. "Did you notice that line of students who marched down the wrong aisle and had to double back around to their seats?"

Meg shrugged. "Dr. Bryant was their line leader, but don't blame us for the mix-up. We did our jobs. That whole scuffle with the air horn was distracting." Dr. Shannon Bryant was the Deaf Studies professor who Cassandra had recently gotten to know a little better. Meg worked with him often. Pointing toward the bathroom stalls, Meg said, "Mommy bladder."

Cassandra had heard air horns several times throughout the program in disregard for signs at the entrance listing commencement etiquette do's and don'ts. An announcement had been repeated during the ceremony requesting that the audience refrain from unruly behavior and everyone had complied. Except for one. Finally, Bob Gregory, the Business Office Director, had beelined over to a well-dressed woman and her disheveled friend in the left seating area and told them to leave.

The young woman had tossed her dark, tightly waved waist-length hair and loudly protested. "We're cheering for our friends! We aren't hurting anyone. Don't be so uptight!" After his stern beckoning gesture, they'd shuffled over the legs of ten people to exit the row.

There's at least one smartass in every audience.

By the time she and her companion had crawled their way to the aisle, the eyeballs of most males in the vicinity were fixed on the young woman's long legs, short skirt, and pretty face. She repeated apologies to each person she stepped around. "Excuse me. Thanks. Hey, how are you? Good to see you. Hi, Professor." The guy with her was dressed in jeans and a wrinkly t-shirt under a black leather jacket. He stood quietly in the aisle waiting for her until Gregory ushered them both out.

Some people had noticed the disruption, but the incident took only half a minute and the ceremony had continued smoothly.

As soon as Cassandra returned to the lobby, Bob Gregory appeared by her side. "Those air horn people were removed by campus security." His nose wrinkled in distaste. "I tried to calm the young lady down and was willing to let her stay for the post-commencement luncheon if she agreed to relinquish the offending device, but she refused."

The way Gregory said *lady* made it clear he did not consider her worthy of the title. "Apparently her mother is some diplomatic la-ti-da and she threatened to complain about her treatment today. Frankly, she was quite disrespectful." His large stomach heaved upwards with his breath and his lower lip formed into a small pout. "Most of these young folks are nowadays. Disrespectful." He nodded to himself as though Cassandra's opinion was unnecessary for the conversation.

It was all she could do not to roll her eyes and tell him, *okay, Boomer*.

"Thanks for letting me know." Cassandra said, "I'll take care of it from here."

Pulling her phone out of her blazer's pocket, she sent a text to the campus security director, Andy Summers. "Hey Andy. Are you still with the couple from the graduation? Where are they now?"

While waiting for a response, Cassandra moved among the luncheon tables, congratulating graduates she recognized and meeting their parents. Small private colleges like Morton had a leg up on the chaotic busyness of her former college, Oahu State, because of intimate events like these.

Her phone vibrated with Andy's text response. "Back at Picotte Hall. Student believes staff shamed her by singling her out."

Fake candlelight blazed brightly overhead in the baroque chandelier, and Cassandra pressed her lips together.

She typed back, "Hang on there. I'll be over in a few."

Cassandra scanned the crowd until she found Cinda Weller. She waited near the doorway for the luncheon buffet line to thin down while chatting with a student and his family.

Cassandra stepped into Cinda's line of sight, nodded her head to the hallway twice, and waited for Cinda to join her outside. "Would you mind going with me to deal with the students who were removed from the ceremony?"

"What was Sela thinking? I could hardly hear the graduates' names with all that racket!"

"You know her? Is she a troublemaker?"

Cinda looked around the lobby and stepped closer to Cassandra. "Not exactly trouble. More like high maintenance. Her mother works in DC for an embassy or something fancy pants. The guy is Daniel Leung, but I haven't had any problems with him. Sela Roberts..." Cinda made a big exhale. "That girl can be a long day."

"Great. Well it might be an even longer day if she raises a stink about being called out." Cassandra often walked the fine line between enforcing rules and letting students express themselves in productive ways.

They claimed their heavy winter coats from the cloakroom. Cinda said, "It's colder than a well digger's butt out there."

Indeed.

Dr. Bryant walked out the main doors the same time she and Cinda were leaving. He made the sign for cold and then pointed toward the banquet room as though he wondered why she and Cinda weren't staying to eat.

Cassandra typed into her phone and showed it to him. "Checking on the students with the air horn."

Bryant laughed and pointed at his ear. "Didn't bother me," he signed in ASL.

Cassandra laughed and waved goodbye while they turned away. Leaves crunched under their boots as they walked past the central square covered in brown grass.

Picotte Hall was only one city block away from the Arts Center, but a stabbing pain on Cassandra's right pinky toe formed halfway there. Cassandra had assumed that her dress boots with 3" heels would be a perfect fit for the ceremony. Since moving to Carson, Cassandra had experienced several catastrophic footwear events, but she wasn't giving up her love of beautiful shoes. No knockoff flats or clunky snow boots yet.

When Cassandra and Cinda made it past the security desk to the residence hall's lobby, Andy Summers was waiting alone, thumbing through his phone, one hand resting on his thick black utility belt.

"Hey Andy. Where did the students go?"

His eyes broke away from the phone and slowly traveled from Cassandra's boots to her face, then lingered on her head. She was still wearing the graduation tam. "We had a friendly chat. I think I convinced them not to file a complaint."

About her age, military-cut blonde hair now covered by a thick navy stocking cap, Andy probably could stand to lose twenty pounds around his middle. Not that she was judging. Because not everyone had inherited their metabolism from Cassandra's parents who moved constantly like worker bees and never gained a pound over their healthy weight.

"My ears are still ringing," Cinda snorted. "*I* should file a complaint."

"You could have texted us before we walked all the way over here."

Andy's ears flushed red. "They literally just left the lobby before you arrived. I thought you'd appreciate not having to deal with Sela and Daniel."

"Okay." Were they really so difficult to handle? "Thanks for the assist. While we're all here, I need to ask you something else." Cassandra stepped to a seating area and perched on the edge of a large ottoman. Andy and Cinda rested on the nearby couch and chair.

"Did either of you see Dr. Nielson at the grad ceremony?"

Identical expressions of skeptical confusion appeared on their faces.

Cinda said, "How much of that Kona coffee did you drink this morning? Dr. Nielson? He and his wife are in Florida."

"I wish," Cassandra breathed quietly to herself. "I didn't see his wife, but Dr. Nielson was in the parent section, all dressed up and enjoying the show. Afterwards, Mr. Hershey told me that Nielson is coming back to work as president for the spring semester."

Andy Summers blew out a soft whistle. "That's good news! Nielson's a good guy."

"Hope nothing is wrong with his family," Cinda said. "Maybe they're in town for the holidays."

Adjusting her boot to relieve the pinch in her shoe, Cassandra stood. "Let's stop at Nielson's office. I don't want to wait until Monday to get the story."

Fifteen minutes later, Cassandra swiped her key card to open the administrative suite and she and Cinda entered the president's office area. The reception area and large desk where the president's assistant normally worked was quiet, grey light penetrating the wall of windows.

Cinda paged through the piles of paper on the desktop.

"Don't snoop, Cinda!" Cassandra stage whispered.

"How else would we find out anything?"

Cassandra's high heels sunk into the plush carpet as she slowly pushed the heavy wooden door separating the entry area from Nielson's old/new office. Finding it unlocked, she opened it wide enough to see the overhead lights were on. Cassandra knocked. "Hello, is anyone in here? Dr. Nielson?"

No one answered. Was Nielson's key card still valid or had Hershey given him a new one already? Although Cassandra had no basis to feel unease, an urgency she couldn't express made her cross boundaries she normally would have respected. Both women pushed inside.

Mismatched furniture and cardboard boxes sat where they'd been since the previous occupant's hasty departure two weeks prior. Cassandra made a circuit of the room, noticing a banker's box containing awards and framed diplomas on the white desk chair. Maybe he'd brought some of his old things from storage and begun unpacking already. A cup of pens, a blank desktop calendar, a Morton College coffee cup, a commemorative keychain, and a pad of yellow sticky notes were the only items on the desk. The top paper on the yellow pad had a few words printed in Nielson's trademark neat handwriting. He had been here at some point that morning.

"Should we check the men's bathroom?"

Cinda was taking this hunt too far and Cassandra hated wasting time. Cassandra's lips formed a line. "No, that's fine. Let's go back to the luncheon. Maybe Nielson is there meeting parents and hanging out with Mr. Hershey."

Turning off the lights and closing the door behind them, they headed downstairs and back to the Performing Arts Center. Cinda said, "Aren't you relieved that Nielson's back? Less work for all of us now that we don't have to do his job plus ours. I thought you liked working for him."

Cassandra had looked forward to working at her own pace without anyone nosing over her shoulder. She thought a minute before answering carefully. "Don't get me wrong, I'm grateful he took a chance and hired me. But Nielson can be..."

"Oh bless his heart, he's a sweet old coot."

Cassandra laughed. "That's one way of putting it. You didn't see him at the graduation this morning. His skin was tan like he'd been outside, but something was off. I need to talk to him." She nodded. "Then I'll adjust to having my boss back."

Chapter Two

The luncheon crowd had thinned, but there were still families lingering at the round tables while small children played hide and seek in the empty corners of the banquet room. One boy a year or two younger than Cassandra's nephew darted out from under the buffet table and slammed into Cassandra's legs. Cassandra grabbed his arms to stabilize them both, then the laughing boy ricocheted off in another direction.

Cassandra didn't see Nielson's gray hair among the remaining faculty and guests. Hershey was also gone. A catering crew in black uniforms methodically moved around the empty tables clearing trash and dishes.

Cinda held out both hands and shrugged. "Maybe you'll have to wait until Monday to see him."

"How can I relax this weekend knowing that come Monday I'm starting over again with my third boss in one semester?" Technically, Nielson was boss number one and the future number three, but she was worked up. No way was Cassandra waiting two more days to get answers. "I understand if you need to take off and get home to your family. I'll go back to the office and see if I can track him down."

"Yeah. If I'm lucky my hubs, Jacob, got Oliver down for a nap and I might be able to finish my Christmas wrapping." Cinda zipped up her coat. "Hey, maybe Nielson went home after commencement."

Cassandra nodded. "I don't think they sold their house yet." She would have noticed a for sale sign when she'd passed it on the way to visiting Cinda's house. "I'll grab my car and follow you, if you don't mind the extra stop."

"You're not giving up, are you," Cinda laughed. "Like a scavenger hunt!"

When they reached the entrance, Marcus Fischer, recently promoted Facilities and Maintenance VP, walked through the double doors holding a small paper. "Oh, perfect timing! I was hoping you hadn't left."

Cassandra pulled up short less than an arm's length in front of him. Heat rushed up Cassandra's neck and she felt embarrassingly pleased to hear the sincerity in his deep voice. "Uh, hey Fischer. Cinda and I were—" Cassandra looked over her shoulder for backup, but Cinda had abandoned her to talk to a couple of staff members packing party decor into plastic tubs.

A head taller than her, but not so big that she had to step back to look up at him, dark-haired, blue-eyed Marcus Fischer wore a green Packers stocking cap and his heavy leather jacket.

Cassandra cleared her throat. "We're on our way out. I could call you later?" She hadn't seen him alone since their winery date weeks ago. More than a colleague, not an official boyfriend, their relationship status was pending.

A clean, outdoor scent clung to him and his cheeks were pink with cold. "No need, I just have a quick update. We consolidated the stragglers and closed the other two residence halls. Some went home with local students or to visit family in other cities over the holidays."

Cassandra wished she hadn't agreed to oversee the international student dorm during the holidays. She winced. So much for any cozy holiday evenings curled up in front of a fire sipping hot cocoa.

The big fantasy she'd imagined since moving to Nebraska was wearing plaid flannel sweats tucked under a soft blanket and watching burning logs. So far, she'd yet to burn a twig in her fireplace. Terrified of doing it wrong and burning the place down, she needed to find a native Midwesterner to set the whole Norman Rockwell scene perfectly.

"Here's the resident assistant's phone number for the Picotte dorm floors," said Fischer. "Lin Chow will probably check in with a final student count for the international floor before she leaves."

Fischer had made it sound like nothing big when he'd asked her to babysit the international students' floor while he joined his family for a Mexican cruise. She'd expected a follow-up plan with specific activities, but finals week had been too hectic. The RA leaving town was an unexpected twist.

For two weeks, Cassandra would be solely responsible for twenty-five 18-to 24-year-old students away from home and family. Shoving the sticky note in her pocket, irritation crept into Cassandra's voice at Fischer's breezy attitude. "How often do I need to stop by Picotte?"

"They might catch a few movies, bake cookies, sleep in late..." said Fischer. "If you just show your face a few times, I'm sure they'll be fine on their own."

But what if they got homesick? Cassandra understood that feeling perfectly. Her stomach still tightened every time she thought about her nephews opening gifts without her and missing the big breakfasts and game nights when everyone gathered at her parents' Waipahu home.

Before Fischer took off, she wanted to touch base about her concern. "Did you see Dr. Nielson at the graduation ceremony?"

"No-Nonsense Nielson? Nope." He gave her a skeptical look. "Why would he be here? He retired to Florida."

Cinda finally stopped chatting and joined them. Cassandra said, "I thought so too, but he was at commencement. In the audience. And afterwards, Chairman Hershey told me that he asked Nielson back to Morton as president next semester."

Cinda shrugged. "I didn't see him either, but..."

Fischer lifted his chin in greeting toward Cinda. "Wow. Didn't expect him back so soon." Dressed in navy khakis, he bounced a little on the balls of his brown ankle boots.

"Totally out of character," Cassandra nodded. "Cinda and I are going to find out what changed his mind."

Fischer's head bobbed, but he edged toward the doors. "Thanks for pinch hitting with the dorm students."

17

She could tell he was already picturing himself body surfing somewhere on a sunny beach and sipping beers at a poolside bar with his brothers-in-law. They waved goodbye and Fischer hopped into his waiting car.

Cassandra scanned the small parking lot behind the Osborne Administration Building. No Ford Taurus. Maybe Nielson was driving a rental.

On the drive to his house, Cassandra replayed their last conversation in her office. "This might seem abrupt, but I've been planning for months, Dr. Sato." Relaxing in the armchair in front of her desk, legs crossed casually, Nielson had left no hint that he'd ever return to Carson. Lines had crinkled around his light blue eyes. "I'm certain that Morton is in good hands. You and the other young faculty are the future of this college, Cassandra. I believe you can be the force for change."

At the time, she'd been touched by his confidence. Now Cassandra wondered what had happened to change Nielson's faith in her leadership.

Cassandra pulled her Honda Accord to the curb behind Cinda's Subaru SUV. One block away from Professor's Row, Nielson's house wasn't a mansion by Nebraska standards, but would cost nearly a million dollars in the Hawaiian real estate market. The two-story Colonial with a portico-covered front door had seen better days. One of the upstairs shutters hung crookedly by a bottom hinge and the front evergreen hedges had overgrown to cover the ground floor windows.

Walking up the driveway with Cinda, Cassandra headed toward the front door.

"I'll check the back yard and peek in the garage," Cinda spoke over her shoulder as she kept walking. A detached two car garage sat behind the house. A small window along the top of the garage door was cracked, a triangle missing from the glass.

Cassandra called after Cinda, "Shouldn't we knock first before you go snoop—." She let her voice fade out as Cinda disappeared around the corner. Cinda acted like a character in a TV sitcom, but Cassandra was really worried. The doorbell was missing the plastic cover, so Cassandra pressed the small round button. A chime echoed from inside, but no footsteps approached. Peering through the narrow side window, the distorted glass blocked her view.

The gray clouds seemed lower than they'd been earlier this morning and the air felt thick. Looking at her smartwatch, Cassandra noted the temperature was thirty degrees. Ears stinging from the cold, she wished she'd traded her graduation tam for a warmer stocking cap.

Maybe the Nielsons had sold their house privately before moving to Florida.

After two minutes, Cinda came around the corner. "No cars in the garage. The sliding deck door is locked and has window blinds. From what I could see of the kitchen, someone left their laptop on the table. Foam takeout containers were piled in the trash and a box of Cap'n Crunch sat on the countertop. Never imagined No-Nonsense Nielson as a Cap'n Crunch man."

"Really, Cinda." Cassandra had heard people use Nielson's nickname ever since she'd arrived in July. Cassandra rolled her eyes. "Spying on his favorite brand of breakfast cereal? We're not analyzing his food quirks for a laugh. I need to know why he came back so I can be ready."

Cinda eyed the neighbors' houses. "Unless you want to knock on doors hoping for nosy neighbors, we'll have to wait until Monday, huh?"

Nielson wasn't in his office, he wasn't at the luncheon, and he wasn't at his house. Cassandra had called his number, but it went straight to voicemail. Small-town Carson didn't exactly offer millions of hiding places. Cassandra's stomach tightened. "We worked together for four months, and I thought he respected me. Something's wrong."

While they walked toward their cars, Cassandra's watch vibrated with a text. She didn't recognize the number, so she pulled her phone out of her jacket pocket.

She slipped off her glove and read the text. "Hi Cassandra, this is Rebecca Nielson. I can't get ahold of Gary. Is he there with you?"

Cassandra stopped abruptly at the end of the driveway and nearly tipped over when Cinda ran into her back. "What the—!" Cassandra grabbed Cinda's arm with her free hand until she regained her balance.

"Hey, what's wrong?" said Cinda.

Becky Nielson had often made treats for the office and had invited Cassandra to join her book club although she'd been too busy to attend. Cassandra showed Cinda the text message.

Cinda's eyes narrowed. "Maybe Nielson and the other board members are off somewhere having a secret strategy meeting."

"Why would they need to have a secret meeting? And why wouldn't his wife know about it?" Cassandra said, "He's only been gone for like, six weeks. Hershey made it sound like Nielson's reinstatement was no big deal."

Cassandra replied to Becky, "No, we're looking for him, too. Where are you?"

Within seconds she responded, "With my sister's family in Iowa. Why are you looking for him?"

Maybe a marital issue had surfaced in Florida, causing a separation. Cassandra didn't want to get in the middle of that.

Cinda had read the message over Cassandra's shoulder and must have had the same thought. "Oops. This sounds like the Nielsons' personal problems that I do not want to know about." She held up her mittened hands. "I'm sure Hershey will send an announcement memo on Monday. Most of the students are gone next week anyway. Winter term classes start after Christmas. Look, I need to get home. Go enjoy the rest of your weekend."

Cinda was right. Cassandra would begin her winter break and deal with Dr. Nielson next week. "Thanks for helping me out. See you Monday."

Cinda drove off, Cassandra buckled her seat belt, and messaged Becky again. "Just catching up with him after graduation. Must have gotten our signals crossed." She added a reassuring happy face emoji.

Cassandra pulled her gloves back on as another moment from Nielson's last conversation swam into her vision. Following her Japanese and Hawaiian cultural traditions, Cassandra had presented Dr. Nielson a going away token. When she had handed him a small koa wood box engraved with a Japanese bonsai motif, his blue eyes had welled up.

"This symbolizes peace and harmony," she had told him. "May you have plenty of both during your retirement."

Wiping away the wetness from his cheek, Nielson's normally gruff voice had softened. "I'm aware that people mistake your confident, calm professionalism for coldness. But it's been a pleasure knowing you these short months. This means so much to me."

Patting his suit pockets, Nielson had stood and cleared his throat. "I'm embarrassed that I have nothing to give you in return." Then he reached into his pants pockets and his keys jingled. "No, wait. I do have one thing." Pulling out his keys, he removed a keychain from the ring and held it out to her. "I received this in October from the Chinese delegation in Hangzhou during our cultural exchange visit. It's a limited edition only for members of our traveling party. The future partnership with the Hangzhou School of Commerce depends on you and the other leaders continuing the work I've begun."

Grasping the heavy die cast metal in the shape of the Leifeng Pagoda with her leather covered palm, Cassandra let out a deep sigh and started her Honda, turning the warm air full blast.

As she drove toward home, large snowflakes drifted from the sky covering the town.

Chapter Three

The first thing that hit Cassandra when she stepped into her kitchen was the ammonia smell. And it wasn't from the wipe-down she'd done Saturday morning before the commencement ceremony.

Walking through the short hallway, Cassandra paused in front of the small black kennel she'd placed in the formal dining room turned office. "Murphy! I was only gone a few hours. Couldn't you hold it, braddah?"

The little white fluff ball stood up and shook himself out, barking his reply. When she reached out to open the kennel, he growled and lunged.

"Hey—" Startled, Cassandra yanked her hand back. "You go on keep that attitude to yourself. I'm trying to let you out."

When he stopped growling, she opened the door. Murphy's black eyes locked onto hers. A suspiciously dark circle had formed on the old towel she'd placed inside the kennel over newspapers. He didn't move.

She tried her nice teacher voice. "Come on, Murphy. I'll take you outside to shishi." No response. She reached inside with one hand, lifting him up and out. "Let's get you cleaned up." His twenty-pound body stiffened, and the growling started again, his upper lip curling to display little doggie fangs.

She dropped him from waist height to the floor and recoiled. Giving up the sugary sweet voice, she switched to local Hawaiian scolding. "Look, brah. You no play nice, you no get sweet talk from me. Enough!"

He barked twice then ran through the kitchen and stood at the side door, yapping impatiently. She hooked the leash on his collar and led him outside. After more than a week, she'd hoped he would have adjusted to his new living arrangement, but this was how it went day after day, no matter how hard she tried to make him feel at home.

 Cassandra normally didn't make impulsive decisions, and she already regretted this one. Murphy's constantly soiled towels and poopy surprises reinforced why she'd never owned a pet. Especially not an ungrateful foster dog. If his owner hadn't been recently placed in a nursing home for dementia patients, Murphy would already have been returned.

Luckily the one thing she and Murphy agreed on was that lingering outside to do his business in the cold was unnecessary. He trotted around to the patch of brown grass that formed her small back yard, lifted a hind leg near the corner of the deck, then immediately headed back toward the house. The falling snow had changed to a nearly opaque white curtain. Her driveway was already lightly covered.

Once inside the kitchen, she turned on the stovetop to heat water for tea and rubbed her arms. Her University of

Hawai'i doctoral robes were still draped over her shoulders, and she couldn't wait to change out of her suit into comfy yoga pants. Making her winter break to do list would have to wait. First, she had to wash the kennel's dirty towel and plug in a room air freshener.

Her watch vibrated. She'd received a message from Dr. Nielson! "Are you in the office? Meet me at the Gas & Sweets in 15 minutes." Then a minute later, "Are you on the way?"

Frowning, she turned off the stovetop and checked the time. She had a few minutes to change clothes and still get to the gas station within the deadline. She tapped the microphone icon and spoke into her watch, "I'll be there in 15." Hitting send, she rushed to her bedroom. Murphy did not follow.

While changing clothes, she realized one nice thing about moving to a town of 8,000 people. No traffic jams to slow her travel time. Although she'd have to take it easy on the snow. Her father had insisted she get all-season tires for the Honda when she'd moved but bringing the car to the auto shop to get them switched was one of the things that hadn't been checked off her list yet.

* * *

Cassandra eyed the goods inside the glass case while sitting at a table on the bakery side of the Gas and Sweets building. One cinnamon sugar donut remained, but several chocolate-covered eclairs rested on a serving tray at eye level. Cassandra's stomach growled, reminding her that she'd skipped the commencement luncheon to track down Dr.

Nielson. It was going on 2:00 p.m. and the Spam musubi she'd eaten for breakfast was long ago digested.

Cassandra checked her phone again. She'd been waiting for twenty minutes. To her right, the plate glass window overlooking the parking lot showed one dirty pickup truck at the gas pumps. Over her left shoulder, she read the cute home decor signs and admired the Christmas display in the gift shop part of the bakery.

Her lips formed a straight line as she texted Dr. Nielson. "I'm at the Sweets shop. Are you still coming?"

Nielson was the one who'd asked for the meeting. Whatever game he was playing didn't bode well for Cassandra's holiday downtime.

Leaving her coat on the back of her chair, she stepped into the gift shop and checked out a rack of hand towels with funny quotes on them. These might make cute gifts for Cinda and Meg. She could pair them with wine from one of the local vineyards and some crackers and cheese. At least this detour wouldn't be a complete waste of her time.

An angry growl came from behind the baked goods case. "If you weren't my daughter you'da been fired long ago."

From where Cassandra hunched over the turning display rack, the stocky man with white hair was intimidatingly close to the baker. Cassandra had to decide whether to show herself or stay half-hidden and leave them to the privacy of their family argument.

His daughter retorted. "How about you stay on the gas station side and leave me alone to manage the shop."

"I can't let my guard down. These idiots are out to get me." The father said, "Haven't I taught you girl that if you don't get the bastards first, they'll get you?"

"All my freaking life, Dad."

"Okay then, we understand each other." The gas station owner grumbled, "Don't disappoint me. You know what happens to jerks who steal from me." He stomped out the double sliding doors toward the gas station store.

Cassandra peeked around the display and spotted the daughter wiping under her eyes. Straightening, Cassandra looked out the window and stepped back to her table but turned when she heard a gasp.

"I didn't know anyone was still in here." The woman's hands fluttered up to cover her mouth. "My father knows I wouldn't steal from my own family." Her hands slid down to rest on her hips.

Cassandra took a step closer to read her name tag. Rhonda wore long, dangling earrings and a flowy peasant top under her white apron. The apron was spotted with flour and a few smudges that looked like jelly donut filling. "I'm sorry he spoke to you that way. I like your shop."

Rhonda beamed at the simple, honest compliment. "Thank you. I've always dreamed of opening my own place, but for now sharing space with my father is the most economical way to go. Someday maybe I'll move to Main Street. Do you work at the college?"

Morton was one of the few large employers in town. "Yeah. I'm Cassandra. I moved here last summer."

Rhonda's eyes narrowed as she took in Cassandra's dark hair and stocking hat pulled to just above her eyebrows.

"Nice to meet you. I'm Rhonda." Her head tilted toward the gas station side, "My father Bob Soukup bought the gas station fifteen years ago after he retired from running the corn processing plant. He's afraid if he retires, he'll just up and die of boredom. Work is his whole life."

Cassandra would never work anywhere until she was in her late seventies, no matter how much she liked the job. Both of her eyebrows raised. "Sounds like his jobs are stressful."

"To family, he's just a grouch. But if you do business with him, don't get on his bad side."

Through the gas station doors and convenience store Mr. Soukup held court behind the elevated cash register, waiting on one customer.

Rhonda made her father sound like a crusty old mobster. Cassandra planned to avoid him.

"See you next time," said Rhonda. "I'm terrible with names, but I'll try to remember yours."

Just as she'd gathered her coat and bag, Cassandra's phone rang. Nielson's voice came through before she'd even said hello. "Sorry, Cassandra. Something's come up and I can't meet you today after all."

She gave the screen a fervent stink eye. "I've been waiting for you for half an hour."

"Sorry for the inconvenience," Nielson said. "Let's meet in my office Monday morning at eight to go over plans for the holiday break and winter term classes."

"I looked for you after graduation. Is something wrong?"

Nielson said, "I've had a lot of time to think the past few weeks, and I'm excited about what we can accomplish during the spring semester. I feel rested and refreshed."

None of his behavior had been his usual No-Nonsense style. His cheery voice sounded forced. Cassandra wasn't convinced. "Did your wife get in touch with you earlier? Becky texted me because she couldn't contact you."

"Becky? My wife, er ... contacted *you*?" He stammered. "Oh, yes, sure we've spoken. I'm heading to Iowa to meet her for the holidays after everything is set up here. Do you know of any cleaning services?"

Somehow, she'd forgotten how maddening the man could be when he was flitting around between subjects. Nielson had wasted her time before when he'd taken on too many projects at once then delegated them to her. "I don't use a cleaning service, Dr. Nielson. If there's nothing else for today, I'm going to drive home before the roads get worse."

"Nope, I'm good now," he assured her. "I look forward to seeing you again Monday. First thing we'll have to do is retrieve my office furniture from storage. My executive desk chair is missing, and it looks like someone splashed hideous white paint on every surface of the presidential suite. I don't know how Dr. Winters worked in there with the blinding whiteness of it all. Luckily, she didn't touch the mahogany bookshelves."

They disconnected. First of all, she was not his lackey and wouldn't be hunting in the storage for his stuff. Secondly, Cassandra was now the owner of his super comfy office chair and she wasn't giving it up.

Several minutes later, she cautiously pulled out of the Gas and Sweets parking lot, shopping and bakery bags resting on the front passenger seat. Two eclairs for her and one cinnamon donut. Maybe Murphy could be bribed into friendship.

* * *

The doorbell roused Cassandra from lightly dozing on the couch in front of an episode of *Fixer Upper*. The transformations Chip could do with plywood and paint. Cassandra's bullet journal already held a wish list of home improvement projects.

Pulling her long sweater around her yoga pants and UH t-shirt, Cassandra flipped on the overhead light in the bungalow's entryway and peeked through the small windows at the top of the outer door. A tall man's gray hair glinted in the light.

"Who is it?" Cassandra called, although she thought she knew.

"It's Gary Nielson. I need to come inside."

Glancing at her watch, Cassandra saw that it was after nine o'clock. Why would Dr. Nielson be at her house? She unlocked the deadbolt and cracked the door open. "I thought we were going to talk Monday?"

Nielson's hand pushed the door open and he stepped inside the entryway. Words tumbled out of his mouth in a barely understandable rush. "I thought it was over. I just want to be left alone."

Anxiety rolled off him in waves. Cassandra took two steps back to give him space. "What are you talking about?"

He closed and locked the front door and turned off the outside porch light. "I swear I don't know why these people won't believe me. I sent Becky to visit her sister for the holidays."

Did he ever just answer a question directly? He often seemed to be in another conversation entirely.

"We looked for you this afternoon. Mr. Hershey said you're accepting the president's job back?" Cassandra searched his shadowed face for answers. Dressed in a heavy canvas field coat, he looked more like a sporty grandpa than a college president. "I saw you at the commencement, but then we missed you."

Sweat or melting snow dripped down from his flat woolen cap. "The texts don't stop. I bought a new phone so they can't find me." His voice trembled slightly. "I can't go to my house."

She'd known he wouldn't disappear after graduation without saying hello unless there was an emergency. What the heck was going on? Cassandra's heart thumped. "Come, sit down." She gestured toward the living room chair. Nielson took off his coat and scarf, hanging them on the wooden pegs in the entry. "Would you like a glass of water?"

Murphy chose that moment to scramble up to Nielson and yap, yap, yap. She scooped him up, although his little legs stuck out stiffly and he wriggled in protest. Taking him through the short hallway, she deposited him in the main bathroom. When she closed the door, his yaps were muffled enough that she could at least hear Nielson talk. Retrieving a glass of water in the kitchen, she met him in the living room where he'd chosen a small side chair not far from the front entryway.

Nielson looked around Cassandra's simply decorated living room from the fireplace, couch and coffee table, to the kennel in the adjoining office area. "I never knew you were a dog person." Nielson gulped half of the water.

The man's attention span was shorter than a chimpanzee's. Looking back at the bathroom door where Murphy's yaps had quieted to a sporadic yip, Cassandra shook her head. "I'm *not* a dog person! He's not mine. I'm watching him. Temporarily. For a—" She was about to say for a friend, but that wasn't true. Dr. Winters and she weren't friends; no longer co-workers, either.

"Are you staying in Carson? And taking your old job back?" Cassandra steered him back to the reason for his visit. "What texts are you talking about?"

"All I know is after we came back from China, I received random texts asking me for the soybean seed formula. I ignored them because I thought they were scammy robocalls." His shaky hand removed his cap and balanced it on a knee.

"So they weren't robocalls? Someone thinks you have a Chinese seed formula."

"But I don't have it. I told them!"

What had he done with the smart-but-sometimes-bumbling boss she'd respected during the fall semester? His anxiety was contagious. "Take a breath, sir." Cassandra didn't even know where to begin. "Have you called the police?"

"Heck no. The police can't help me." He babbled out short bursts as thoughts occurred to him. "I just got back to Carson last night. I thought everything had been settled in Florida. Maybe there's a local spy."

Spies? Maybe he'd had a mental breakdown in Florida? "Okay, let's think about this a minute. What did you mean when you said you thought it had been settled in Florida?"

"A few weeks ago, the USDA contacted me in Florida when I applied for a job at the plant repository there. Someone in the Chinese government reported a missing proprietary file of a high-yield soybean seed formula after Morton College's visit touring Hangzhou. My name was flagged during a background check. I assured them that no one in our group would steal government secrets."

Nielson had bungled into minor misunderstandings before, but agricultural espionage was an entirely different level. Cassandra's legs felt a little wobbly, so she sunk into her desk chair. "Let me make sure I understand this right. Either the US government or Chinese spies are searching for missing proprietary soybean research. They think *you* have it, and they keep texting you?"

Nielson's shoulders raised into a small shrug and he slowly nodded. "How would I have it?"

Even the appearance of impropriety between anyone representing Morton College and stolen scientific data would be devastating for their reputation. "As far as you know, you didn't actually bring anything home from China that you weren't supposed to." Cassandra used a calm voice like the ones on her favorite yoga tutorial videos.

"I'm just a simple retired guy from Nowhere, Nebraska." He looked down at his wet shoes dripping on her wood floor. "I want my quiet life back."

"Okay, that's good." She smiled kindly, exuding positive warmth toward him. "Do you know who's sending the texts?"

Frowning, he said, "Tell me everything you know about the Chinese mafia."

He had an annoying habit of mistaking her ethnicity for Chinese, no matter how many times she set him straight. Maybe he assumed the Japanese Yakuza and the Chinese triads were the same thing. She closed her eyes and wished for more patience. "If you think organized criminals are texting, you should call the sheriff."

He placed the empty glass on the coffee table and turned toward her lighted Christmas tree. Murphy had stopped barking and the house was quiet while Nielson considered his alternatives.

"I promised Chairman Hershey that I'd come back. I'm contacting everyone who went on the trip in October and asking if they can help us clear this up."

Why had Hershey even offered Nielson the job again? After the earlier death and injuries this semester, Morton College needed to avoid any connection to legal problems or another scandal. "This weekend would be a good time to re-think all your options, Dr. Nielson. Morton needs stable leadership during the spring semester."

He stood and slipped his coat off the peg in her entry. Wrapping his scarf around his neck, he said, "I'm sorry for bothering you, Cassandra. I'm sure this is all a simple misunderstanding." His voice shook slightly, and she was sure the moisture on his forehead was sweat. "When I come back to work full-time, everything will be better."

Cassandra didn't share Nielson's blithe trust that a few phone calls would clear up this mess.

Once Nielson bundled up and left, Cassandra went back to the kitchen and spied the bakery bag with the uneaten eclair resting on her countertop ready for the next day's breakfast. Her willpower lasted about 90 seconds before she snuck a hand inside, ripped off half the pastry, and savored the sugar rush after the first bite.

Thirty minutes later, she was ready to try sleeping. She turned off all the lights and changed into pajamas before a soft whine sounded through the door on her bedroom's side of the Jack and Jill bathroom.

She'd forgotten Murphy! Wrenching open the door, Cassandra gasped, "Oh!"

Murphy had unraveled a full toilet paper roll all over the tub, toilet, and floor, then torn it to shreds. He sat on the bathmat, his white fur blending in with the heaping white pile that half-buried him up to his collar's jaunty plaid bowtie.

Fall semester had been more overwhelming than she'd ever imagined. Housebreaking a pet might be more than she could handle. "I don't think this is gonna work, Murph," she whispered.

Melancholy brown eyes gazed into hers until her own eyes filled with tears.

Chapter Four

Cassandra wished she had Dorothy's ruby slippers that she could click together to instantly transport her home. Her *real* home. Gazing out the bay window in the so-called sunroom of her chilly bungalow, she could barely breathe at the sight of so much stark whiteness. Snow covered the hedges under the window, her front yard, the pristinely smooth road, and every leafless tree of the neighbors' homes across the street.

Sunday had been quiet. She'd done a slow and easy yoga session, laundry, and worked on a puzzle she'd found on her basement storage shelves. An old owner of the house must have forgotten to move them out because in the back corner Cassandra had found a stack of 1970s era puzzles. A cold afternoon inside seemed like the perfect time to distract herself. Piecing together a western sunset over the Grand Canyon reminded her of spending time at puzzles with her Grandma when she was a little girl.

She'd even baked a batch of soft chocolate chip cookies before settling in with a Harry Potter movie marathon.

There had only been a couple inches of slushy snow on the roads when she'd gone to bed.

Now Cassandra wanted completely out. Back to Oahu's tropical paradise where "winter" meant 75 degrees and partly cloudy azure skies. Intellectually, she had known about winter weather. But watching holiday movies and reading regional articles hadn't prepared her for this, this... blizzard. A couple of weeks ago, her first snowfall had been light, fluffy, and beautiful then melted after 12 hours.

She plodded to the kitchen in her stocking feet to make Kona coffee. While the Keurig worked its magic, she pulled on a second hoodie over her pajamas and tapped the central heat up a few degrees. Meg had cautioned her once about setting her thermostat too high in the winter which would lead to eye-popping utility bills in January.

Meg and Connor! Her best friends lived on an acreage in the country about 30 miles away. What if they lost power? Maybe she should have offered to let them stay with her.

A while later, Meg's makeup-free face appeared on Cassandra's FaceTime app. "Hey sistah," Cassandra waved at the iPad screen. "You look... natural." Messy red hair drooped in a bun piled on top of Meg's head and her ratty sweatshirt looked big enough to fit her husband, Connor.

"Between the snow excitement and pre-Christmas jitters, Tony woke up early and *someone* forgot to re-stock the decaf coffee." Meg hooked a thumb in the direction of the kitchen and mouthed the word *Connor*.

From off-camera, Cassandra heard Connor's voice, "And to make it up, *someone* is helping their delightful son cook a delicious Eggs Benedict breakfast for his favorite pregnant and pleasantly non-demanding wife."

Cassandra wrapped her hands around her warm mug until the heat from the coffee seeped into them and traveled up her arms. Involuntarily, she inhaled the dark, rich scent of her favorite roast.

"Do not laugh! I see your nostrils flaring," Meg warned.

Meg's face zoomed closer to her laptop camera until Cassandra's screen was filled with wide open green eyes and lightly freckled skin normally camouflaged by concealer. Meg said, "I'm stranded on an arctic oasis with a house full of testosterone, and you're over there in your quiet little bungalow with your fully caffeinated brew picturing Waikiki beach."

"When I interviewed here in July, not even you accurately described this... this..." Seated at the small table in her sunroom, Cassandra gestured her arm to encompass the bay window and vast tundra outside. "I don't even know a word for sub-zero windy snow covering every— I can't even see my mailbox!" Through the cloudy haze she could hardly make out the shape at the end of the driveway. She wouldn't be able to receive mail until spring!

No need to panic. She'd be able to leave her house in days, maybe a week? Cassandra said, "It's after noon. Why's the sky so heavy looking? Is more snow coming?" The tightness in her chest couldn't simply be the dull ache that had underlined the days leading up to her first Christmas away from home.

"Snowpocalypse," Meg backed away from the camera and nodded. "That's the word. This here's a classic example of Nebraska in December. Do you never watch television?"

"I researched, but I thought with warm clothes, I'd be fine. How do you people work in the wintertime? Does everyone just stay home until March?" Her voice got higher and louder than she'd intended. "I don't have enough clothes in my whole closet for this."

"Don't be such a diva." Meg popped a quick smooch on Connor's cheek as he deposited a heaping plate in front of her on their kitchen table. Scattered mail, a pile of folded laundry, and a half-finished puzzle covered everything except the little space in front of Meg. She dug in like she hadn't eaten in days.

Connor sat next to her, rested an arm on the back of Meg's chair, and smiled like a man who cherished the daily chaos of his family life.

"I bet this is the worst storm you've ever seen in your life, right?" Cassandra asked Connor. When he shook his head no, she gasped, "Tell me it's not going to get worse."

His dimpled smile epitomized the Midwestern all-American farm boy. "When I was six years old, a surprise blizzard hit in October the day before Halloween. My back yard had a neck-high snow drift, our dog didn't know where to pee, we missed four days of school, and a tree branch fell on my dad's car."

Yeah, none of those things had happened during her childhood. Cassandra's head shook slowly.

Connor said, "Our neighborhood's streets were blocked by tree limbs because ice clung to leaves that hadn't fallen yet, cracking branches with the heavy weight. The mayor canceled Halloween. I was so disappointed; I wore my Batman costume around the house for a week."

Cassandra clamped her mouth shut. She'd never really thought about snow doing major property damage like that. Of course, she'd seen TV news coverage of blizzards showing people shoveling, sledding, and making snowmen. Making a snowman was her second private winter fantasy, right before coming inside to cocoon by the fire and drink hot cocoa.

Murphy woke from his nap on the living room rug, trotted into the sunroom, and yapped twice. Cassandra's back clenched.

Meg cooed over the video, "Hey Murph'! How ya doing, buddy? Is your new Mom spoiling you?"

Murphy whined. Earlier, Cassandra had given him a scoop of food which he'd ignored. Every time she'd tried to pet him, he either growled or scooted out of her reach.

"He hates me." A loud motor fired up nearby, the sound carried in the quiet stillness of the neighborhood. Murphy yapped again, louder now over the din of the motor.

Meg's voice cut out a few times and it was obviously time to hang up. "Just give him a little time," Meg advised.

"Maybe you guys should take him. You already have Burt. You know how to care for a pet."

"Gotta go now. We're still on for Christmas Eve," Meg nearly shouted.

Cassandra hooked the leash up to Murphy's collar and led him out the side door to do his business. Wind howled around the corner of the house and Murphy soon became nearly invisible. The drifts were deeper than his little white body. With each step he was up to his black nose in snow.

Little ice chunks bit into Cassandra's cheeks and her eyes watered. The snowblower noises now came from both directions. Even though it was Monday, she didn't plan on going into work. She'd have to tackle the driveway at some point but wasn't feeling it yet.

Gratitude flashed through her when she saw a trace of yellow snow where Murphy had been standing. Evidence that he'd managed to accomplish his task.

"Good boy!" She praised, scooped him up, and carried him inside. He must have been relieved to return to the warm house, because for the first time he didn't growl or squirm out of her arms. When he wasn't all defensive and rigid, his hair was silky soft. Wrapping him in a towel, she gently dried his paws and body.

* * *

Cassandra perched on the edge of her couch folding clean clothes and watching *Friends* when her doorbell chimed. Murphy scrambled over to the door and barked a few times.

Assuming a delivery person was dropping off Christmas gifts she'd ordered online, Cassandra ignored the doorbell and figured she'd pick them up when she finished folding the clothes.

The doorbell rang again, and Murphy trotted back to the couch. His eyebrows raised at her like he was saying, *isn't it customary to answer that noise?*

Springing up so quickly she knocked over a pile of folded towels, she cursed under her breath and unlocked the door.

Standing on her front porch in full winter uniform was Deputy Tate, although he'd traded his brown campaign hat for a warmer brown stocking hat with a Saunders County Sheriff patch. Frowning, she opened the door and invited him inside.

"Thank you, Dr. Sato." He brushed droplets of snow and water off his coat sleeve, then stood at formal military attention. So large he could have been an NFL linebacker, he filled her entryway.

Murphy turned and ran to the kitchen. Coward.

"Deputy Tate. This is . . . unexpected."

Had she missed some kind of evacuation order because of the weather? He was a bit younger than Cassandra but had the commanding authority vibe that came with his job.

"Ma'am, I'm following up on a matter. We'd appreciate it if you could answer some questions."

Ma'am? She wasn't *that* much older than him. She laughed nervously. "Yes, of course. I was supposed to go to work, but with the—" Cassandra pointed toward the front door and the snowy outside world. "With the emergency weather, I called the office and cancelled. I mean, there's no classes. Everyone's kind of on holiday already . . ." Her voice actually squeaked. Why was she intimidated by him? They'd worked together before when one of the deaf students had died mysteriously. He was a really nice, very smart guy.

His broad face was serious. "Did you speak to anyone? When you called this morning?"

Was she in trouble for something? Her stomach contracted. She couldn't imagine what she'd done wrong by calling in to work. "No one answered, so I left a voicemail. I figured they both stayed home. What's wrong?"

Tate's eyes closed for a second longer than a blink and he exhaled a big breath. "Dr. Sato, I regret to inform you that Gary Nielson is dead."

Dr. Nielson. Cassandra's stomach flipped and her legs wobbled. "Wait, *what*? Are you sure?"

Tate reached out to steady her upper arms, then guided her back two steps to the chair in her living room. "We're following up with his calendar and acquaintances as part of our investigation and saw a note that he had a meeting scheduled with you this morning."

"That can't be right." Instinctively, she bent over as a wave of light-headedness rushed up the back of her neck. After a minute of steady breathing, she cautiously raised her face. "We were supposed to meet at eight, but I couldn't drive in this snow. When he didn't return my call, I assumed we'd catch up tomorrow."

Tate looked down at his heavy work boots where small pools of water had formed in the same spot Nielson himself had stood 48 hours earlier. Two heartbeats passed before Tate raised his head.

Cassandra asked, "What happened?"

Nielson had often ridden an emotional roller coaster but seemed more stressed out than usual when he'd stopped over on Saturday night. Unless, . . . what if he'd taken his own life? "Did he . . .?"

Tate waved that idea away with a flip of his large hand. "Still under investigation."

"Can't you tell me anything?" Forming coherent sentences was difficult.

"His assistant, Julie, gave us your name and address. We tried contacting the other administrators but everyone else seems to be out of town or unavailable. I'd like to ask you a few questions."

What she needed were answers. Cassandra looked down at her University of Hawai'i hoodie, feeling underdressed and ill-prepared for this moment. Her eyes teared up and she couldn't speak over the knot in her throat. She nodded.

"What was your meeting about this morning?" Tate asked.

"I found out at graduation on Saturday that Dr. Nielson moved back to work at Morton for spring semester. We were supposed to discuss how to divide administrative responsibilities for holiday break and the winter term classes."

"Where was your meeting planned? How many people are left on campus now?"

"We closed three dorms and left one open for out-of-town students who need a place to stay. A skeleton crew of cafeteria and cleaning staff. Normally there's almost 4,000 students, but we're down to less than a hundred over the holidays." She wiped under her eye using the cuff of her sweatshirt. "Can't you even tell me how he died? Was it at Morton?"

"Still under—"

Cassandra held up her hand, "—investigation. I got that part. I just can't believe he's gone." He had been like a goofy, out-of-touch, well-meaning uncle to her during the short time they'd worked together.

Murphy quietly padded over to Tate's leg and bumped it with his head like a cat. Tate absentmindedly scratched his ear. "Do you know when Nielson came back to Carson?"

"No. I was surprised to see him at graduation. I know he'd been in his office before then because I saw some of his things in a box. I wanted to talk to him, but he must have left right after the ceremony."

If she were completely honest, she was a touch miffed that Tate kept repeating "it's still under investigation." Nielson had acted weird—even for him—on Saturday night. Without knowing how he died, she was reluctant to share anything negative now that he was gone.

Tate adjusted his hat. "Since you're the only administrator still here, we'll be in touch if we need anything else from Morton."

Cassandra would find out soon enough. She nibbled her lower lip.

News traveled fast in Carson.

Chapter Five

As soon as Deputy Tate's four-wheel drive SUV pulled out of her driveway, Cassandra called Cinda. "I just heard the strangest news. Dr. Nielson passed away." Saying the words out loud made her throat close up again.

"Well, now that makes sense." Cinda said.

It made no sense at all.

"The boys and I were outside shoveling the driveway a while ago and I saw the fire truck and ambulance go down the street. Maybe they stopped at Nielson's house."

Cassandra's mother would have walked down to see for herself if emergency vehicles had stopped on her street. "Did you see anything?"

"Nah. Justin hit Simon in the face with a snowball and his nose was bleeding. We went inside and I got distracted. You could call Andy. He knows those sheriff guys." Cassandra could hear the boys talking loudly in the background. Cinda said, "Sorry, I gotta go break this up before anyone gets an eye poked out."

A few minutes later, Cassandra was knee deep in her snowy driveway bundled like Ralphie in *A Christmas Story*.

Between her teary eyes, the stinging wind, and her runny nose, the scarf wrapped several times around her face was clammy wet. Her heartrate raced from shoveling the heavy snow.

Her concern about Dr. Nielson wouldn't go away, and she wanted to drive by his house to see what had happened. She must have inherited the nosiness gene from her mother.

She'd finished about one-third of her driveway when a Good Samaritan dressed like the abominable snowman in coveralls roared down the sidewalk. Pushing a large snowblower, he adjusted the metal chute to blow snow toward the yard and away from the wind. Within ten minutes he'd neatly cleared her entire driveway and the walkway to her front door. After shoveling off the front porch, Cassandra nearly fell to her knees in gratitude.

He shut off the engine when she walked up to him. The instant silence was disconcerting. Removing dark wrap-around sunglasses, he tugged down his scarf and revealed a movie star handsome face.

Cassandra's head jerked back slightly in surprise. She'd assumed by his friendly wave and the familiar way he walked behind the snowblower that it was her next-door neighbor Mr. Gill, but it wasn't him. Mr. Gorgeous held out a gloved hand and shook hers. "You must be Cassandra?"

Tongue-tied, Cassandra had just nodded. Where had he come from? Most of the homes surrounding hers were inhabited by retired baby boomers, young couples with small children, and college kids. She would have noticed this guy out raking leaves in the fall.

"Sean Gill." He pointed at the two-story Craftsman-style house on the other side of her driveway. "I'm staying with my parents for the holidays. You're the chocolate chip cookie baker, right? You'll have to join us for game night. Beware if my mother suggests Scrabble though. She never loses."

"Cassandra Sato." Her voice finally started working again. "Thanks for your help. My driveway is long." She wanted to smack her forehead. You'd think with a PhD she'd be able to speak in sentences longer than five words.

* * *

Backing down her driveway was easy, but the streets were packed with snow and Cassandra drove slowly. A Saunders County Sheriff car was parked in Nielson's driveway. More cars parked along the curb on both sides of the street making Cassandra wonder how the fire truck had squeezed between them.

She didn't know what she'd hoped to learn, but the house looked the same as it had when she and Cinda had stopped here Saturday with the addition of yellow crime scene tape blocking the front walkway. When Cassandra took her foot off the brake and eased it onto the gas pedal again, Deputy Tate appeared around the side of the house and locked eyes with her while she gawked.

"Busted!" she muttered and looked straight ahead. When she pulled up even with the sheriff's car, there he stood arms crossed over his chest. She pulled in behind a car along the curb, blocking half the driveway.

A blast of cold air poured inside when she rolled down the passenger window. Tate leaned his head closer. "Dr. Sato. I thought I made it clear that we are still investigating Gary Nielson's death. We don't need your help."

Ouch. He'd never used that tone with her before when they'd worked together. "I heard that Dr. Nielson had a medical issue," she stretched the truth. "I need to know what to tell Mr. Hershey from the board of directors when I call him. It's important I keep Morton officials informed."

"Nielson was a well-known person in town. All the more reason for us to keep details of our investigation confidential until we make an official statement." He held up his hands like he was frustrated with her. "Look. I understand you need to do your job, too. I can tell you he didn't die of natural causes. I really can't say more."

Cassandra told Tate goodbye and pulled away from the curb. She was already out on the roads, might as well stop at the Student Affairs office and pick up her laptop. She could outline her sections for the telecommunications grant or access her other documents from home and not completely waste a workday.

Thirty minutes later, Cassandra paused in her office doorway holding her laptop case when Andy Summers entered the darkened main office and held a drink holder with two cardboard cups out to her. "Decaf macchiato or Poor Man's Mocha?"

Normally there would be a student worker holding down the front desk and answering phones. But when Cassandra had called to cancel her meeting with Nielson, she'd also sent out a group text to the students telling them to stay home, too. Her officemate, the Assistant Director George Hansen, had prescheduled his vacation during the next two weeks. He did so little work on a good day that his absence wasn't noteworthy.

"Andy! How did you know I'd be here?" Cassandra pointed at the decaf cup.

"Saw your car in the parking lot. The Student Center's coffee shop is open during winter break." Andy handed the coffee over, unzipping his heavy Carhartt canvas jacket. "I'm actually kind of impressed that you drove to the office with this storm. I half-expected a phone call asking for a ride."

Cassandra scoffed. "I'd still be in yoga pants cleaning my house if Deputy Tate hadn't come over."

"Yeah, that's too bad about Nielson."

Each time someone said his name, a new pang of grief hit her, Cassandra reached into her tote bag for her office keys. "Wait! You knew about Dr. Nielson and didn't call me?"

"It's an active police investigation, Cass. They have rules."

"But we're friends. And Dr. Nielson might be our boss. I don't actually know whether he signed a new contract."

"Either way, it looks like you're the boss this week," said Andy. "I heard the forensics people had a heck of a time driving up from Lincoln with the road conditions. So weird, the president's job has been like a revolving door the past couple of months. We'll find out more when the autopsy is finished."

She remembered now that Andy had worked for the sheriff's office before becoming Morton's security director.

He obviously had the inside scoop. "Look, I know you can't tell me confidential details, but you can at the very least tell me how Dr. Nielson died. Deputy Tate only said it wasn't from natural causes, but I need to notify key people with the college that he's not coming back."

Andy's eyes got that longing stare she recognized. The one when he wrestled between his desire to follow the rules of his job and the crush he had on her. Their friendship had been platonic all semester, but if she gave him the go ahead, she knew he'd be happy to change that status. "You'll probably read this in the newspaper soon. Someone robbed Nielson's house. Maybe they'd watched the house and counted on it being vacant, not knowing he was in town last weekend. Looks like he surprised the robbers and they shot him."

Cassandra had assumed he died from a car accident, or another sudden injury. Knowing it was violent made her heartsick. "Oh, that's terrible!"

Now that Nielson was gone, she wanted to remember him in the best light possible and overlook his personal quirks, including his weird visit Saturday night. Good thing she hadn't mentioned it to Deputy Tate earlier. She'd let the poor man rest in peace.

"Thanks for the coffee. I've had enough caffeine, but I'm always cold."

Andy said, "I thought you might need a pick me up. I stopped home to let Buckley out. He's not used to being in the kennel all day and I was worried." Andy had adopted his stray dog a couple of weeks ago, and whenever he mentioned Buckley, Andy's eyes lit up with happiness.

"Don't feel bad," said Cassandra. She'd agreed to take on Murphy a few days after Andy had rescued Buckley. "Murphy has accidents all the time. I do laundry almost every day to keep up with him."

"Oh, no. Buckley is pretty well house broken, but I just worry that he's lonely when I'm gone for more than a couple of hours. Normally I bring him to work with me, but with this snow I didn't think that was a great idea."

When Cassandra glanced at her office door, Nielson's cheery postcard taped below her name plate made her sinuses sting with unshed tears. "I imagined Dr. Nielson was having a great time in Florida." Nielson's outfit was straight out of an outdoor catalog's sale page with the multi-pocketed vest, khaki camp shorts, and sandals with crew length socks. Cassandra grabbed a tissue from a nearby desk and wiped under her eyes. "Look at this hat." She touched the photo. The floppy fishing hat had a thin plaid ribbon on the brim and several feathery lures stuck along the top.

"I just don't understand how this happened, Andy. Nielson spent his whole career serving others, loving his role as an academic. I want more answers."

"We'll find out more when they run the fingerprints and do the autopsy."

"I'm headed back home now. I just stopped in to get my laptop."

Andy waited while she locked the main office and walked her to the bottom of the stairwell. "I know you liked Dr. Nielson." He leaned over and gently tapped her coffee cup in a little toasting motion. "I'm sorry for your loss."

"It's hard to process." She wanted to remember Nielson's twinkly eyes and fatherly smile.

She had so many questions about Nielson's time in retirement and why he'd come back to town. Waiting was not her thing, but this time she had no choice.

* * *

Long past the time when Cassandra normally fell asleep, she leaned against a pillow propped up against her headboard, flipped through articles on her iPad, and wondered when there would be a local notice about Dr. Nielson's death. More snow was predicted overnight. She might have to shovel again before she could go into work the next morning.

She'd tried distracting herself by scrolling through super organized closets and storage solutions on Pinterest. Nothing was as calming as rows of color-coded hanging shirts and perfectly folded stacks in a large closet. Her own walk-in closet, though good-sized for the age of the house, was barely functional with one hanging rod and a high shelf she couldn't reach without a stepladder. One of the projects she'd looked forward to tackling over winter break was installing lower rods to accommodate shirts and jackets and stacking shoe shelves.

Instead of drifting to sleep dreaming of perfectly aligned plastic shoe containers in rows, Cassandra kept thinking about Dr. Nielson. She'd seen him in the graduation audience for an hour and their conversation at her house was less than fifteen minutes long. Cassandra felt unsettled about his sudden death.

Nothing had hit the newspapers yet. Maybe the sheriff's office hadn't finished notifying all his next of kin. Cassandra would wait a day or more and check in with them again.

Normally Cassandra didn't give up so easily. Her Chinese zodiac sign was an Ox, after all. She was crafty enough to find another way to get more details about the robbery and his death.

Cassandra had started the semester with a planner full of dreams and visions for what her life would be like in Nebraska. But dealing with unpredictable bosses, a student's untimely death, and scary student injuries had hijacked her careful goal setting. It felt like a run of bad luck.

Traditionally for good luck in the American New Year, her family baked mochi. Maybe she should go full-on Japanese old lady and do the whole good luck menu. Cassandra didn't want to become the next person who would have the bad luck.

Chapter Six

Bad luck came for her before she even had a chance to shop at the market for baking supplies. The noise was as loud as a gunshot but lasted longer. Cassandra had only been asleep a few hours. At first, she thought the noise was in a dream. Blinking, she wiped her eyes and stilled under the warm comforter listening to the wind rustle the bush outside her bedroom window. Heavy gusts came in waves like water on the beach.

Murphy was the one who had convinced her to get out of bed. His intermittent barking finally prompted Cassandra to push the covers off, slide her feet into sheepskin slippers, and grip the baseball bat. Not that she expected a bad guy on the other side of her bedroom door.

"Murphy, I heard it too. I know it was loud, but it's just the wind." Standing in the darkened office, she peered through the kennel. Maybe he had messed on his towel again. So far all of his "accidents" had been during the day. She was profoundly grateful that he usually slept through the night uninterrupted.

Nothing smelled bad. "Shhh." She placed a finger over her mouth as though he were a toddler. Turning to go back to her room, she shivered in her house's cool air. She hadn't realized how cold it was during the night while she was tucked into her warm bed.

Murphy whined. Maybe he needed to pee now that he was awake. Maybe she did too.

Grabbing a fleece blanket from the back of the couch, she wrapped it tightly around her and opened his kennel. Unlocking the front door, she let him out to do his business quickly and return right back inside.

Only Murphy had other plans. After he lifted his leg on the snow pile she'd shoveled that morning, he ran around the side of the house down the driveway toward the back yard.

"Oh dog, you are killin' me, brah!"

Cassandra chased after him still wearing her sheepskin slippers, the blanket trailing behind like a superhero's cape. "Mur-phy, come here," she whispered angrily. She didn't want to wake the neighbors at 3:00 a.m. Squinting into the unnaturally bright night from the snow's reflection, she couldn't see the dog.

Fresh snow came down in sideways gusts and covered the driveway. She did not have the patience for this.

Stomping back into the house, she traded her slippers for the taller suede snow boots sitting on a plastic tray by the back door and threw on her puffy parka. When she yanked open the side door, a hooded guy stood in the driveway looking at her house.

A startled yelp escaped her lips at the same time the figure held out his hands to her calmly. "Cassandra. It's Sean Gill."

"What the heck, you scared the crap out of me!"

"Are you okay? Did you hear that noise?" He cautiously stepped closer.

"Wait—you heard it too? I thought maybe I was overreacting to the wind." Cassandra headed for the corner toward the back yard to find the dog. "I let Murphy out to go to the bathroom, but he ran off. He must be back here somewhere."

Gill squatted and in an encouraging voice called, "Murphy! C'mere boy!"

"I tried that, but he's stubborn."

First, she heard his collar jangling then saw him trot toward them on the driveway. Only instead of heading for the person who had been feeding him, sheltering him, and changing his wet kennel, he rubbed up against Gill's shins and barked in satisfaction when he patted Murphy's white head. Gill reached down and picked up the dog. Again, no barking or fuss.

Cassandra had reached the back door when she heard Gill. "Oh... *that* was the noise. A tree smashed your roof, Cassandra!"

His tone of voice had Cassandra's immediate attention. She boomeranged back around the corner of the house and looked up. One of the gorgeous old cottonwood trees that had provided cool shade over her backyard during the hot summer had broken apart and a large branch had landed on the opposite back corner of her house and deck.

"Oh no!" Cassandra stood on the edge of the back yard in the mostly shoveled driveway and pressed her hands together. Her head shook back and forth. Maybe the tree was simply resting on her roof, but she wouldn't know for sure until morning when they could see better.

"Want me to come in and check it out?" Gill asked.

Small towns were famous for being safe at 3:00 a.m., but that didn't mean she needed to let a stranger inside her house. Cassandra hesitated. Shivering from head to toe, she cleared her negative thoughts. This was her kind neighbors' son. He had no hidden agenda.

Cassandra nodded and they went inside, bringing Murphy along.

Gill removed his snow boots by the back door and followed Cassandra up the spiral wooden staircase to the second floor. "My parent's house has the same design. We called these the Stairs of Death because all three of us kids fell down them at some time growing up."

The first door opened onto a spare bedroom where Cassandra intended to put guests some day when she got organized and actually bought an extra mattress set. Everything inside looked the way Cassandra had left it. The upstairs bathroom, too, was untouched.

A blast of cold air reached Cassandra as soon as she opened the third door to the empty bedroom. Reflecting snow revealed a large hole in the ceiling with tree branches poking through. Plaster chunks and debris littered the floor and bowing attic beams clung to exposed ceiling drywall which had been punctured by the offending tree branch. The branch itself was maybe 20 inches diameter and the smaller pieces had sheared off as it smashed through her roof.

She hit the light switch, but nothing happened. She had no electricity.

No wonder the house had felt cold when she'd first gotten out of bed. Cassandra slowly raised her hands to cover her mouth. What was she supposed to do now?

Gill was already halfway down the steps. "I'll grab a tarp from my parents' garage. If we cover your boxes and close the bedroom door, it should protect your stuff from getting too wet until morning."

"A tarp! Yes, good idea." Cassandra mobilized into action. She shoved cardboard boxes into the corner as far away from the hole as possible.

Thirty minutes later, her hickory floors were covered in a blue tarp anchored by boxes. An extra blanket was stuffed under the door crack of the spare bedroom to keep the cold air inside. Sean Gill had promised to be back when it was daylight.

Cassandra lay on the couch, covered in two fleece blankets and pulled up Netflix on her iPad. Grateful for long battery life and cell service, she turned the volume to a low murmur. When she was nearly asleep, a cold nose bumped the fingers resting on the edge of the couch. Opening her eyes, Murphy's face was inches away from hers, staring expectantly.

She scooted further back into the couch leaving enough space for him to jump up and curl into a small ball in front of her. Within minutes, he snored lightly. She had intended to have a strict "no furniture" rule when she'd agreed to take him in. But this *one time* his warm weight cuddled against her felt good.

* * *

"Look, miss, I'm truly sorry we can't do much for you today. You've already protected the floor." Mid-morning on Tuesday, the temperature was at least 20 degrees colder in her spare room than the rest of the house.

Despite having his name—Norm—hand-lettered in black sharpie on a patch over his heart, the coverall wearing handyman had not given the small-town-looking-out-for-a-fellow-resident response Cassandra had expected. "Norm. Uh... Don't you know another guy you can call and cut that thing down?" She pleaded with the massive, dark-haired repairman whose brown work boots dripped melted snow on her kitchen floor.

Normally, she would be irritated at his rudeness coming inside her house wearing wet shoes. But his wet shoes seemed the least of her problems. She'd also left a voicemail at the power company to report her outage.

"Actually, I *am* the other guy. My two other workers are helping customers across town. Yours wasn't the only tree that got taken out by last night's wind."

"Well, okay. But when can you come back and fix it?" Taking shallow breaths, she stared at a deep white scar on Norm's cheek.

"We might be able to stop by tomorrow afternoon and put plywood over the hole until we can get a more permanent solution figured out." Norm jotted notes on a work order attached to his clipboard. "Christmas is on Friday. It's gonna be a while before the whole thing's fixed."

Her eyes welled up with unwanted tears while she calculated the money and time it would take to fix this. She'd used all of her savings for the down payment and wasn't prepared to pay an insurance deductible so soon after moving in. One of the attractive features of her back yard had been the large cottonwood tree offering shade to her deck and house. Was a fallen tree branch an Act of God or was it covered? As long as no lasting damage happened to her floors or belongings, she could wait a few days.

Maybe she should have ignored her brother's advice to jump into the affordable Nebraska housing market. She'd lived a privileged, sheltered life until this point. Her father had taken care of her insurance needs before the move.

Buying a house was risky, but she'd craved the marker of success so badly. Most of her high school and college classmates still lived with their parents or shared tiny condos with several friends. Even married couples with children usually lived with grandparents for years while they saved up money toward a down payment or waited until their own parents passed away and the family home was transferred to their names.

As soon as it was a reasonable hour back home, she would call Keoni. He'd reassure her that she'd made the right decision.

Cassandra stood on the front porch watching Norm back his truck down the driveway, revealing a man standing on the neighbors' porch. He waved and gave her a smile.

Sean Gill looked like a good night's sleep. She self-consciously patted her ponytail thinking she looked like a rumpled zombie.

"How'd it go?" he called across the driveway.

In daylight without mascara, she felt vulnerable. Like the makeup she normally wore was the competent mask she showed the world. Absent contour and color, she was younger, more unsure of her decisions. "Norm can't fix it right away, but he'll call me back this afternoon."

Cassandra couldn't force herself to sound optimistic. She was too busy beating herself up.

Gill said, "I haven't lived in town for a while, but one of my old high school buddies runs a small painting and remodeling crew. I could call him for you."

Cassandra was frustrated enough that she jumped at the chance. "You know, yes I'd like that. Norm told me he was backed up. I guess there's been tree damage all over town."

Gill waved and gave a thumbs up as he ducked inside his house. She'd have to stay home until the hole was covered and she could clean up the mess. It was only Tuesday, but already the week felt like a sinking ship.

Chapter Seven

Cassandra really wanted to call her brother, but the time difference made that rude. In the meantime, Cassandra called the O'Briens while Hawai'i still slept.

A man's voice answered. "Hey, Connor. I was calling Meg, but you'd maybe be a better person for me to talk to."

"Were you wondering about the merits of the flea flicker versus the fumblerooski?"

The involuntary temptation to bang her head was strong. She looked at her phone like, *what*?

Oh wait, Connor had made a lame joke. "Ha, ha. No football emergencies here, but I was wondering if you know anything about tree branches falling on roofs. How long does it usually take to get electricity turned back on when you have an outage?"

"What... are you serious! A tree branch crushed your house. Do you need me to come over? Are you hurt?" He switched into knight in shining armor mode immediately.

Before Cassandra could answer, he was talking to Meg in the background. "Cass's house got damaged by a tree branch from the storm. I'll go over there and fix her up."

"I'm fine!" Cassandra shouted into the phone before he alerted the whole countryside and roused the volunteer fire department to come to her rescue. "I've got a tarp on the floor. I found some help. You don't have to come over. I just wanted to talk to Meg."

"Oh. Why didn't you say so?" he passed the phone to Meg.

"What happened? The storm wasn't that bad."

Cassandra's voice wavered although she tried to just give the facts. "Middle of the night. A huge cracking noise woke me and the dog up. I grabbed the baseball bat next to my bed and hurried into the office but couldn't figure out what made the noise."

"Why do you have a baseball bat next to your bed?"

Duh. Meg should know why. "Because, my Halloween stalker guy. What if he comes back? You don't just forget something like that and go back to normal living. Anyway,..." She stamped her foot on the kitchen floor in frustration. "Focus here."

"I liked that tree, but it looked a little tall and close to the house." Meg's voice turned away from the phone to Connor who must have been standing close by, "Didn't I tell you that, honey?"

"It would have been nice if you'd told ME that the tree was too tall and close to my house. Because right now half of it is actually lying on top of my house. One branch poked right through the roof. And it made a huge mess."

"Wow that totally sucks. Especially so close to Christmas. There's no way anyone is going to fix it right away. Hey, . . . I already invited you over for Christmas Eve. Why don't you come early and sleep here?"

"No, I'm fine. I don't want to impose. The damage is upstairs. I'll be good." She had more blankets. Even to her own ears it rang hollow.

Cassandra was actually less optimistic than she acted for Meg.

It had turned out that working from home wasn't very productive. Wearing three layers of sweatshirts and thick socks for warmth had made Cassandra look and feel like a hibernating polar bear. After her phone calls, the nearby couch called her name. Four hours of sleep hadn't been enough.

Her phone ringing roused her from her nap, and she answered the call from an unknown local number. "Is this Cassandra Sato? This is Wendy from the power company. You reported an outage in your area? We have restored power to everyone on your block already."

After thanking the woman for the update, they hung up. Cassandra flipped the lights on, but nothing happened. She stared at the offending light switch and stretched her achy back wondering what to do next.

She didn't have to think long because Sean Gill rapped on the back door. "Hey, my friend is on his way over to temporarily cover the hole in your roof."

On the ground behind him was a large yellow ladder and a coil of rope.

"That's great. Thanks so much."

How was he so perky fresh after the interrupted night's sleep? Cassandra felt hung over and funky from not showering.

Sean Gill was too good to be true. She'd only seen him wearing a thick hooded winter parka and hat, but the parts of his face she could see were well put together. Even Fischer wasn't as dazzling.

Looking for a distraction, she called her brother in Hawai'i. Thankfully Keoni didn't annoy her by teasing her like she'd made a mistake becoming a homeowner.

"No worries, Cass. You had no way of knowing the tree was going to fall on your house. Don't blame yourself."

"Did they not inspect those things before I signed the closing papers? Maybe the tree was already damaged and if I had known I would've had it removed."

"You can beat yourself up all day, but you can't change it, sis. Call the insurance phone number to make a claim. Your repair guy might not do anything until you get word from the adjuster that his estimate is approved. Sometimes they make you get several estimates."

"There's like 4,000 people besides our college in this whole town, brah. I don't even know how many businesses do home repairs."

Cassandra leaned against the kitchen counter, ate her PB&J sandwich, and listened to the ladder thudding against the side of her house, then footsteps on her roof.

She paced into the sunroom and stared out the bay window. A team of neighborhood helping hands had traded their snowblowers for chainsaws. The men walked up and down the block cutting fallen tree limbs to clear driveways and the roads.

Half an hour later Sean was in her kitchen, hands on his hips, his expression grim.

Her eyes squinted and she braced herself for the estimate.

"We've got plywood nailed down to roughly cover the hole. The tree took out a corner of your attic, but my buddy Craig says he can fix it."

That didn't sound awful. Or too expensive.

"That was the good news. You ready for the bad news?"

She inhaled a big cleansing breath and nodded.

"The tree clipped the power line that feeds into your house. My parents only lost power for an hour. Yours is still out because they have to come repair the line from the street."

She couldn't stay in the house with no electricity. Meg had invited her over there, but she didn't want to be a burden. Her office had a couch, but no place to shower.

"I'm waiting for a call back from the power company." Her heart fluttered with anxiety that everything was happening at once. Cassandra folded her arms over her stomach to hide a shiver. "When can you guys fix the roof?"

"Realistically? After Christmas weekend. We'll have to order the attic beams from Omaha."

All the home improvement and decorating projects Cassandra thought she'd tackle over break were now pushed aside by Mother Nature. Disappointment rendered her speechless.

"Do you have somewhere you can stay for a few days? Maybe a week."

She'd grown attached to her small, old-fashioned kitchen and the ancient wallpaper she'd planned to scrape off this weekend. "I have somewhere in mind."

Sean's voice softened like he had noticed how much this upset her. "Not to assume that you can't figure it out, ... but do you want my help turning off the water and opening the kitchen cabinets so your pipes don't freeze?"

All this week needed was a burst water pipe. She led him to the basement. "Show me what to do."

After Sean and his friend left, Cassandra folded clothes and considered various scenarios in her head. She packed three days' worth of items into her bag. That would last her until Christmas.

She was tempted to call in favors, but she was a grown woman. She'd already talked to Sean and her brother. It was time to follow her instincts. After making a call to the Picotte Residential Assistant to confirm that there were extra rooms available in the students' dorm, Cassandra decided to stay there until repairs were complete.

Staying in the residence hall had the added benefit of giving her an opportunity to get to know the students better. The day had been so exhausting, Cassandra would unpack, hunker down in the warm room, and go to sleep early. She would make the best of a difficult situation.

It wasn't until she'd tucked her overnight bag in the trunk of her car and returned inside that she noticed Murphy sitting quietly in the hallway. He'd watched her packing and carrying her stuff from bedroom and bathroom to the back door without making a peep.

She couldn't very well foist her new foster dog off on someone else. He'd have to come with her. Most likely there was a no pets allowed rule in on-campus housing.

Who better to break the rules than the acting college administrator? She'd keep him on the down low.

Crossing her arms over her chest, she let his leash dangle from one hand as they faced each other. "You know how to be a good boy when you feel like it, right?"

Murphy barked once, sharply.

"I'm going to take that as a yes."

Chapter Eight

Sleeping on campus meant that Cassandra was showered, dressed and in her office by 6:30 a.m. just like her usual routine. The campus maintenance staff had plowed the sidewalks and Cassandra only had to walk from Picotte Hall to the Osborne building. She had plenty to catch up on after two days at home. A quiet morning was the perfect time to finalize the spring's student activities master calendar and tweak updates to the Student Code of Conduct and handbook for later approval at the next department meeting. She craved some semblance of routine to make her feel grounded.

Murphy was used to spending the days following his owner around an office building. So that was one piece of luck. He seemed happier in the office basking in the glow of attention from Cassandra's student worker Bridget who was scheduled for today and half of Christmas Eve.

At noon, Cassandra asked Bridget to keep an eye on Murphy while she walked to Picotte looking for lunch. Her last sight of Murphy as she stepped out the door was him nuzzling Bridget's neck while she scratched under his chin.

Cassandra swore Murphy peeked an eye open long enough to give her a smug grin.

Picotte was the oldest out of the four campus dorms with small residential wings enclosing a central courtyard. The traditional style reminded Cassandra of a cross between Oxford and Hogwarts.

What she found inside Picotte surprised even her. The common room looked like something out of the movie Old School. Greasy pizza boxes stacked up in one corner, overflowing trash bins filled with beer cans and large glass liquor bottles gave off a stale smell of neglect. Two students stretched out on the L-shaped couch in front of the TV where they watched a movie featuring skimpy swimsuit-clad Spring Breakers partying.

Her eyebrows must have shot to her hairline.

Around the corner in the shared kitchen area was even worse. Cassandra flipped the light switch on and squeaked as a cockroach scurried under the sink's cabinet. Dirty dishes and takeout containers littered the sink and nearby countertop.

How could 25 students eating in the cafeteria for most of their meals make this mess in only four days?

Pulling the fire alarm was very tempting, but now that she knew those local fire department guys were all volunteers, she wouldn't waste their time. They'd hurry into town, hop into their truck, and drive over to this slum, just so she could make a point.

Gingerly, Cassandra opened the pantry door and found a mop and bucket, one spray bottle of bleach cleanser, and a box of rubber gloves.

Putting on a pair of gloves, she walked up and down the hallway knocking on every door, shouting as she went. "Hello! Time to wake up! Let's go! Out here."

Within minutes a small group was assembled in the common room in various stages of dress.

"What the—"

They all looked like zombies with dark circles around their eyes, hair sticking up or pulled back into dirty ponytails.

"Who are you? I don't hafta wake up."

"I'm on winter break, dude."

Cassandra waited for them to stop complaining.

"You're not my mom. You can't tell me when to come out."

They were going to wish she was their mom by the time Cassandra was done here. Their moms were probably much nicer people.

Her blue gloved hands held a mop and the bucket, a box of trash bags sat nearby on the table. Cassandra said, "Of course I'm not your mother. This is my job. If your mothers were here, none of you would be trashing this place. What is wrong with you all?"

Yelling at them wasn't going to accomplish anything. She took a big breath. "I'm going to be living here for the next week. My house got damaged by the storm the other night." Taking two steps, she handed the mop to a heavy kid with a week's worth of scraggly beard. "And I don't live in a hovel. Starting today, neither will you."

She handed the bucket to a girl who had to put down her phone to accept it.

"Why are you making *me* do the mopping?" she sneered. "I didn't eat none of the pizza."

"Don't worry. Everyone will help. We won't leave out anyone." Picking up the trash bags, she passed out a couple to the nearest students. "Everyone else, come get a trash bag and gloves." Cassandra handed a quiet girl who looked familiar the spray cleaner and a roll of paper towels. "Jasmine, right? You can start wiping down the counters and fridge."

Holding up her phone, Cassandra used it to take a 'before' video and made sure to get the faces of everyone in the room. Most of their expressions were annoyed, appalled, or angry. "I'm setting a timer for 20 minutes. You'd better hustle your butts and get this whole thing cleaned up. No slinking off to hide in your rooms either. I will write you up if you disappear."

Working with middle schoolers during her first job out of college had prepared Cassandra for difficult young adults for life. She clapped her hands together. "Ready, set, GO!"

Standing in the hallway screaming at them to work during the timer was what Cassandra really wanted to do. Instead, she forced herself to step into her own room and dig around her bag until she found her emergency stash of energy bars. No lunch food and a kitchen with bugs was emergency enough for her to call that today's lunch.

Cassandra's home was meticulously spotless, just like her mother's and her gran's before then. But credit for her current by the book strictness had started with her brother, Keoni. She rarely admitted that it had taken her overprotective brother setting her straight, instead of her own maturity and realization that things had needed to change.

The summer before she had met Paul Watanabe in college, Cassandra went off the rails, falling in with a crowd of partying surfers who drank and smoked weed. She followed along, and it almost cost her bachelor's degree. While partying one night, she bumped into a group of teachers from the middle school where she would student teach the next semester. Cassandra had been so out of it she didn't remember the end of the night. The next morning, Keoni woke her up at dawn, ignored her monster hangover, and warned about throwing away her future. From that day forward, she got herself together by dropping the loser friends. Within a few months, she began student teaching, met Paul, and became the disciplined person who wouldn't spend a week in a pig sty residence hall, no matter how uncool she seemed.

After Paul had died, Cassandra talked to Keoni about that summer night and he confided what he'd kept secret. Keoni had been out at the beach with some friends and arrived home after midnight to find Cassandra passed out on the front yard in a heap, reeking of alcohol and pot. Her clothes were dirty and ripped. He picked her up, carried her inside and set her in the shower, then helped her dress before dumping her in bed. She passed out again. He left the house, found her best friend, Tami, and told her that Cassandra wasn't hanging out with them anymore. "If Cassandra calls you, make an excuse for why you can't see her."

Cassandra had wondered that summer and occasionally through the years why her friends had suddenly become distant, never realizing it had been her brother's doing.

The Picotte dorm room smelled faintly of disinfectant. Judging from the institutional cement block walls and weird shelving in the closet, she suspected the space had previously been a cleaning closet.

Once she'd used the bathroom and eaten her energy bar, Cassandra went back to the common room. The air contained a satisfying bleach smell, the trash was empty.

Sullen young adults stomped around throwing away junk, plumping couch cushions, and someone had even located a vacuum cleaner that they were using to suck up a week's worth of crumbs from the industrial carpet.

Everyone had taken her threat of being written up to heart. Or maybe they also were tired of living in squalor. All except for a couple lying on a corner couch on the far end of the common area by a ping pong table.

Cassandra approached, taking in the young woman's expensive lounge pants and tunic, her dark, twisted hair piled high on her head and held in place with a colorful scarf wrapped around it several times.

The guy had a faint mustache, dark rimmed glasses, and a black t-shirt advertising an 80's heavy metal band. His eyes were glued to his phone and he didn't even see Cassandra until she was right up next to them.

Hands on her hips, she challenged them with both eyebrows raised. The guy darted a look at the girl, then eased forward as if to get up. She held him back with a palm on his shoulder. He looked uncomfortably stuck between two women with opposing agendas.

"Don't, Daniel. She can't make us do nothin'. We pay our college fees. They have janitors and people who're supposed to clean our floor. I don't take orders like a child." She held herself regally, like a woman used to people listening to her, not the other way around.

When he looked back at Cassandra, his half-smile wasn't filled with nearly as much bravado as the young lady's British accent. Not exactly UK British. Maybe a Caribbean island?

Cassandra's lips pressed into a flat line. She, too, was used to people following her directions. The girl's face was familiar. "I've seen you before."

The guy's too. Several seconds later, she remembered them from the graduation ceremony. "You're the couple with the air horn from last Saturday morning, right? Sela and Daniel."

Although the girl's face looked less glamorous today, she was still beautiful. Her dark eyebrows weren't as well-defined without the pencil filling them in, her skin tone was uneven without concealer or foundation, and her normal-sized eyelashes not nearly as thick as they'd been with full extensions.

Now that she'd recognized them, Daniel seemed more nervous. "We didn't mean any harm Saturday. We told security that we were just cheering for our friends." He spoke in standard American English without any accent that Cassandra recognized.

Cassandra wasn't a complete grinch. She smiled. "I get it, really. It's just that graduation is a family event and not everyone appreciated the noise and interruptions."

Sela still looked at Cassandra like she had three heads.

"But here's the thing." Cassandra lowered her voice enough that the couple had to lean in to hear her. It was an old teacher's trick. "The cleaners are down to a skeleton crew over the holidays so they can be home with their families. And while we're away from our families, this is where we hang out during break. No one wants to live with cockroaches and stale food. If we keep everything picked up, we can do more fun stuff together."

Sela said, "The dance party was Monday night. You missed it."

That moment, a guy wearing a ball cap passed by the community room heading down the hallway pushing a keg on a cart.

Cassandra ran after him. "Hey, wait! Excuse me! What's this?"

The keg guy pulled out his phone, looking up and down the hallway with wide eyes. "Uh . . . I'm dropping this off for my friend."

She held her hand out like a stop sign, then pointed toward the exit. "Hey braddah, we're a dry campus."

At his blank stare, Cassandra added, "No alcohol on campus." She pulled out her phone and snapped a photo of his face. "What's your name?"

Frowning, he returned the phone to his back pocket. "You don't have to be testy." He looked down at the dirty cart's wheels in indecision.

"No way," she insisted. "No kegs. *Out* before I call security."

He shrugged, let out a sigh, and rolled out the way he came.

The timer's alarm went off. The students put away the cleaning supplies and stood together expectantly in the area between the kitchen and common room.

"Looks much better now, thanks," Cassandra enthused. "I'm pretty sure there's decorating supplies in the storage closet. If I can find a Christmas tree and some decorations, would any of you be up for decorating it together later? We could watch *Elf* or something and make some snacks?"

Jasmine's face lit up. "I love *Elf*!"

The others looked more skeptical.

"This ain't some family movie," said the heavy kid with the scraggly beard. Cassandra couldn't tell from his accent which country he was from. Maybe Canada? "We're all stuck here in the middle of nowhere. This is more like *Lord of the Flies* than *Elf*."

"I get that you're all far from home during the holidays. But if we want to have fun, we have to make it fun."

"It was going to be fun until someone stopped the keg guy."

Several of them snickered.

"You don't all have to get smashed to have a good time. Come on! I'll find the decorations and leave the boxes on the counter here. Maybe I can stop at the store and pick up some groceries. You can all write ingredients on a list, and I'll bring them back with me after work tonight?"

DEAD OF *Winter Break*

A Japanese student nodded. "Are we going to have an authentic American Christmas?"

Another student said, "You're not my mom. Stop acting like my mom. This is so lame."

"You don't have to help if you don't want. I'm not assuming everyone celebrates Christmas." Cassandra shrugged, "Personally, I've always liked the twinkly lights on the tree." She zipped up her coat to go back to the office and wrote her phone number on a notepad. "Seriously. If you guys write a shopping list and send me a photo, I'll stop after work and bring the food home from the market. Anything. Cookie dough." She eyed the large stone-faced fireplace and bookshelves that took up almost an entire wall of the common room. "Hot cocoa. Hey, is there any wood for that fireplace?"

"There's a big pile around the back of the hall." The Japanese student's strong accent forced her to listen to him carefully. "I can bring some logs inside." The excitement vibrated off him in waves.

A quick visual check around the room showed several other students had put down their phones and turned their eyes toward her with anticipation.

"Mate," said a curly blonde-haired kid with permanent tan lines where his sunglasses would normally sit, whose accent reminded Cassandra of an Australian surfer. "I already told you there's no KFC in Carson, Nebraska. Real Americans don't eat KFC for Christmas, dude."

Cassandra laughed quietly. "I'll see what I can find." She didn't know when the KFC for Christmas myth had started in Japan, but it was fantastic.

Walking to her office, Cassandra hoped the international students would take her up on the American Christmas Night In idea. She'd seen Keoni use bribery to work magic on her nephews' behavior. Crossing fingers, it worked on college kids, too.

Chapter Nine

Cassandra returned to her office and opened the student handbook draft to make final changes. Bridget, the student worker in the front office, carried in two small wrapped gifts with cards and placed them on the edge of Cassandra's desk. "One's from me, and the other looks like a Secret Santa gift."

"Thank you! You didn't have to do that." She gently squeezed the rectangular box. "Dark chocolate?" she guessed.

Bridget smiled. "Thanks for the coffee gift card. I can always use that."

Cassandra tucked the gifts away to open on Christmas day, loving the anticipation and surprise. Before she'd even written a full paragraph on the handbook, Andy called. "Hey, just checking in. Did your house get fixed?"

"Not yet. I ended up moving in with the international students in Picotte Hall." Her phone rested on the desktop with FaceTime opened which meant Andy looked at her ceiling while she topped off her Morton travel cup with filtered water from her mini fridge.

"You moved? I didn't think the hole in your roof was that big."

"It's pretty bad. Some of the attic rafters broke. My neighbors' son got it boarded up. But the tree branch took out the power line to my house."

"Where's Murphy?" he asked.

She had left him in his kennel at the dorm this morning. "Murphy came with me to the residence hall. He likes the attention from the other students and seems used to hanging out in an office during the day."

"I brought Buckley to work with me, too, but he doesn't like sitting. Maybe because he was a stray. He seems more active than we can be right now with the snow. He'll love it when the weather is better, and we can walk all over campus together."

Having never owned a pet before, every small detail was new to Cassandra. "If I keep Murphy, I'll have to buy a second kennel for him in my office. He can nap while I'm out of the office at meetings."

"What do you mean, 'if you keep Murphy'? I thought you already adopted him."

"I promised to try it out. If he isn't housebroken soon, I can't keep him. It's a lot of work washing the towels and cleaning up his messes all the time." He'd been accident-free for two days because she came back every few hours to let him outside.

"I can take him while you're in the dorms."

"Thanks, but not necessary." She'd made a promise and wouldn't give up too easily. "I'm bringing him to the O'Briens' house tomorrow. They have a dog too, and their son Tony will love playing with Murphy."

Anticipation warmed her at the thought of spending a day with Tony, Meg, and Connor. Tony's busyness would keep her mind off of Nielson's death, and the homesickness that swamped her every time she looked at the Wyland underwater ocean print in her office.

"What have you heard about Nielson since Monday?" The newspaper only had a one paragraph bit in the police report saying that a 71-year-old man had been found dead in his home and that police were investigating. "I thought news traveled fast in small towns. I thought we'd know more by now."

Andy shook his head and grunted a small laugh. "Not when everyone's busy chopping fallen tree branches and shoveling snow. It's been less than 48 hours. Nielson came home early and interrupted some robbers. An awful tragedy. Open and shut. Why are you so interested?"

"Isn't it enough that I knew him? I left a voicemail for Becky, Dr. Nielson's wife, but she hasn't called me back. She must be very upset."

"I didn't realize you two were that close."

He seemed skeptical. Or maybe Cassandra was just feeling edgy.

"I've met her several times before and wanted to give her my condolences." Cassandra propped the phone against a book so she could see Andy better. "We just texted each other Saturday after graduation."

Andy frowned. "On Saturday? For what?"

Time moved in slow motion while Cassandra considered that telling the truth would lead her down a path she'd intended to keep quiet out of respect for Nielson's memory.

Saving his wife grief was a valid reason to lie. But it still felt wrong.

"Cinda and I wanted to chat with Dr. Nielson after graduation. We stopped at his office and his house but missed him. Becky texted me and asked if I knew where her husband was. We didn't know either."

"Wasn't it strange that she asked you?"

"Becky had my phone number because she'd invited me to join her book club and had texted me once or twice before. I didn't think it was weird. Sometimes Nielson mixed up his appointments or agendas. And maybe she thought I knew."

Now was the moment when she should admit that she'd spoken to Nielson later at her house.

Instead she let Andy talk. "Well, the autopsy will tell the sheriff more details about the weapon. The state patrol will run any fingerprints through their system."

Cassandra closed her eyes and counted to three. "Andy, is there any way the police are wrong about Dr. Nielson?"

"Wrong about what?" He frowned. "Over a third of homicides go unsolved every year. They aren't going to solve this in an hour like on NCIS."

"I'm just trying to understand if police are certain it was a simple robbery. When Nielson stopped at my house Saturday night, he acted jumpy and told me he'd sent his wife to Iowa for safety. Someone had sent him threatening texts. I encouraged him to contact the sheriff."

Andy leaned in closer to the camera which made Cassandra instinctively back away from her phone. "What the heck? Why didn't you tell Tate?"

"Don't take that tone with me," Cassandra chided. "Deputy Tate told me several times to mind my own business, and he didn't need my assistance with his investigation. You told me before that Nielson surprised the robbers. I didn't want to make a big deal out of nothing."

"But you still called his wife to ask more questions and do your own—"

First Deputy Tate assumed she was nosing her way into their investigation and now Andy implied the same thing. "I told you, I called Becky to tell her how sorry I am that she lost her husband!" Cassandra's voice rose to match Andy's volume. "I've been thinking about it for two days now and I'm worried. Most of what Nielson said was gibberish. He mentioned the October exchange trip to China, talking to someone from the USDA, and a proprietary soybean formula. He said someone followed him. Like a local spy. I thought he was crazy."

"You have to tell Deputy Tate so he can follow up with Becky."

"Will a call from law enforcement spook her?"

"If the government has already been in touch with Nielson, she is correct to be spooked," said Andy. "Someone shot her husband and until we find out more, she should be careful."

That's what Cassandra was afraid of. If it wasn't a simple robbery, then Carson had a killer on the loose and Cassandra was one of the last people to talk to Gary Nielson.

There was one more thing she needed to know. "I never asked before, but you said Nielson was shot. Like where on his body?" Cassandra's stomach really couldn't take squeamish details, but she had to know enough to be helpful. She hunched up her shoulders. "Was he executed?"

"I shouldn't say any more. Why do you want to know?"

Cassandra didn't like his tone but wasn't going to argue with Andy. "Because I don't want anyone else on campus or in town to get hurt. We need to make sure that Nielson's last actions help catch the person who did this."

Andy shrugged. "I'm not a detective. But from the police report, it didn't look like an execution."

A big breath oozed out of Cassandra's lungs and she felt a teeny bit better knowing someone didn't kill Nielson in cold blood. Which was a strange thing to think because the circumstances didn't change the outcome. Her former boss was still dead.

"It was bad luck," Andy pointed to his thigh. "The bullet hit his thigh. Nicked the femoral artery."

"Could it have been an accident?"

"I'm not sure *your* definition," said Andy. "But when someone aims a gun at a person and pulls the trigger, it's tough to call it an accident."

Cassandra glared at Andy. "Sarcasm is unnecessary. What if the person who shot Nielson intended to warn him? I mean, who aims for the thigh?"

"Hard to say," Summers shrugged. "Poor guy would have lived if he'd gotten medical help right away. He tried to save himself using his own tie as a tourniquet."

Summers' description of the crime scene was more graphic than Cassandra had envisioned. Digested granola bar raised up her esophagus and into the back of her mouth. "I'd better call Mr. Hershey again."

Andy moved closer to the camera so that one large eye and half his nose filled her screen. "Cassandra, the sheriff is running the main investigation. He won't appreciate your interference."

She didn't want to say the word *lawsuit* out loud, but it loomed large in the back of her head. "I'm not interfering with the police. I'm doing my job. We need to make sure whatever Nielson did after the graduation had nothing to do with Morton College."

Not long after hanging up with Andy, Mr. Hershey returned her call. "Good morning, Cassandra. Horrible luck about this business with Gary Nielson. He had just returned to Carson."

There was background kitchen and talking sounds on the line. "Yes, I was very sad to hear about it, too. Although I saw him at the graduation Saturday, I wasn't sure how many people knew he was back in town."

Hershey said, "He'd only been away for a short time. Once the newspapers write a longer story, his death will be the talk of town. He was an important person in our community. Let's be cautious about our characterization of this tragedy, even amongst ourselves. We don't want to attract undue attention to Morton. Again."

"Our security director mentioned that police believe someone robbed his house and Dr. Nielson surprised them." Cassandra didn't want to mention that it might not have been a random robbery until she had more than her intuition for proof.

Hershey was silent for several moments. "I see. Truly tragic."

Finally, she'd gotten through to Hershey that they were talking about a real man's *life* ending. Her relief lasted a nanosecond.

"We hadn't signed a contract yet," said Hershey. "The board only made the offer to him on Thursday last week. That offer was confidential, so crossing fingers there's no reason for the media to shine a negative light on Morton. If anything, we will get sympathetic coverage from the loss of our long-time professor and president."

This whole discussion felt disjointed. She was worried about the robbery, but the board wanted to use a man's death to score points in the media.

She asked, "What else do you need me to do over winter break?"

"I'm in Colorado at our family's ski condo, and I won't be back in Carson until the semester begins. We can keep in touch over break by email or phone in an emergency. I need you to liaison with the local law enforcement, talk to the press, and deal with any student issues over winter term. I'm confident you can handle the reins during this slow time."

His backhanded confidence was underwhelming. "I'll keep in touch, sir."

"Happy Holidays, Cassandra." She shook her head after hanging up. Little did he know that her house was a disaster, she was sleeping in a dorm room, and she worried that Dr. Nielson's death was more complicated than the police suspected.

Chapter Ten

"Thank you for seeing me Dr. Zimmerman. I was shocked when you called me back right away. I thought everyone had left town."

They sat across from each other at the Sweets side of the Gas & Sweets. Since meeting the woman who managed the bakery, Cassandra wanted to support her business venture as much as possible. Rhonda cleaned the large coffee machines behind the counter and refilled bins. The yeasty smell of baking bread was intoxicating. Soft holiday music floated down from the ceiling speakers.

Cassandra had met Terrance Zimmerman through his work on the Faculty Senate as well as in his role as an Ag Science professor. Every time she'd talked to him, he gave her his full attention like he had nowhere else to be in that moment.

"Not me. My family lives in Connecticut and my wife went to visit her folks in Alabama." His closely cropped hairline started midway on the top of his head, and a sparse beard grew along his jawline. "She travels every two years for the holidays. Now that the kids moved away, our holidays are quiet."

Cassandra loved all the craziness of a lively house over the holidays. In Hawai'i her brother's boys came over and bounced on the furniture, her sister brought her toddler daughter. There were park outings and board games played well past bedtimes.

"I haven't seen you since the party at Dr. Bergstrom's house in November. You've had quite an active first semester." Zimmerman's long legs stretched out to the side of their bistro table, his phone peeking out from one of the cargo pockets on his khaki pants.

"You and Dr. Nielson worked together on the agreement between the local farmers and the college to supply beef to our cafeterias." Cassandra asked, "Did you work on other special projects together?"

Zimmerman chuckled. "You saw the cattle farm close up, didn't you?"

Probably he was right, and it was funny. Zimmerman had had a front row seat to Cassandra's cartwheeling fall into a cowpie and ruined suit from her first outing to a local farmer's cattle operation.

Through the open double doors, Cassandra saw Bob Soukup in the convenience store side of the station. White hair visible under his seed corn truckers' hat, he sat at a booth with three elderly men playing cards. A high-school aged girl worked the register for the trickle of customers. Even from far away, Cassandra saw the deep frown lines permanently imprinted on his forehead.

"Dr. Nielson's passing hits me hard. We weren't just colleagues, we were friends. He took me turkey hunting a couple of times. It's so hard to believe he's really gone." He looked off to the side and Cassandra waited a few moments. He said, "How can I help you today?"

Cassandra snapped her eyes back to Zimmerman and met his smile with one of her own. When Nielson had mentioned that he'd been accused of having a proprietary soybean formula, Cassandra had written it off as one of his famous conversational tangents. "I know this is kind of crazy. I wanted to ask someone who could help a city girl rule out this line of thinking..."

He sipped his coffee and nodded for her to continue.

"I saw Dr. Nielson before he died, and he mentioned something odd about proprietary soybean seeds. "

Zimmerman's thin, dark eyebrow raised. "You saw Dr. Nielson before he died?"

"Briefly, on Saturday."

"Soybeans are one of my research interests, but I don't know what concern Nielson would have about it. Didn't he move to Florida?"

Hopefully he was right that Nielson's death had nothing to do with soybeans. "Maybe I misunderstood him, and probably there's nothing to his soybean rantings... I just thought you might know about any commercial or corporate agreements involving the college that I should be concerned about? The police are following up on the physical evidence. I'm assisting them with the academic connections."

"Anything related to soybean seeds studies or grants is under my purview or Rich Johnson, the other faculty member in our department." He shook his head and smiled. "You don't think I had anything to do about it, do you?"

Kind of an odd thing to say. Cassandra gave him an awkward smile. "I just want to understand Morton's potential liability if evidence reveals a connection. Can you give me a crash course on soybean engineering?"

"I can't imagine how a genetically engineered proprietary soybean seed would be significant..." He adjusted his wire-rimmed bifocals and looked off to the side. "But you said Nielson mentioned them before he died. Well, as you might know, there's a good bit of competition among companies and trade partners for agriculture products. I'm sure you've read about food shortages, tariffs, etc."

Truthfully, this wasn't her area of expertise. She made an, "Mmm hmm," murmur.

"Basically, it comes down to this. Large companies that sell corn or soybean seeds to farmers have complex in-house laboratories to develop the best seeds possible. This is an ongoing process."

Zimmerman let out a breath. Cassandra could tell he was trying not to treat her like a complete novice, and she appreciated that. For time's sake, she needed the condensed version.

"It's similar to how pharmaceutical companies develop new medicines through years of testing and trials until they come up with the best product to help the most people while causing the least amount of harm to patients."

When Cassandra nodded that she understood the comparison, he continued, "Companies cross breed soybean plants and develop patented processes where they make seeds that are resistant to pesticides and diseases. When a farmer plants the seed, they can spray pesticides that kill weeds or insects. Everything except the soybean plant. This produces a bean that grows better even in extreme weather conditions, and over several iterations improves the plant. The more soybeans a plant produces, the more a farmer yields, the more money the farmer earns. Soybeans feed the world. You can imagine these high performing seeds are an important commodity to trade with other countries. For example, China has to feed 1.4 billion people. Figuring out how to do it at scale and cost effectively means all the difference to their country's economic success."

Meaning high yield, drought resistant soybean research and production were deadly important issues. She asked, "Is that one of the reasons our country clashes with the Chinese government in our trade and tariff agreements?"

"Yes, it's a major issue. Another problem is corporate espionage. There have been multiple lawsuits and arrests of people spying on farms in Iowa or another farmland. Seeds are stolen, then reverse engineered. They use our research investments to duplicate or improve yields in their fields. Soybeans are a very competitive commodity with big money at stake." He frowned, "Although it's a stretch to imagine that Dr. Nielson has anything to do with them."

Cassandra didn't want to say too much and run afoul of Deputy Tate. "Remember Nielsen's cultural exchange trip to

China in October? I wonder if Morton's research was part of their discussions?"

Loud voices carrying into the bakery distracted Cassandra enough to lean forward to see the card players' booth. Soukup stood at the end of the table pointing his sausage-sized index finger at the man to his left. Slapping his cards on the table, he stalked toward the back of the store, his back as straight as his stooped shoulders would allow.

Rhonda walked over with a coffee carafe offering refills. Several customers had purchased cookies or bread while she and Zimmerman had been meeting, but they were the only ones seated at a table.

Rhonda said, "If he scares away our best customers, we'll both be bankrupt soon."

"Is he always this crabby?" Cassandra frowned, "I'm surprised his friends play cards with him."

"Arguing is what makes Dad feel alive. He'll debate anyone about any topic whether or not he has any idea of the facts."

Cassandra slowly shook her head, then turned back to Zimmerman.

Zimmerman returned to the China trip topic. "Our specific research projects might not have been part of their discussions but would be an attraction to future students enrolling in a Education Exchange year at Morton."

"Soybean seeds are potentially a much more complicated crop than what I had pictured." Nielson had specifically mentioned talking to someone in the USDA because the Chinese government had reported a security breach.

After listening to Professor Zimmerman, that didn't sound so far-fetched now. Cassandra wrote a note in her journal to follow up with the IT department and ask about unusual cyber activity after Nielson's trip to China.

She'd read about foreign countries and corporations hacking into college IT systems. If someone suspected Morton personnel were involved in a security breach, they might investigate through unofficial channels as well as formal complaints.

Zimmerman raised his eyebrows. "Agricultural economic espionage is a growing threat. Biotech piracy is big trouble for both the private and public industries." He seemed uneasy. "Not that I'm suggesting Nielson or anyone at Morton did anything wrong. But anything with that much money at stake has a dark, seedy side, if you will."

Cassandra blinked then made an awkward laugh at his agriculture joke. She was going to have to dig more into the October trip to China. She needed names of everyone who'd gone and their exact itinerary,

"Several of my graduate students work on research projects developing better corn and soybean seeds."

Turning to a new page in her notebook, she said, "I know that Dr. Nielson as president signed any large grant applications and agreements. So he knew about your department's soybean research. You teach along with Professor Johnson, supervising the graduate assistants and staff?"

Zimmerman said, "Our department is fairly small. I can give you a list." He slid his phone out from his pants' pocket. While he typed the names, he read them to Cassandra. "Just me and one other tenured faculty member, three graduate assistants who maintain our test plants and data collection, plus several work study students."

He texted the list to her phone.

Cassandra sipped coffee while she read the names. "I've met this Daniel Leung. He's your grad student?"

"I worked with him." Zimmerman frowned. "If you want to learn more about our research, you may want to contact another student. I'm not sure Leung will be with our department next semester."

Bad feelings between them? Cassandra waited for the silence to become uncomfortable.

After several beats Zimmerman said, "Daniel Leung and I had a difference of opinion, and he's asked for my colleague to be assigned his new thesis chair."

That was vague. "What kind of difference?" Cassandra didn't judge other people without a reason and so far, every time she'd talked to Zimmerman, he'd been kind and reasonable.

Now that he mentioned it, Cassandra remembered seeing a complaint addressed to academic affairs regarding Dr. Zimmerman. The student had claimed the research was his intellectual property, and that Zimmerman had stolen it.

Years in academia had taught Cassandra to view the problem of who gets research credit from both sides of the situation. Many graduate students in vulnerable positions were grossly taken advantage of intellectually and sometimes sexually at the hands of unscrupulous professors who wielded power and future job recommendations like currency.

One bad reference could spoil a new academic's ability to find a good job at the next level or to get tenure. On the other hand, many students cried foul when they were only privy to a small portion of the data collection and didn't deserve to have their names included on a published paper by a tenured professor with a PhD.

"He did some background research on my lit review. He didn't earn a contributing credit on the paper."

Cassandra nodded, not in agreement but that she understood his position.

"Leung is a pretty smart kid. I'd be happy to work with him in the future after he's completed his master's thesis. But I think he has aspirations in commercial industry, not in becoming a tenured professor."

After a few more minutes, Cassandra had enough information. Andy Summers had been correct earlier when he'd urged her to tell Deputy Tate about Nielson's visit Saturday night. She'd thought the soybean seeds were just a unique Nebraska thing, but now she felt sure it was more serious.

Once she had more details, she would insist that the police pay attention to her lead. For one thing, she wanted to see who else had signed off on any research contracts besides Nielson. She hated to think that one of Morton's own faculty could be greedy enough to hurt Nielson but had to admit it was a possibility.

Back in her car, Cassandra felt better when she saw a text from one of the Picotte students. The "night in" was a go. She had a shopping list and at least a few students willing to hang out with her instead of binge drinking themselves into oblivion.

She wasn't always serious. Tonight, she'd fulfill her own midwestern Christmas wish, too.

Chapter Eleven

When Cassandra returned from the food market, a group was gathered in the common room. They'd already been served their cafeteria meal at five and would likely be hungry again by eight. Most of them scrolled through their phones, but three guys wearing large headphones sat on the floor in front of the big screen playing a video game.

The mood of the room was hopeful, but they avoided eye contact like they didn't believe she'd deliver on her promises. What had the resident assistant done here to enable such an unhealthy dynamic? She'd check into that later when everyone came back to campus.

While Cassandra went to her room to get Murphy and bring him outside to make shishi, two volunteers put flavored waters and soft drinks in the fridge and set the takeout buckets of fried chicken, potato salad, raw veggies, chips and dips along the countertop.

Within minutes, all 25 students were chatting happily in the makeshift buffet line while they filled paper plates with food and chose drinks.

The Japanese student gushed, "Thank you!"

"Sorry it's not real KFC, but the local market makes pretty good fried chicken." She handed him a sports drink bottle. "What's your name?"

"Akira Higashi, Dr. Sato-san. From Tokyo." Cassandra returned his slight bow in greeting. "I am grateful you tried."

After dinner and clean up, the students gathered chairs and cushions then chose movies to stream, starting with *Elf*. Wearing her flannel pajamas, Cassandra suggested *It's a Wonderful Life*, but a loud group had outvoted her.

Cassandra chose a spot at the corner of a long couch next to Sela Roberts who was on a nearby chair snuggled up to Murphy and scratching under his ears. Face resting in a blissful near smile, he raised one eyelid and regarded her with what Cassandra swore was a patronizing stare.

Cassandra said, "Every time I try to pet him, he ducks out of the way and runs into another room."

Sela glared at her silently, her low-cut tank top revealing more breast than Cassandra usually spotted away from Waikiki beach. Sitting on the floor in front of Sela's chair, her friend Daniel gazed over his shoulder at Sela like he wished he could get a fraction of the attention Sela heaped on the dog.

"You're Sela, right?" Cassandra smiled and looked between them. "And Daniel Leung, yes? Where are you from?" She was curious about his research disagreement with Professor Zimmerman, but there was no way to ask about it in a professional way in this setting.

Daniel nodded, "I grew up in San Francisco with my mother, but most of my family lives in Beijing."

Sela answered, "Trinidad and Tobago. Then Virginia for high school."

"I moved from Hawai'i in August. This is my first big snowstorm. It's more than I expected." Cassandra gestured out the window, which was still bright with the snow's reflection, even though it was nighttime. "Why didn't you go back to San Francisco to be with your mother over the holidays?"

Daniel shrugged. "I stopped at my mother's for the weekend in November when we came back from China. I couldn't afford another plane ticket again so soon."

"Oh, you must have travelled with Dr. Nielson's group to China?"

"For my international business class. That's how Sela and I met." Daniel waited several beats for Sela to add more details. Finally, she deigned to nod at him but said nothing.

Standing, he brushed off his sweatpants. "I'm getting a drink. Want anything?"

Sela shook her head. He headed down the hall to the rooms.

"For the record, he's not my boyfriend. We just know each other. He's not my type."

Cassandra guessed that Daniel thought he was her type. Although, what young guy wouldn't want to date a beautiful, confident woman with a cool Caribbean accent?

Cassandra sipped hot cocoa from her mug. "Is everything okay? You seem annoyed."

She blinked hard once. She didn't seem used to people using the direct approach with her. She leaned forward.

"He just tries too hard; you know what I mean?" Her eyes followed the back of Daniel as he walked down the hallway.

Most men who approached Cassandra with romantic intentions quickly learned she wasn't interested. Cassandra nodded slightly.

Did Sela think Cassandra was trying too hard, too? She had that air of superiority that only twenty-somethings who know it all can achieve.

Sela said, "Now his cousin, Jason, was hot. A Chinese businessman. More mature. Daniel brought him as a guest to one of the dinners on our trip."

Ouch. That didn't bode well for Daniel. Cassandra changed topics. "What was your favorite part of the visit to China?"

"West Lake was pretty cool." Her voice was friendlier now that Daniel was gone. "When we were there it rained, and I didn't get to take the boat ride to the pagoda. The food took some getting used to though."

"Were you around Dr. Nielson very much during the visit?"

"Not really. They had some fancy receptions and dinners. My mother arranged an invitation for us to the ambassador's residence for a cocktail party. Nielson must have met with college reps while we toured campus and met the students."

Sela obviously assumed everyone knew about her mother's embassy job and would be suitably impressed.

"It sounds like it was a great trip." Cassandra said, "Maybe you didn't know, but Dr. Nielson died Sunday."

There had been a brief article in the statewide newspapers Wednesday morning, but it was short on details about how he died.

Sela nodded. "Someone shot him, right? Don't they have fingerprints or DNA? I talked to him in China a few times because of my mother's job. He was kind of weird."

"Weird like your goofy grandpa, or another kind?"

"Weird like he wanted to make a good impression but every time he opened his mouth, he said something old-fashioned." Sela met Cassandra's eyes. "Or he'd tell a story but get the facts wrong. Everyone in the room knew he didn't know what he was talking about, but they were too polite to correct him. It was kind of embarrassing to be around him. Like an old dad trying to sound cool."

Cassandra was impressed by Sela's perceptive description of Nielson.

"Some things he said were even racist or chauvinistic. But you could tell he was oblivious to how it sounded to other people. Everyone would look at each other with pained expressions and then a tour assistant would take his elbow and steer him off to see an ancient vase before the Chinese folks realized what he'd really said."

That had happened here at Morton College a few times at the major donor dinners. Nielson's strength was his sincerity and intensity. He wanted the best for the students and college, although his methods could be painfully awkward.

"You know Sela, there's a cool group of women leaders on campus who will get together for meetings and mentoring type trainings in the spring. It's called the Women of

Tomorrow. I can email you the next time we meet if you want to check us out."

Sela didn't say no right away, which Cassandra took as a win. "Maybe. My mother's on my back to do more stuff for my resume." Sela's mother the diplomat. Cassandra wondered why Sela's family sent their daughter to such a small-town college when they could probably have afforded an expensive urban university experience for her. Cassandra nodded. "Yeah, you can let me know."

"You'll meet other female faculty and community leaders who could be good contacts for when you apply for internships." Including Sela would add another interesting perspective to the group. Cassandra would love to have a full room at the next event.

Daniel came back and folded himself into his spot on the floor in front of Sela. He must have overheard Sela talking about Nielson.

"Nielson wasn't nearly as bad as that other jerk." Daniel offered Sela a bowl of microwave popcorn.

She took it without even a thank you and scooped up a handful of popcorn. Murphy jumped off her lap and wandered through the tangle of bodies and legs of the students stretched out on the floor watching the beginning of *Elf* at the North Pole.

Her darkly painted eyebrows met together in a frown. "Which—oh the guy from the gas station? I forget his name."

Cassandra described Bob Soukup, "Tall, white-haired guy, like 70 years old?" She had heard that Soukup was an important Morton donor and a former town councilman.

"Probably. He talked down to Dr. Nielson and us and you could tell the whole time he was there he didn't want any Chinese cooties to touch him. His face was always screwed up like the place smelled bad. I don't think the other adults liked him either."

A couple of students glared at Cassandra and Sela in a non-verbal shush. Cassandra wanted to find out more but stopped and watched the movie.

Soukup's angle might be important. Cassandra would need a work-around for his famous grumpiness.

Chapter Twelve

Cassandra only had until noon to get the emergency management software grant outline ready and clear her desk before the long Christmas weekend. While she missed the student workers' antics, the quiet meant she'd actually get stuff done. The board of directors had authorized a temporary contract while they sought funds for a more permanent solution to updating Morton's communication system making it more accessible to all students and faculty.

She tried Becky Nielson again in Iowa, ready to leave another voicemail. When she answered on the second ring, Cassandra scooped up her phone. "Becky, this is Cassandra Sato. Thanks for taking my call. I've been thinking about you and hope you are okay."

"Thank you for calling and for your thoughts." Her voice was so quiet, Cassandra pressed the phone's volume all the way up. "It's been a long week, but on the other hand, it feels like I'm going to walk into the kitchen and find him sitting at the table drinking coffee out of his favorite stained mug that he refused to part with." She made a half-hearted laugh.

"I just want you to know how sad everyone is here at Morton, and I hope you got the flowers we sent."

"We did, dear, and that was very thoughtful of you. Gary and I had looked forward to our new Florida adventure. That wasn't in the cards." Cassandra heard a sniffle. "It's been good for me to be near family."

Cassandra itched to ask Mrs. Nielson more questions about their time in Florida but resisted the urge. "We haven't planned a formal memorial yet because everyone is out of town over the holidays. But we'd like to host something next semester when it fits with your schedule. Dr. Nielson was a key person at Morton for such a long time."

"It was lovely of you to call. You know Gary thought very highly of you. I remember when he first mentioned you, I thought he was crazy. I said, 'No one moves from Hawai'i to Nebraska for a job.' But he was a stubborn old man and he told me, "No harm in asking. She'll shake this place up.""

Cassandra's eyes burned and a lump formed in her throat. She laughed a bit, "Yes, he could be stubborn, but he had a good heart."

After they hung up, Cassandra sat quietly collecting herself wiping under her eyes with a tissue. Besides her fiancé, Paul, and her grandfather, she hadn't really known many people who had died. This whole experience was exhausting.

Her phone buzzed with a text from Andy. "Hey. My mother wanted me to let you know you're welcome to eat dinner with our family one night over break."

Cassandra hesitated. She enjoyed her friendship with Andy and usually thought of him as a younger brother, although there had been moments the past few months where her feelings had been a bit muddled.

During her pause, he added, "My mom thought you might like a home cooked meal since you're so far from your family during the holidays."

The power of homesickness had been even worse than she'd anticipated. She looked forward to spending Christmas at the O'Briens' house and getting some good quality family time with her Nebraska ohana.

Fischer was out of town. And they'd only been on two dates. Colleagues mentioned coworkers to their parents sometimes. Cassandra had told her mother about Cinda and Meg and Nielson. Not Fischer or Andy though. She typed back, "That's very thoughtful but the next few days are pretty full. Maybe we could plan something next week?"

He didn't respond for several minutes. Had she hurt his feelings? Her previous rule of keeping a distance from male colleagues had been safer and simpler than juggling the egos of two guys at once.

"Okay I'll text you next week."

"Have fun with your family."

"I will. I'll get the nieces all wound up then let their parents deal with them later." He added, "I got Buckley his own stocking. He's going to love the big chew toy. Merry Christmas!"

"Merry Christmas."

Cassandra hadn't even thought of Murphy and Christmas. Bribing him with donuts had worked pretty well. Maybe she could improve his behavior with a few well-timed toys.

At closing time, Cassandra quietly admired her tidy office while reflecting on the emotional ups and downs of her first semester. Her email inbox was at zero. That feeling of completion was so rare. Cassandra inhaled the feeling of contentment that washed over her.

***

About half of the Picotte students sprawled on the couches, chairs, and floor of the common room around the big screen TV where they'd all been engrossed in a *Home Alone* marathon on the classic movie channel. In between movies, everyone stood up to get a snack or drink and planned to meet back again in 20 minutes to watch the next movie. Murphy made himself at home in the lap of anyone willing to pet him.

The refrigerator looked considerably emptier than the night before. The housing department and resident assistant had arranged for The Home Team, a local bar and grill, to cater a full Christmas Day dinner for the students on the floor.

Cassandra grabbed a can of Diet Coke and practically crashed into Shannon Bryant and Daniel Leung coming around the corner from the kitchen.

"Dr. Bryant!" Cassandra looked up and down the hall in confusion. She wasn't aware of any deaf students left on campus.

"Hello!" He signed. "You said you moved into Picotte Hall, but I didn't know where exactly to find you." He looked around and nodded. "I met him near the front door, and he showed me where to find you." Bryant rested a hand on Leung's shoulder and patted it twice.

"Thanks man. Daniel, right?" Bryant used his voice. "Nice to meet you." Then they did a little fist bump, bro hug thing before Daniel peeled off to forage in the kitchen.

Cassandra gestured for them to move to a small table in the common room. She liked the challenge of signing without Meg nearby to interpret. It forced Cassandra to practice her ASL. Her stomach fluttered nervously. "Sure. Good idea."

"I'm driving to Minneapolis this afternoon. I got your outline in the email." When it took Cassandra three tries reading his fingerspelling to understand Minneapolis, he pulled out his phone, tapped a message in the notes app, then turned it toward her. "I can do the research on the text-based emergency management systems. Can you make the comparative tables using the examples we found from similar sized institutions? I can ask my buddy for referrals."

The relief she felt was immediate. No way would she have understood all of that if he'd signed it to her. She really needed to study ASL more over the break. She wondered if any of the Picotte students took his classes and would practice with her.

Cassandra tapped the microphone on her Notes app and spoke into her phone, "Andy Summers already gathered corporate data for us. We only have to change the format and verify the content is still current." Her words displayed as text while she spoke. She handed her phone to Bryant to read.

He replied, "I'll be back in town Monday when my winter term Deaf Literature class begins. We could meet for coffee to go over what we have, and I can give you your first tutoring lesson in ASL then, too."

She didn't remember seeing that course in the catalog before. "Deaf Literature?"

"It's a special short course during winter term. ASL storytelling, ASL poetry, and a bit of history. Why don't you join the registered students and audit my course?"

Cassandra glanced over at the large sectional sofa which was filling up with students ready to watch the next movie. Her plans for winter break had already completely shifted. She might as well make the best of it and learn something new. "I'd be interested in auditing the class, even if I can't attend them all."

Jasmine entered the common room and stopped short when she saw Cassandra and Bryant. "Dr. Bryant?" she signed. When he smiled and waved at Jasmine, her face flushed red.

Bryant said, "Great. I'll email you the details." Bryant handed her his phone again with a new message. "On the grant. Your outline looks good. If you can do the introduction and conclusion, I'll put together the middle points."

"It's a deal," Cassandra signed. "Thanks for stopping here. Have a safe trip home."

Bryant first wished Cassandra, "Merry Christmas," then turned and signed to Jasmine, "Merry Christmas!" He waved at a few other students and walked down the hallway.

Sela, seated on the far end of the couch craned her neck to watch his backside departing. Cassandra chuckled and turned to see what about him captivated Sela. His dark hair and fiercely dark eyebrows, while making him handsome, also kind of scared Cassandra. Or maybe it was just the prospect of embarrassing herself by signing badly to him that made her armpits drip sweat every time she met with him. Cassandra chose a spot on the couch near Sela.

Jasmine said, "How do you know him? He's my ASL professor. I could watch him all day!"

Sela wore another expensive looking lounging ensemble, her hair wrapped in a brown scarf. "I was going to take Spanish, but maybe I'll have to change my language class. Is he your boyfriend?" Suddenly Sela seemed interested in Cassandra as a person instead of simply as annoying college staff.

Cassandra laughed. "Nah, we're working on a project together." She couldn't even say they were friends, exactly. Colleagues would sound stuffy to the women. "Do you like his ASL classes? I'm trying to learn."

"Sitting in his class is the best three hours of my week. He's so hot," said Jasmine.

"Maybe we can practice signing to each other this week? I need more—" Cassandra frowned and tried to remember the sign for practice. She knew her right hand was supposed to move somehow on her left pointer finger.

Jasmine made a pointing handshape with her left hand and an "E" handshape with her right. She moved the E part along her left finger. "This is how you sign practice."

111

Cassandra didn't want to be just the mean disciplinarian all the time. Hope that this week wouldn't be a total loss lifted her mood. If talking to popular professors made her more likeable and interesting in their eyes, then she would build from there.

Daniel Leung returned to the seating area carrying a bag of Doritos and a bottle of water. He first looked at the space between Cassandra and Sela, presumably judging if there was room for him to squeeze in next to her without making it obvious. His eyes roamed the few open spaces, rejecting each one in turn.

Cassandra read the disappointment on his face. Popping up, she said, "I'm sorry Daniel you were sitting here, and I stole your seat. I have to get something out of my room. I might miss the beginning of the next movie."

The gratitude started in his eyes and traveled to his smile. He fought it though and pressed his lips together and nodded his head. "Oh, hey thanks." But he beelined over there before anyone else could think of sitting next to Sela.

Cassandra's quick trip into her room turned into a couple hours of reading and emails. Fishing a granola bar out of her bag, she called home. Her family would be preparing for a huge meal and gift opening around the Christmas tree at her parents' house.

"Hello Cassandra!" her mother yelled into the iPad Cassandra had bought for them. Behind her head, colored lights twinkled on the tree among homemade ornaments she and her siblings had proudly brought home every year from elementary school. Her mother decorated the tree exactly the same every year, right down to the lighted star on top.

The Satos weren't big on the Christian story of Jesus' birth, but they loved the gift giving and big family meals.

"Hello Mom!" Cassandra waved.

Suddenly the screen whirled in a jerky one hundred eighty degree turn that encompassed a bunch of blurry people calling back. "Hey Cassandra! Auntie look at my pajamas! Hey Sis!"

Cassandra's stomach lurched like a roller coaster ride. "Mom! Can you put the iPad on the table?" Her sister Kathy stood over the kitchen counter ironing the tablecloths for their special meal.

Keoni aimed the iPad at their sister Sarah's daughter. "Watch this new trick! Diana is walking!"

The last time Cassandra had seen Diana she hadn't been able to crawl. Her niece would grow up without her in their daily lives. After only ten minutes, Cassandra invented an excuse to hang up. Tears formed in her eyes.

She'd accomplished so much in the past year. She was proud of herself for making her big move to Nebraska and buying her own house. (Which she'd be a lot happier about once it was repaired.) Getting everything Cassandra had worked and planned for didn't feel as happy as she'd imagined. Letting go of her family a little at a time hurt more than she expected. She'd chosen this life, but that didn't make it easier.

When Cassandra emerged, the common room was dark because no one had turned on any table lamps. The spot where Sela had been sitting was now open, so Cassandra sat next to Daniel Leung.

"Hey Daniel. Is Sela coming back?"

"I dunno." He was sulky.

She felt sulky too. "Everything okay? Are you bummed about not going anywhere for break?"

He shrugged. "Not really. It's been a long week."

She completely agreed. "What's your major?" She knew he studied with Dr. Zimmerman but didn't think he'd want to know that she knew that much about him.

"Biology's my major, but mostly I study agriculture."

"I see. Morton seems like a good place to learn about plants and farms. Did you and Sela go to China in October as part of a class?"

"Sela plays violin and performed during the trip." He shrugged, "They invited me because I speak some Mandarin. No way a lowly grad student like me would be able to afford plane tickets to Hangzhou without the college's support. Unlike Sela, some of us don't have a trust fund paying for our every whim."

Daniel's voice held contempt. Cassandra raised an eyebrow. "I got the impression you liked Sela. Maybe I was wrong?"

"Not very many people really like Sela. Most of the people who call themselves her friends just hang around to get free rides in her Mercedes."

Chapter Thirteen

Meg met Cassandra at the front door early Christmas morning, taking her coat and scarf to hang in the hall closet. Leaning in quietly, Meg whispered, "Heads up. Tony is teetering on the edge of giving up Santa this year. He's full of questions."

"And how are you answering these questions?" Cassandra asked.

"We've always followed my mother's old axiom, 'You have to believe to receive.' Connor thinks he's old enough to get the full story, but I'm not ready to stop yet."

"Did someone at school spoil it for him?"

"Whoa there, Auntie!" Meg tugged gently on her arm. "This is just normal kid stuff. He's ten years old and connecting the dots. His brain can't figure out how it all works logically, but his heart still wants to believe."

"Ohhh. Ok I get that." Cassandra assured her. "I can take care of Tony."

Murphy scratched at the door of his kennel and Cassandra set it on the floor of the entry hall. "I grabbed a clean towel for inside the kennel. We could stick him in the basement for a few hours to nap."

Meg's eyes bulged out like she thought Cassandra was a three-headed unicorn. "How do you not love those sad brown eyes, Cass? He's so sweet. So you have to do a little more laundry. Suck it up, wahine."

Cassandra's hand inched toward the wire door and Murphy growled. "Are you sure you want me to let the beast out?"

"Of course! Murphy's smaller than Burt. He won't be any trouble." She opened the door, reached inside, and pulled him out in one fluid motion. His pink tongue licked Meg's cheek when she held him up to snuggle her face.

A shiver of disgust went down Cassandra's back. Why did people let animals lick their face?

Placing him on the floor, Meg went to the kitchen and Murphy followed, white tail wagging like he owned the place. Burt, their German shorthair was last in the happy little train, nose in Murphy's private parts checking him out.

Cassandra unpacked her large shopping bag with wrapped gifts and placed them under the Christmas tree. Tony must have been the main tree decorator. Everything under five feet high was covered with silver tinsel clumps and homemade ornaments using Popsicle sticks, glue, green yarn and photos of him at various ages. The tree's upper regions shined with a few strands of tinsel and glass ornaments hung in a more organized format.

Michiko Sato had sent a package to the O'Briens' house directly. Cassandra had asked her mom to buy Hawaiian chocolates and shortbread cookies dipped in chocolate.

When she heard Tony's excited voice and loud footsteps running down the hallway, Cassandra called, "Make sure Tony doesn't eat all my bacon!" Smiling, she paused for a moment in front of the family photo collage in the hallway next to the bathroom. Holidays were meant to be shared with family. Even if it's calabash family instead of blood relatives.

Skinny arms gently shoved her toward the kitchen. Tony said, "Auntie, hurry up and eat breakfast so we can open presents."

Cassandra reached around his back for a quick one-armed hug. Tony's hair smelled sugary like cereal.

From the kitchen, Meg called, "Did you tell her Merry Christmas first? Where are your manners?"

Tony repeated dutifully, "Merry Christmas, Auntie Cass!" He hadn't changed out of the SpongeBob pajamas he'd worn to bed. Without Cassandra, SpongeBob probably would have been too babyish for Tony. But given Cassandra's obsession with the hilarious series since her college days, she used every gift-giving opportunity to encourage it in her godson, including the birthday pjs he now wore.

Meg came around the large kitchen island and handed Cassandra a large mug of coffee. "Thanks for coming so early. Connor's in the shower."

"Hey brah," Cassandra sat with Tony on the cushy sectional in front of the tree. Excitement radiated from him.

"What's this I hear you're too old for Santa Claus?" Cassandra heard Meg's exasperated gasp behind her but chose to ignore her. The direct approach had always worked with her own nephews. Why quit now?

Tony's innocent blue eyes looked straight at hers, "I'm in fifth grade, Auntie Cass. I know about Santa," he tried to sound confident, but there was still a note of question in his tone.

"Well, I'm a little older than fifth grade. Maybe I can help you out. Is there anything you don't know about Santa that you want to ask me?"

His eyes glanced over his shoulder toward the kitchen where his mother was making eggs. He lowered his voice, "How does he bring toys over the ocean to children in Hawai'i? His sleigh can't reach that far."

"Good question. See, it's part magic and part technology. Back when I was a keiki, Santa brought the presents on a big airplane to the islands. Then I think he used his sleigh to get around to the individual houses. Most houses in Hawai'i don't have a fireplace so we left the back door open on Christmas Eve so he could get inside. If that didn't work, he used magic."

Tony's head nodded while he considered. She smiled at his round face framed by wavy reddish-brown hair cut shorter over his ears. The Meg half of him was light freckles dotting his nose and the tops of his cheeks. The Connor half was his tall, lean build; he was big for his age.

"Auntie Michiko told me that back in her time Santa came by boat." Cassandra played the game completely. "The gifts came on one of the big container ships that bring everything across the ocean from the mainland. Maybe his sleigh was on the ship too, I dunno. Anyway, he and the reindeer came by boat.

Tony's smile said that he was still skeptical about Santa himself, but he craved the stories about how it all worked. He wanted to be in on the secret.

"If you visit Hawai'i around Thanksgiving time, you'll see the town parades, just like here on the mainland. We have high school bands, those giant balloons and fire trucks just like you. Except at the parade's end there's a truck pulling a trailer with a huge motorboat and a guy dressed up in a Santa suit, wearing a lei, yelling 'ho ho ho' and flashing the shaka, hang loose, sign to all the keiki.

"One time, I remember it was super-hot and instead of the regular Santa on the boat, the guy was wearing red board shorts, a bright red Aloha shirt with his long white beard and Santa hat and riding a big Harley Davidson motorcycle. That time I thought was kind of weird. I'm a purist about my Santas," Cassandra explained matter of fact.

Tony digested all that for a few seconds and asked, "So if the Hawaiian Santa wears leis and flashes the shaka sign, then what about the other countries? On TV, they say Santa goes all around the world. So is it different Santas or the same one?"

"You're a pretty smart kid for noticing that Tony. Obviously, delivering presents to all the children in the world in 24 hours is a huge job. I mean he has the elves, but I think there's a lot of logistical questions to consider. Like you said: does he wear different outfits depending on which country he's in? He can speak all those foreign languages. Does Google help him update the naughty and nice list now so the elves can work on other projects? It's good that you're trying to figure it all out. Better than turning your brain into mush playing video games all day." She messed up his hair.

Cassandra moved to the stove where Meg was smiling down at the frying pan while she stirred scrambled eggs. They did a subtle fist bump.

"You're such a good Auntie. I hope someday you have your own keiki so you can be a mom too."

"I love being an Auntie for my brother and sister and for you too. I can't handle my own kids right now. But that's okay cuz I get them when they're all cute and cuddly. When they start puking on the carpet from eating too much junk food, then the parents get 'em and I escape to my quiet, clean home." Cassandra laughed. "... Or I will. When my home is again quiet. And clean. With a whole roof." She blew out a big sigh. What a time to be homeless.

"One of my clearest Christmas memories as a kid was when my sister and mother and I traveled to Boston to visit family." Meg sprinkled shredded cheese over the pan. "My father must've taken the boys to the cabin for hunting. I don't remember that part. I was eight and my sister would've been six. A huge ice storm in Chicago delayed our connecting flight to Boston. We got bored sitting at the airport gate for hours, so we walked down the concourse to one of the gift shops. My sister had snacked all afternoon on junk food. Next thing I know, she vomits a huge gross puddle of pink right in the middle of O'Hare."

Cassandra snorted a little. Meg's poor mother!

"She lost it two or three times. My mother found someone to clean up the messes behind us and marched the two of us, plus our little roller suitcases and bags back to the gate. She parked my sister in the corner and covered her up with a winter coat while she slept it off and they de-iced the plane. It was epic."

Her stomach retched a little just listening. Every time Cassandra had been around her nephews while they were sick, or college students who'd partied too much and lost it in a building, Cassandra had fought back her own strong urge to vomit. She wasn't cut out for cleaning smelly bodily fluids.

"Do you have a favorite Christmas memory?" asked Meg while she refilled her water glass and came around the kitchen island to sit on a stool next to Cassandra.

The heady scents of freshly baked cinnamon rolls and roasted coffee beans emphasized the feeling that the kitchen really was the heart of a home. "In our family, New Year's is a bigger holiday than Christmas, but we still have family dinner and exchange gifts. One year I really wanted one of those realistic baby dolls that you fed a bottle and it had cloth diapers that got wet so you had to change the diaper?"

"Daisy Diaper? I had one of those too!"

"Yep. I came around the living room corner on Christmas morning and saw the big pile of wrapped gifts under the tree. Right on top were three Daisy Diaper dolls—one for my sisters, too—wearing matching beautiful Hawaiian mu'umu'u. The dolls had a little plastic flower over their right ears. Later that morning, we opened the packages and found dresses for my sisters and me that matched our dolls exactly! My mother had sewn everything on her machine."

"I love handmade gifts! I'll have to remember to do more things like that for my kids. Maybe this one will be a girl." Meg rubbed her little baby bump. "I taught Tony how to do his own laundry and make breakfast. When the baby comes, he needs to be more independent."

"Sounds like an elaborate plan to get breakfast in bed."

After breakfast and gift opening, Tony disappeared with an armful of boxes to his bedroom to sort through his loot and change clothes.

Connor sat on the floor near the tree putting together a chest of drawers they had ordered from an assemble it yourself furniture company.

Cassandra had switched to water and joined Meg in the kitchen. She had mentioned her ambivalence about Andy's dinner invitation to Meg. Then Meg teased her about juggling Fischer and Andy.

"Why can't you just answer the question? Why must you mock me?" Cassandra rolled her eyes and chopped apples for the pie crust Meg rolled out between two pieces of wax paper.

The O'Briens planned to leave mid-afternoon to his family's house for the rest of the weekend. Meg said, "Has it occurred to you that Andy's mom might be the Bohemian version of your mother? Remember how Mama Sato invited us for Sunday dinner at your family's house not long after we started working together at Oahu State College?"

Cassandra smiled. Ten years had gone by so quickly. Wait. If Tony was ten, then it was more like 12 years ago since she and Meg had begun careers together in adjacent offices. Meg had been the newcomer then. "I told stories about you, Kimo, and Joan so often that Mom wanted to meet you all." She gathered the apple chunks into a bowl, sprinkled sugar and cinnamon on top, and gently mixed them together. "You and Connor showed up to eat at 6:00 p.m. sharp."

"No one had warned us about Hawai'i time. How were we supposed to know we'd be the only guests there for the first hour?" Meg dumped everything in the bottom crust. "Remember, military guys believe if you're on time, you're late?"

"And then you walked right past the huge pile of rubber slippers outside the front door and stepped into the house wearing your fancy mainland boots." Cassandra laughed and sipped some water.

"I thought your mother's eyes would pop right out of her head at our rudeness!" Meg threw up her hands like Mrs. Sato and copied her voice, "Ay-ee! You must be O'Briens from the mainland!" She made a turnaround motion with her finger. "Shoes out on the front step, sweetie. No shoes in the house." Meg's face was red with remembered embarrassment. "And it was my first encounter with some of the local foods! Spam musubi, tako poke..."

"Connor impressed my dad by how well he could hold his sake, though." Cassandra leaned against the counter and watched Meg assemble the pie. Two pumpkin pies already baking filled the airy kitchen with a warm cinnamon scent.

"They used to sneak all kinds of stuff when he was overseas in Iraq. Plus, he's Irish." Meg shrugged, then dusted off her hands.

Cassandra grabbed a cloth from the sink and helped wipe down the counters.

Meg said, "I hope you go to the Summers' house. You can start practicing your life goal for the new year. Say yes!"

Cassandra's life goal for the new year was not say yes. If anything, it was just keep swimming.

"I've already said yes too often lately." Cassandra rolled her eyes. "I told Fischer yes when I agreed to supervise the international student floor over break. I told one of my student workers she could leave a Rubbermaid tote in my office containing all her valuables."

Meg did a palms up, "Huh?"

"Apparently her roommate has property boundary issues and she wanted her stuff in a safe place over break."

"Any news about when they're holding Dr. Nielson's memorial service?" asked Meg.

"The investigation is moving at turtle speed. I'll probably read about it in the newspaper just like you, because they aren't telling me any details." Cassandra frowned. "When I talked to his wife, I told her Morton would like to hold something next semester when everyone's back on campus. She didn't mention funeral plans or anything yet."

"You said someone threatened Nielson? Maybe his wife is afraid to come to Carson?"

"Possibly," Cassandra said. "Everyone in Carson seems pretty average, though. Except that grouchy Mr. Soukup from the Gas & Sweet."

"Everyone says he knows where the bodies are buried." Meg laughed, "Seriously, though. This semester is the craziest I've seen here since my first year when the students played football in the fountain using a greased watermelon."

"Unfortunately, grumpiness doesn't prove murder. If it did, my officemate, Old George, would get life in prison." Cassandra frowned. "Hey, wait... Bob Soukup went to China along with a combination of donors, students, and even a music ensemble. Dr. Nielson told me the harassing texts and stuff started after that trip in October. He had planned on contacting the students. Now that he's gone, we should check them out. We might find a link."

"Whoa there," Meg said. "What's this *we* stuff? Andy or the sheriff can follow up."

Cassandra gazed at the oven timer counting down the minutes until the pie was baked. The problem Cassandra had been mulling for several days began to sort itself into a more organized puzzle. Starting with Nielson and China, leading to the soybeans. A few names came up repeatedly.

Meg's hand waved in front of Cassandra's eyes like an annoying fly. "I said, hello!"

"Listen, I offered to help the sheriff's office understand Nielson's connections to Morton, but Tate wasn't interested in my information. I even asked Professor Zimmerman about the soybean seed research that Nielson had mentioned."

"It's like you're not even listening to me!" Meg held out both palms like stop signs. "Why did you meet with Zimmerman? He didn't go to China."

"No, but Zimmerman is the ag expert, right? After talking to him, I think the sheriff needs to ask more questions. I didn't know anything before about soybeans, but now I realize they're a valuable commodity. When I get back to my office, I'm looking up the rest of the travel party."

"Earlier, you told me people asked you to do them too many favors over break. Investigating Dr. Nielson's death is not your responsibility! Remember you promised to bring a few students over to help us redecorate the office and baby room?"

"I'm happy to help you! That's not really a favor. You're family."

Meg said, "Good. But why are you talking about suspicious texts and studying the economic ramifications of soybean research?"

Cassandra frowned. "We need to know what happened to Dr. Nielson. What if it had to do with the threats he got or the Chinese government's accusations? It's my job to protect the students and the college's reputation."

"Oh puleeze," scoffed Meg. "Give the travel names from the China trip to Andy and let the police folks do their jobs. I seriously doubt there's a nefarious Chinese spy ring operating in Carson, Nebraska. Get real."

"I *am* getting real," Cassandra's voice raised. Which felt strange because she hardly ever got upset. But Meg was as close as a sister to her and pushed back more than most people tried. "We didn't think there was a pharmaceutical conspiracy at Morton either, but lo and behold . . ."

Meg's eyes tilted up toward the ceiling. "Cass. This isn't the same thing. Let the professionals do their jobs."

Okay, that was uncalled for. Cassandra sucked in her cheeks. "You know, you're right, Meg." The timer beeped. Meg removed the perfectly browned apple pie and set it to cool on the countertop. "You folks need to leave soon if you're going to visit Connor's family this afternoon. I'm going back to Picotte Hall and do *my* job. Because I'm a professional, too."

She forced herself to keep her cool while she told Connor and Tony goodbye, then got her coat from the hall closet, and slipped on her boots.

Meg followed her toward the front door. "Cass don't be mad. Every time you get involved in these weird investigations you end up being the one who pisses off the bad guys. I don't want you getting hurt."

"I'm fine," she lied. "Thanks for breakfast. Have a good afternoon." With dignified poise, she closed the front door behind her.

Cassandra made it all the way to her car before her eyes filled. Frustration, homesickness, maybe a little fear of failure. A teeny voice in the middle of her chest whispered that Meg had a point. There were other, qualified people who might be able to figure it out without her.

But could they? She had a unique skill set as a college administrator. She had access to the student database and the travel schedule. Didn't she owe Dr. Nielson's family her expertise? She would tell Deputy Tate what she knew about Saturday night and the China trip's connection to Nielson's distress before his death.

Her leather gloved fingers cleared the wetness from her eyes so she could see the road. Starting the car, she shifted into reverse and backed near the driveway's end.

Hitting the brake, she banged on the steering wheel, shifted into drive, and pulled forward. Slid the gear into park. Opened the car door and marched back to the O'Briens' front door. Just as her foot cleared the top step, the brown door opened and there sat Murphy, plaid bowtie slightly askew, his kennel nearby. Meg stood in shadow behind him, holding the end of his leash.

Cassandra glanced up just long enough to catch the faint smirk on Meg's face. Reaching out, she accepted the leash and the kennel. "Merry Christmas."

Making an about face, Cassandra and Murphy trotted to her car.

Chapter Fourteen

Spilled beer and grease smells hit Cassandra's nostrils before she entered the kitchen. The Picotte students had been up to their former shenanigans, stuffing frozen pizza boxes and empty beer cans into the overflowing trash bin. Was no one else offended by the stench?

She set her laundry basket on the counter. Leash in one hand, her other paused on the fridge door handle. She really wanted a diet soda before driving over to her house. More importantly, she didn't want to confront whatever nasty stuff they'd left in the fridge. Did she dare look inside? How thirsty was she, really?

To the right, an open case of bottled water made the decision easy. She just didn't have the energy right now to get all worked up about the mess and drag everyone's sleeping butts out to the deserted common area to clean.

There'd be plenty of time later this afternoon when she got back from her house. By then, maybe she could muster more indignation. Cassandra had never worked in the housing department. Never been a resident assistant. Twelve years ago, she'd been a dorm resident at UH, but she didn't remember this smell. Hers had been an all-female hall, but these students seemed less considerate than she'd been in her time.

It felt like babysitting recalcitrant toddlers. A vision of 25 students pouting on timeout chairs made her laugh.

Throwing a water bottle on top of her clothes, Cassandra led Murphy out the side door. The power company had left her a voicemail saying they'd reconnected the line to her house. She planned to tidy up while she did laundry. Technically, with electricity she could move home, but she wanted to wait until the roof repairs were completed first.

Less than five minutes later, Cassandra pulled into her driveway and muscled the laundry basket on one hip while she and Murphy entered the back door of the bungalow. Hanging the leash and her coat on hooks, she carefully carried the laundry basket down the steep stairs to the basement.

Basements were such a cool invention. Rarely seen in Hawai'i because of the rocky ground, the extra space was a novelty. As Cassandra sorted the colors from the whites and added the clothes from the bottom of her laundry chute, Murphy sniffed around the corners of the unfinished area.

Soft music played nearby. Cassandra turned her head. Where was the noise coming from? It stopped. She turned the washer on and picked up a bag of dog food to bring upstairs and refill the plastic food container. At the bottom of the stairs, she held still. The music had started again.

As Cassandra stepped back toward the washing machine, the noise grew louder. Stopping under the laundry chute, she peered up into the darkness. Definitely coming from inside the house. Maybe she'd left an alarm on speaker in her bedroom by mistake.

Or maybe, someone was playing music. She scanned the storage boxes for a weapon. Murphy sensed her change in mood and hunched nearby, his head lowered. "Are you a good guard dog, Murph'? That would be 10 points for Slytherin, brah."

Finding a long umbrella, Cassandra gripped the wooden handle and climbed cautiously up the stairs to the kitchen. Murphy didn't follow. So much for the guard dog theory.

In the hallway on the other end of the kitchen, she paused, umbrella over her shoulder like a baseball bat. Peeking into the living room, she didn't see anything amiss. Creeping up the wooden steps, she made it halfway before one of them squeaked. Cassandra froze. Her heart thumped.

The last time the stalker had broken into her house, Andy had scolded her for not running outside and calling police right away.

Her phone was still in her coat pocket by the back door where she'd left it hanging on the hook. She could run downstairs, grab the phone and call from the driveway without being discovered.

Closing her eyes, she listened carefully. What if she'd forgotten to turn off a speaker? The police would come rushing to her aid, for nothing. That would be so embarrassing.

She blew a breath through pursed lips and walked the last four steps like a normal person instead of sneaking through her own home. All three doors were closed, but the music was coming from the spare room with the tree damage. She was acting ridiculous. Just be a grown woman, for godssakes.

Turning the doorknob, Cassandra opened the door. And screamed. And peed a little. And threw the umbrella hard at the man standing in the center of the room under the hole in the ceiling, his mouth open in surprise.

The umbrella bounced off his hip and landed on the floor next to a portable speaker playing You're a Mean One, Mr. Grinch.

Murphy rushed in, barking and growling. When he made it to the guy's snow boots, he stopped barking and wagged his tail.

Horrible guard dog.

"Sean!"

"Cassandra!"

"What the heck!"

"I didn't know you were coming home today."

"Obviously." Cassandra leaned heavily against the doorframe and clutched her heart. "You scared me."

Cassandra's breathing slowed from panicked to annoyed. All the hanging ceiling chunks had been broken off and stacked against the wall or stuffed into trash bags. The broken attic beams were sawed off. Large white wires poked through the ceiling hole. A small toolbox brimmed with parts and gadgets next to the fallen umbrella.

"Did you think I had broken into your house?"

"I heard the music. I didn't know which jerk had broken in. I've had issues before." She planted a hand on her hip and glared.

A faint smile played on his mouth. "I bet you have." He bent over and retrieved the umbrella. "Interesting weapon of choice."

Her eyes squinted as she grabbed it back from him. She was tempted to smack the side of his head with it like her mother used to do to her brother when he was a pain in the—.

He held up a hand. "I'm sorry. That just came out. I don't know you well enough to know whether you have issues or not." His head bowed once apologetically.

In reply, she folded her arms across her chest.

"Look, I had a couple of hours free and thought I'd get a head start cleaning up and replacing the wiring you'll need before my buddy fixes the drywall in your ceiling."

A large coil of white wiring sat at his feet and a pair of pliers were stuffed into his back packet.

"Also, my mom is going through the closet in my old bedroom and keeps asking me stuff like do I want to save my fourth-grade poetry project. Or the clay pot I made freshman year in art theory class."

"You're hiding."

"Guilty."

"And there's nowhere else in town you could think of to hide out from your mother."

Could he even fix the wiring without burning down the place? He looked like a desk jockey, not a handyman.

"How'd you get inside?"

She had changed the locks after the last creep had broken in.

Holding up a familiar keychain, he said, "Uh... you gave my parents a key."

"Oh, right." His very nice parents, Mr. and Mrs. Gill. "I gave the key to your parents. You just don't go inside someone's house without permission."

She didn't trust him. He was working an angle. Maybe it was the big city arrogance.

"You're right. That was my bad. Sorry I startled you."

Retreating downstairs to her bedroom, Cassandra packed for a few more days at Picotte. There were no events to dress up for, so she folded jeans and comfortable pants paired with warm, simple tops and replenished the toiletries bag.

Wearing two hoodies to keep warm, she was curled up on the chair in her kitchen reading news on her iPad when the teapot whistled. While the electricity was now on, there was no point turning the furnace up higher when she wasn't staying more than a couple of hours in the house.

Sean appeared at the bottom of the stairs holding his small red toolbox. "Teatime? Mind if I join you?"

Her eyes narrowed into a mild stink eye. "Have a seat, brah." Probably she shouldn't antagonize the guy who'd offered to help her.

His face colored. "You having a bad day?"

She laughed, "Pff. Bad week, ... pretty crappy month." Her emotions were still raw about losing Nielson. She gestured vaguely in the direction of her broken roof. "I need a new year. A clean slate."

Cassandra got out an extra robin's egg blue cup and poured hot water into both. Grabbing a small basket with teabags, she set everything on the small gate leg table that rested against the wall on the long end of her galley kitchen.

Murphy rubbed up against Sean's dark jeans like a cat and lay at his feet with a contented sigh.

For the first time, she studied Sean without his heavy coat and hat covering everything. Light brown hair cropped close on the sides, but longer on top and messy in front. Thin nose. One of those tiny chin dimples with a couple days' worth of whiskers along the outer edge of his jaw.

"So what do you do at Morton College?" he asked.

His thick pullover sweatshirt looked expensive. Whatever his job, he must be successful because she could spot quality clothes. Most of the people she'd met in Nebraska wore mid-priced clothes from local department stores.

"Vice President of Student Affairs."

His eyebrows raised like he was impressed. When most people heard her title and guessed her age, they wore a similar expression.

"I just moved here in August. I like it so far. Big difference compared to Hawai'i."

Again, his eyes widened. She knew her story was unusual.

"I can imagine," he said. "My mother used to work in the financial aid office before she retired."

"I've met a lot of nice people like your parents so far. I still have a way to go until it feels like home."

He dunked the tea bag up and down in his cup. "I heard about Dr. Nielson. You must have worked closely with him."

"He hired me. He was my boss before he retired in November."

"My mother was pretty upset. I guess they worked together for a long time. Morton is like a small town or a big family."

Cassandra laughed. "Maybe a dysfunctional family. Lots of big personalities. Each with their own agenda." She shrugged. "Myself included."

"The news said they haven't arrested anyone. Do you know if they have any suspects?"

"I'm not exactly in the loop with the sheriff's office."

"No? I heard you were involved with resolving the research lab death and another student's injury since you moved to Carson."

Had he been asking around about her? She was flattered, but ...

"My mom is a big gossip." He hit her with a full smile, exposing teeth that were an orthodontist's dream. "When she found out I was helping with your roof, I got the full dossier on your background."

Cassandra hadn't chatted with Sean's mother often. She'd brought over a few batches of cookies and exchanged smiles and waves across the driveway. But they weren't best pals. Actually, she and Mr. Gill had chatted outside more often. He gave advice about eliminating weeds from her front yard or trimming the dead part of the hedge that grew alongside her garage.

"Did she mention I happened to be in the wrong place at the right time? I'm only doing my job, protecting the students, helping the college solve issues as they come up."

"The newspaper said Nielson surprised a robbery in progress at his house."

Cassandra still hadn't told Deputy Tate her hunch that it wasn't a simple robbery. She'd tried calling the sheriff's office earlier that morning but with the holiday shutdown, no one had answered. She would wait until Monday and try him again.

Sean's attention was flattering. She said, "I read the same thing."

The way his eyebrow lifted told her that he heard the skepticism in her voice. She hesitated.

Should she let it slip that she worried his death wasn't random? Sean didn't even live here. He'd return to his home soon. "Nielson was an important person in Carson and to the college. Even though I only knew him for a few months, I respected his loyalty to this place." She sipped her tea. "Now he's gone. I'm chasing loose threads trying to understand how this happened."

"You're helping the police?"

Cassandra imagined Nielson's sweaty forehead, his twitchy movements that Saturday night he stopped at her house. "Just covering bases at Morton. I briefly spoke to his wife a couple of days ago."

He finished his tea and sat back against the wall. "Wonder why his wife wasn't with him in Carson."

"Yeah, I have no idea either," she lied. "One person's name who keeps coming up is Bob Soukup."

"He's been a crusty old man since I was a kid. You know the big ethanol plant on the edge of town? He used to be the plant manager until he retired. Everyone remembers him. He knows where all the bodies are buried."

"I've heard other people say that too! For real?"

His long slim fingers rested on the edge of the tabletop. "I don't know. Kids make up stories in a small town. I used to tease my youngest brother that he'd better make my bed, or I'd have Old Man Soukup kidnap him and chop him into pieces. Dopey kid stuff, you know?"

"Older brothers are mean." Cassandra shook her head.

Cassandra didn't want to spill any secrets, so she changed the subject. "Tell me about living in DC? I kind of miss living on Oahu with all the people. Not the traffic though."

"Yeah, the traffic is awful. I take the subway so I can listen to podcasts or work during my commute. I like it."

"Where do you work?"

"In an office building in Maryland. A small health inspection service under Homeland Security."

The washing machine beeped alerting her to switch the loads in the dryer. She stood, "Excuse me."

"Hey, I'm going home before my mother donates my home run baseball collection. It was great talking to you. I meant what I said before about joining us for game night. My brothers left so it's me and the parents. You're welcome to come over."

"You just want competition for your mom in Scrabble."

"You caught me. Losing every time is embarrassing."

"It's tempting to stay here instead of the dorm. I miss my house even though it's freezing in here."

Gill stood and put on his coat. "Home is most comfortable," he nodded. "I thought you were in charge of the students this weekend?"

Cassandra said, "Talking about Scrabble gave me an idea for something I can do with them."

"Undermine their self-esteem?"

Gill stroked Murphy's head and under his ears a few seconds before standing up to leave. Murphy's tongue hung out in unabashed adoration.

"I meant we could play games. Last week, we watched movies. I'm stealing your family game night idea."

After what she'd seen this morning, she couldn't leave the students unsupervised. She needed to stick it out a few more days until the RA returned to full duty. Cassandra didn't want anything bad to happen on her watch.

When he left, Cassandra felt lighter than she had in a couple of days. The refreshing way he accepted her for who she was. Gill wasn't trying to date her or jockey for political power at work. It was great to just hang out with someone for a change.

She placed ingredients for her famous chocolate chip cookies in a bag. Baking together would be a great way to chat with some of the students, although it sounded corny. The smell should entice them out of their rooms. Throwing in a couple decks of playing cards, she didn't care if people thought playing old-fashioned games like trumps or poker was nerdy because it reminded her of what her family was probably doing at home.

* * *

Teaching and learning variations of poker with six students filled Saturday evening with laughter and fun. Background music played from a portable speaker on the end table. For the first time in weeks, Cassandra forgot her personal problems and relaxed.

Not everyone had been interested in poker, but several students watched or joined them in the common room talking on the couches. Everyone spent so much screen time nowadays that opportunities to hang out in small groups seemed like a novelty. Other students passed in and out on the way to parties or to go out. The college bar on Main Street was probably the only other business open late on Saturday night.

Taking a break, Cassandra rifled through the kitchen's cupboards for something salty. She'd already eaten two chocolate chip cookies they'd baked earlier. Craving something crunchy, she found a large bag of white cheddar popcorn and grabbed a paper towel roll to share while they played cards at a long table between the kitchen and the commons.

A loud door slammed and laughing male voices carried toward the common room from the east end of the floor. Akira Higashi and another Japanese guy slowly came toward the table where Cassandra and the card players sat.

Bundled into similar black winter coats and stocking caps over jeans and converse high tops, their laughter made Cassandra smile in anticipation of hearing the story behind their good spirits. "Aloha guys, howzit going?"

Akira recognized her. Right away his eyes widened, and his smile slipped, like he thought she'd punish them for having a good time. His hands appeared empty. It didn't look like they were doing anything wrong.

"Dr. Sato-san," they nodded respectfully.

"Did you have a fun night?"

A couple of the students she'd been playing with weren't back from their snack and bathroom break, but four other students sat around the table, scrolling on their phones or talking.

"We did, sensei." Cassandra didn't remember the taller student's name. He couldn't keep the straight act going and broke into peals of laughter so hard he stopped walking. Leaning on the couch for support, he crossed an arm under his stomach and laughed until he coughed. Akira patted him hard on the back. They'd been drinking but weren't weaving or slurring their words.

A girl named Maria came down the hallway, rounded the corner, and saw Akira and his friend. She said, "Akira! I saw the photos you posted! You partied with the football guys, for real?"

The taller friend dropped into one empty armchair and Akira sat on the arm of the couch.

Cassandra sipped from her diet soda and dumped a small pile of popcorn into a paper towel on the table.

Akira nodded, "Those two big linemen guys are in my chemistry class and always call me Little Boy."

Maria laughed, "I know they pump iron for hours a day. Maybe it's the farm water that grows them so big and fat."

Akira's friend said, "They drink that cheap beer that tastes like flavored water and think they're studs. Always teasing us in the team sports class."

To be honest, Akira and his friend would never be musclebound giants, even if they took steroids. Cassandra knew rude bullying happened even in college, but wished she had the power to make it stop.

"Last week, they mocked us about drinking saké. They said, '*Rice wine*? What is that crap?'" Akira laughed again and pulled out a water bottle from his coat pocket to sip.

"My boyfriend could kick their butts for you," offered Maria.

"Tonight, we showed them Japanese hospitality. We invited the football players over to Tanaka's house for a party." Akira pushed his long bangs back away from his face. "When we offered them some saké, the football players laughed even harder, seeing that the saké is served in very tiny cups that only allow you to sip the alcohol."

Cassandra was well aware of the alcohol content of saké. She smiled and ate popcorn.

Akira stuck out his chest and lowered his voice in a credible imitation of an American Midwestern accent. "The football players said, 'Oooh…you drink your rice wine out of tiny cups. What? You can't handle more?' They laughed very hard at us."

Akira's friend nodded. "We simply smiled and served our new friends saké. They said the saké was so smooth that it was like drinking warm water."

Maria looked at her phone. "It's 11:30. They stuck with you guys pretty well, eh?"

The men laughed again. "Not at all. They passed out drunk two hours ago. We left them on the couches to sleep it off at Tanaka's house…and we continued to drink our saké!"

Relieved that this cultural lesson took place off campus, Cassandra laughed with the rest of the students. She loved a good underdog story.

Chapter Fifteen

Wearing rubber slippahs, Cassandra carried shampoo, her toothbrush, and toothpaste back to her room after taking the fastest shower since her undergrad dorm days at the University of Hawai'i. More than ten years had passed since she'd shared a large bathroom with multiple women, loud music and clouds of hairspray. Much as she wanted to be the cool older sister in the hall, she was fast becoming the old maid who longed for her quiet house.

Besides being her friend and occasional date, Marcus Fischer happened to be VP of Facilities and Maintenance. They would be having a serious discussion about the deep cleaning of communal bathrooms when he returned from vacation. Whatever the schedule, clearly it wasn't frequent enough. She was grateful for her footwear protection from the slimy greenish gunk that grew in the corner of the tiled shower stall.

Cassandra had barely closed the dorm door when her phone chirped on the bedside table. Scooping it up, she dropped the toiletries on the twin bed and tightened the towel across her chest. "Hello?"

Sunday morning phone calls were never happy news.

Cassandra had slept in late this morning and eased through a short yoga stretch routine after staying awake late the night before with the students. Getting extra sleep in the dorm was challenging because of doors closing at all hours of the night and loud voices in the hallway. Even Murphy was a better floormate than some of these kids.

Just thinking that made her cringe at how out of touch she sounded to herself.

The screen displayed Andy Summers name. "Hey Cassandra. Sorry to bother you. There was a break-in at the Osborne Admin Building. Looks like someone hit Dr. Nielson's office."

Her watch on its charger showed almost 11:00 a.m.

"A break in? Oh—I'll be right there." She disconnected, raced over to her weekender bag, and rummaged for jeans and a sweater. Her hair was still wet, so she fixed it into a low bun and pulled on a hat that matched her puffy winter coat.

She shut Murphy in his kennel in her room. She'd only be away a short time.

Slipping on low suede boots, Cassandra emerged from the fourth-floor elevator of the admin wing within fifteen minutes.

Andy met her just inside the door and steered her away from the president's reception and office areas. Several campus security and sheriff's office people were already inside.

"Thanks for coming so quickly."

"It's just a few minutes from Picotte to here."

Andy's face was grim, as though he was personally insulted that someone had broken into campus over the weekend.

Cassandra frowned slightly. "How did you find out about this?"

Andy gestured to a tall muscular guy in a Morton campus security uniform who took photos of the president's office. "Jackson was on weekend duty and noticed the unauthorized access to this office. Whoever it was had a valid key card to enter the building but not for the office. Since we are between presidents at the moment, it's hard to know if anything is missing. After we finish with photos and fingerprints, we'll go over the video footage."

Deputy Tate joined Cassandra and Andy. For a normal college incident, Andy would take care of it himself if there were no injuries or big-ticket items stolen. Cassandra raised an eyebrow at Andy.

Andy answered her eyebrow with a meaningful stare. "I called Tate because I thought this burglary could be related to Dr. Nielson's death."

Now was her opening. "I tried calling you yesterday, deputy. Do you know when Dr. Nielson was killed?"

She had to tilt her head back to look into Tate's frowning face. When he started shaking his head, she put up a palm to stop him. "I know it's an active investigation, but I've been trying to tell you all week that I don't think Nielson's death was simply because he surprised a robber in his house."

Andy had worked for the sheriff's office before taking the job at Morton and seemed to be respected by the local officers. Andy said, "Let's go down the hall to the conference room. You need to hear Dr. Sato's story."

At first Tate looked impatient to get on with their investigation of the office. Then he sighed and the three made their way to the large conference table.

So many thoughts fought for priority that Cassandra took a few moments to choose where to start. "Cinda and I stopped here on Saturday morning after graduation when we were looking for Dr. Nielson. The lights were on and a few half-opened boxes hadn't been there the last time I saw the office. It seemed like he had been here earlier but stepped out for a few minutes. Once your guys are done taking photos, I could tell you if the office looks different today."

Deputy Tate nodded and made a note in his small book. "Why were you looking for Dr. Nielson?"

"Just to say hello and have a chat," Cassandra shrugged. "I was surprised to see him at graduation and wanted to talk to him." She didn't think Mr. Hershey wanted the world to know he had asked Nielson back as interim president while they searched for his permanent replacement.

One of Andy's officers knocked on the conference room doorway. "There's a woman here to see you."

Before Andy even answered, Cinda's head peeked around the guy's back. Cassandra had texted her on the walk over to Osborne about the break-in. Cinda waved hello and flashed Andy her big smile.

"Thanks, Pete. Let her—"

"Hey y'all." Cinda set her lidded cup on the table and rolled a chair next to Cassandra's.

Andy said, "Deputy Scott Tate, meet Cinda Weller, Counseling and Career Services Director."

Cinda reached across the table and shook Tate's hand. Tate looked distracted. After a few seconds he flipped backwards a few pages in his book. He leaned forward and commanded more authority than you'd expect from a guy who was still in his late twenties. "Cinda Weller, why were your fingerprints found on the sliding glass door on the back of Gary Nielson's house?"

Cassandra and Cinda exchanged a long look while Cassandra tried to send telepathic waves for her not to get them both in trouble for snooping around.

Cinda laughed and unzipped her coat. She sipped from her cup in what Cassandra recognized as a stalling method. "Well of course you found my fingerprints, Deputy. I probably leaned on the door when I was knocking Saturday."

Tate said, "Was there something wrong with the front door?"

"No one answered the front door, so I tried the back. Did Dr. Nielson die on Sunday? Because I, for one, am grateful I did not see his dead body and a bunch of blood."

"That explains the extra footprints in the snow." Ignoring Cinda's question, Tate flipped another page. "What time were you at the house?"

Cassandra and Cinda looked at each other and shrugged. "Maybe 11:30 or Noon."

"When you were at his house, did you notice anything out of the ordinary?"

Cinda shook her head. "Well, definitely he'd been there before Saturday. And his cereal choices were odd." Her face turned red.

The only way Cinda or Cassandra would know what kind of cereal he preferred was if they'd peeked in the doors and windows.

Cassandra cleared her throat. "Did you find anything useful on Nielson's laptop?"

Andy and Tate both looked surprised.

"Let me guess," Cassandra said. "You didn't find a laptop at his house?"

Tate's voice rose. "We didn't. I wish you'd told me this earlier, Dr. Sato."

He was kidding, right? Both of Cassandra's eyebrows flew up to her hairline. "I have tried multiple times to talk to you this week, but you were too busy investigating."

She spoke as politely as possible because she really did believe he was a good guy just doing his job, but his unwillingness to include her from the beginning still grated.

"The robber trashed the place." On a big sigh, Tate added more details about the house. "The cupboards were emptied, boxes strewn around the kitchen. The couch cushions were cut open, boxes dumped onto the floor. Weirdly the robbers didn't take the big TV, desktop computer, or jewelry."

"And now they've broken into the college." Cassandra's thoughts might not have been welcome before, but now Morton was involved and that was her responsibility. She said, "Suppose whatever the killer thought he'd find on the laptop wasn't there? So, he checked the Morton office instead."

Tate frowned. "Look, Dr. Sato, we can take it from here."

Cassandra felt a nudge from Andy's elbow. "Tell him about Saturday night."

She pursed her lips off to the side. "Gary Nielson stopped at my house on Saturday night. He seemed spooked by someone who had sent him texts and he said he felt scared. Then on Monday, you told me it seemed like a pretty obvious case of him interrupting robbers at his house."

Tate's chin dropped to his chest. He was normally a smart guy, so he probably recognized that by cutting her off, he'd missed some crucial information. He said, "Why didn't—"

"I did call—"

"You tried to call me. I know." He held up a hand. "Let's start over. Tell me what happened when Nielson came to your house."

A few minutes later she had filled him in on the Chinese government reporting a security breach, the USDA interview, and the threatening texts. "Oh, and Mr. Hershey, the chairman of the Morton College board, asked Nielson to come back and work as president during the spring semester. He wanted Nielson to ensure no one from the college had been involved in the security lapse during the trip to China."

Cassandra sat silently for a full thirty seconds after she'd finished talking while Tate took notes in his book. No way she could repress the tiny feeling of satisfaction in being right about helping the investigation. She knew stuff they didn't, and it was about time Tate acknowledged it.

"When will Nielson's body be released by the coroner's office? Won't Becky and her family come and pick him up?" Cassandra made a mental note to try to meet up with Becky in person. She wanted to know more about Nielson's meeting with the USDA people in Florida and the soybean formula. Probably Cassandra wouldn't be mentioning any of that to the deputy.

Andy kept shifting his weight in the seat next to her. He couldn't seem to get comfortable, but she couldn't guess why.

When the police finished asking questions about what they had seen at Nielson's house and in his office on Saturday, Cassandra and Cinda walked outside and stood on the pathway.

Cassandra's coat was completely zipped up, but she still shivered, "I don't like this. It was bad enough that someone shot Nielson dead. Now our offices are targeted."

"I assume it's the same people who broke into his house," said Cinda. "I felt better when I imagined the bad guys had escaped town."

Cassandra said, "When Mrs. Nielson arrives from Iowa, I want to see her and ask more about what happened in Florida. Nielson mentioned his new job last Saturday at my house. We need to know more about his contact with the U.S.D.A."

Before returning to Picotte, Cassandra drove to her house to pick up the extra dog food she'd forgotten to grab the day before. She let herself in the front door and hung her tote bag on the entryway hook.

Coming fully into the office and living room, Cassandra gasped. "Holy crap! What a mess!"

Every single couch cushion was thrown on the floor. When Cassandra picked up a cushion and flipped it over, stuffing spilled out of a gaping diagonal cut. The coffee table was turned on its side. The glass-topped end table had been knocked on end and Cassandra's plumeria plant rested on its side on the floor.

Her home had been ransacked, again! Chicken skin snaked up her arms.

Luckily, the plant had been jostled but most of the dirt remained inside the pot. Cassandra had been babying the plant from Paul's funeral ever since the college nursery had fixed it up in October.

Running into her bedroom, she found pillows and the comforter heaped in the middle of the bed, but intact. The nightstand drawers were open, the contents dumped on the floor.

This must have happened after the break-in at Morton College. What if she'd been home instead of sleeping at Picotte Hall? Her breath came in short bursts. The last time her house had been broken into, she'd borrowed one of Fischer's anxiety pills to quell her nausea and fear. But Fischer was gone, and she needed to get herself together without relying on medication.

Okay, this time she did really need to leave the house to preserve evidence. What if the thief was still inside? She was already dialing 9-1-1 before she reached the front door.

Waiting in her car, Cassandra turned on the engine, blasted the heater, and flipped on the seat warmer before she texted Andy. Slowly her heart rate returned to normal.

Ten minutes later, she startled when Andy rapped on the car window. "Hey, are you okay? I was still at the Osborne building."

"Yes. I only looked in the living room and my bedroom. I haven't checked the rest."

Hustling inside, Andy took the curved wooden staircase two steps at a time. Cassandra waited in the kitchen while the upstairs bedroom doors opened and closed, then the bathroom. The kitchen was hardly disturbed except the chairs were knocked to the floor.

She and Andy checked the basement. "All clear."

"I don't know why I'm dragged into this. Nielson retired six weeks ago." Cassandra's face felt hot. Her voice came out louder than normal. "This isn't right."

"You should probably call your insurance agent tomorrow first thing to file a claim."

"I met the deductible already on the roof. My agent is gonna hate me."

"I noticed your back door lock was damaged pretty badly. You'll have to replace it. You might want to check into a full security system. Especially after what happened in October."

They'd taken out every drawer in her large wooden desk and dumped out her file folders. No amount of browsing on Pinterest was going to make this organizational nightmare go away soon.

"What were they looking for?"

Summers scratched his head through his knit hat. "Let's assume it's about the soybean seeds. You had your laptop with you so they couldn't steal it. But they're also looking in drawers and couch cushions."

"The main question I want an answer for is why my house? I didn't even go to China." The upended kitchen chairs bothered her sense of order. She tucked shaky hands in her coat pockets to avoid disturbing evidence by setting them upright. "We need to figure out what's going on before someone else's house is next. Or worse, what if they target another person from the trip?"

Summers checked in to update Deputy Tate. While he talked, Cassandra gingerly stepped around the living room looking for a pattern to what was ruined or missing.

A knock on the front door made her heart skip. Cassandra glanced back at the kitchen where Summers was still on the phone. "That was fast."

Sean Gill stood on the front step, no winter coat. His button-down preppy shirt was untucked, same jeans as the day before, and were those sheepskin slippers on his feet?

"Are you hurt?"

While she stood there holding the door open, her jaw loose in confusion, letting all the outside cold air into her already chilled house, Gill took it as an invitation to step inside.

"How did you know?" Cassandra scanned her driveway and up and down the street but saw only her car and Andy's behind it.

"We heard the police scanner. Major neighborhood watch failure on our part." Gill stopped just inside the living room, mouth set. "I can't believe I didn't notice someone breaking in."

Her temple throbbed and she rubbed it absently. "I don't know. Maybe it was overnight."

Seriously? Her neighbors sat around listening to the police scanner. Cassandra frowned. "I suspect it was the same people who broke into my former boss's place last week. The deputy told me his house was trashed like mine."

She'd spent so much time and money this semester designing the simple, calm modern space she now called home. Foreboding heaviness settled on her chest like a brick.

"Which door did they use?" asked Gill.

Cassandra felt uneasy. He didn't write anything in a little notebook, but he sounded a lot like Tate, only more experienced.

Not for the first time she wanted to know more about Sean Gill. "Our campus security guy said the back door lock was broken."

Andy Summers came into the living room. "Tate's sending the techs here as soon as they're done at Morton. Then I'll help you fix—" He broke off when he saw Sean Gill. "Well, now wait a minute."

Judging from their expressions, they recognized each other. Also, they didn't seem like old buddies.

"Summers." Sean did that thing where he jerked his chin up to acknowledge Andy's presence. "Hold your horses. I'll take care of the locks."

Cassandra looked from one to the other. Summers was a couple of inches shorter and quite a bit heavier than the wiry-framed Gill. She guessed that Gill looked a little older.

Andy's light brown eyes flicked between her and Gill. "Sean."

Cassandra stared at the little chin dimple on her neighbors' son's face. A guilty twinge fluttered. She chastised herself for worrying about hurting Andy's feelings when she wasn't doing anything wrong.

"I gotta head back to my office and start the paperwork." Andy frowned at Sean and said, "You should stay outside or in the entryway and don't touch anything. After they're done, you can make a list of what's missing or broken."

Summers stared at Gill for several heartbeats, then nodded his head once. As though some secret guy conversation had just happened at a frequency only they understood.

As soon as Summers left, Gill said, "Your boyfriend isn't a fan of mine."

Cassandra looked over her shoulder toward the kitchen where Andy had left. "We're just friends."

She sounded like Sela talking about Daniel Leung. Why did people assume that spending time with a member of the opposite sex meant you must be dating?

If she were completely honest, she'd acknowledge that Andy probably did think of her that way, even if she was keeping things strictly platonic. "You know each other?"

"Summers went to high school with my younger brother."

There was more to the story than Gill let on. She recognized antagonism when she felt it. "Where's your brother now?"

"Lives in the big city of Omaha."

Maybe he said that sarcastically. She didn't know him well enough to be sure.

"The police will need time to process your house for fingerprints and collect info for the reports. We won't be able to work on your roof for a couple more days."

Of course, it would make a delay. Just what Cassandra needed. "Luckily, I've got a place to sleep. The resident assistant is back tomorrow, but it won't hurt if I'm there too."

If she'd been home, instead of leaving her house unattended with the lights off while she baked cookies with students, maybe the thieves would have left her place alone. Part of her wished she'd been here to chase the idiots out of her house last night. However, the brainy part of her felt grateful. If the same people who killed Nielson had done this, being gone was safer.

She asked, "I don't suppose any of your high school friends own a security company?"

Gill punched some numbers on his phone and paced in the kitchen. "Craig is on his way over now. He said he'll stop and buy you a new back door lock. I'll take a photo of yours so he can match it as closely as possible."

"You didn't have to do that. I could've gone to the hardware store tomorrow."

A few minutes after Sean Gill left, the sheriff's and the technicians' cars pulled into Cassandra's driveway and on the street in front of her house. Like a traveling road show.

While the police worked, Cassandra stayed in her kitchen to avoid the cold outside or interfering with the crime scene in her living room.

She made hot tea. She browsed on her iPad. She called Cinda to tell her what had happened.

"Want me to help you clean up?" Cinda offered.

"I can handle the house, but I'll need you tomorrow." Cassandra said, "This has got to stop before anyone else gets hurt."

"I'm so sorry about your house, Cass. At least your roof is fixed though, right?"

"Pffh," Cassandra's blood pressure rose again. "The neighbor, Sean Gill, said he's waiting for parts and for his friends to be available. I walked in on him yesterday afternoon."

"Walked in on him doing what?" Cinda's voice was interested in the latest gossip.

"Working on the wiring in my ceiling. He just let himself into my house like it's no big deal. He probably sneaks over at night to watch TV and spill potato chip crumbs on my couch." She was overreacting but couldn't stop herself.

"Eh, maybe not a big deal. That's kind of a small-town thing. Some people don't even lock their doors, or they'll leave their keys in the car overnight."

Cassandra was not some people. "All I'm saying, he should communicate better about expectations."

"It's not like he's a professional carpenter. You have a hunky neighborhood stud at your disposal and you're mad about it?"

Cinda was right. Sean wasn't the enemy.

"After I realized my house was ransacked, Andy came over first. When Sean stopped over, they had a bizarre bro conversation. Like super polite, but with an undercurrent of tension. One of them said, hold your horses. The other seemed mad about it."

"Hold your horses aren't fighting words." Cinda said. "Good thing you're friends with me. I speak Midwestern. If one of them says, listen here, pal, then you should duck out of arm's reach because someone's about to get punched."

After hanging up with Cinda, Cassandra felt sweat drip down her side. She sighed. A large glass of Chardonnay sounded better than decaffeinated chamomile.

By the time the police left and Cassandra had time alone to walk slowly around the house, she was worn out. The jerks had even slashed Murphy's brand-new dog bed. That was just too much. Tears of frustration formed in her eyes, but she wiped them away.

She was a homeowner now. Through good times and bad. Although she'd had enough bad times.

Chapter Sixteen

Cassandra took a long sip out of her large takeout coffee cup and waited for Dr. Bryant to get his order from the barista on the bakery side of the Gas & Sweets. He settled himself into the chair opposite her at the industrial style bistro table.

Her heart raced in anticipation of doing the whole conversation in ASL without being able to rely on Meg to interpret. She'd brought her iPad with her in case she needed to bail at some point and type everything out on the notes app. But she intended to try harder this time. They'd exchanged emails of their draft grant proposal. Now they needed to hash the bits out in person. She could do this. The night before she'd spent an hour with Jasmine in the common room looking up vocabulary words on an online ASL website and practicing together.

Cassandra's cheeks burned with self-consciousness. "Good morning!" Her hands shook slightly.

"Hi Cassandra!" Bryant saluted back at her.

He offered her a blueberry muffin from a small brown cardboard box he placed on the center of the table. She waved him off. If she ate anything, she'd be in danger of throwing it back up from nerves.

"You look beautiful, as always," he signed. He kind of moved his mouth a little when he made the signs and his hands moved slower and more precisely than when he was talking to Meg. She didn't have to ask him to repeat.

Maybe this wouldn't be impossible after all! She let out a breath she hadn't realized she'd been holding. Cassandra held up the stack of notes she'd printed out. "Work on these?" She laid three pages side by side on the tabletop and pointed to the summary at the top of the first page.

Bryant nodded and scooted his chair around so they could lean in together and read at the same time. A warm vanilla scent clung to his clothes. Enough to notice, but not completely distracting her from the task at hand.

Quietly, they read together. Cassandra checked his eyes a couple of times, guessing where he was following on the page. With a colleague who hears, she would have talked while they were both looking down. But she with him, she needed to wait until they made eye contact again.

Bryant pointed halfway down the page at a list of potential companies where they could order the emergency text alert equipment. "We need more numbers here. If the costs are one lump sum or monthly." Cassandra made notes in the margins. "And this is where we add the campus comparisons from similar institutions."

Between his gestures to the page and his slow signing, Cassandra actually understood him. She was so proud of herself! And shocked. She couldn't help a huge self-satisfied grin from forming on her face.

Bryant's head tilted a little like he was amused. "If I had known numbers made you so happy, I would have talked accounting to you all the time."

"H-A!" Cassandra fingerspelled. "I don't love numbers. But I understood what you signed. I was surprised!"

He wrote a note next to the paragraph they had discussed. He turned a few pages and pointed again. "This is where we should put the project idea for the Deaf Studies entrepreneur-style competition." He had to fingerspell E-N-T-E-R-P-R-E-N-E-U-R three times and finally he wrote it on the paper because Cassandra still didn't understand him.

Her lips pursed together in frustration. Her back was damp with perspiration.

Bryant said, "You're fine. That was a long word. You've been studying ASL? You're doing a good job."

"I studied phrases with your student, Jasmine. But you are faster."

"Spend more time with me and you will learn." He raised his eyebrows up and down in a flirty way. His chiseled cheeks and striking brown eyes made her blush involuntarily.

She ignored his teasing. He was at least ten years older than her. "I could learn more if you tutored me." She really wanted to improve her sign skills to communicate with the students in her office too. "Could we meet for coffee every week?"

His dark eyebrows met, and he straightened in the chair. "I don't date hearing women."

Cassandra's smile slipped. She thought they were just bantering playfully. "Wait! I wasn't flirting—" She didn't know that sign so she fingerspelled it slowly.

Bryant put both palms down in front of his chest and then wiggled his fingers slightly. Kind of like eyelashes fluttering.

Cassandra copied his sign. "—Flirting. I wasn't flirting with you. I don't want to D-A-T-E you." She shook her head to make sure he understood.

Her no dating at work policy had always been her fallback. Until Fischer. And they'd only been on two dates, so that didn't really count yet, did it?

Again, Bryant's face became more serious, like she'd offended him. "Is it because I'm deaf?"

She couldn't tell if he was messing with her. But there was a tiny hint of playfulness in his brown eyes. "Stop teasing me."

Bryant ruffled his dark hair a little and straightened the collar on his quarter zip sweater. On second thought, he did look offended. "Am I too old? What is it? I've looked in the mirror. I know I'm irresistible. How is this not working on you?" He moved one hand in a small circle in front of his face.

Warily, she sat back and studied him more. He was handsome and he knew it with that self-assured way guys do.

Bryant signed, "It's that Fischer dude. I've seen you look at him."

Okay, now she *knew* he was teasing her. He finally smiled completely.

She laughed. "I thought you don't date hearing women?"

"I don't."

She didn't know the signs for mischievous or impish. "You're... bad."

Shaking her head, Cassandra picked up the next page in their proposal.

Once they'd made it through the grant proposal notes, Cassandra felt comfortable enough to break off a bite of the blueberry muffin.

Bryant signed, "That's sad about President Nielson dying."

Unless he'd read the local paper's website while he was gone, he probably didn't know the details. She looked out the window into the deserted parking lot. The Monday after Christmas and most people were probably staying home.

She wanted to tell him about the shooting and everything, but she didn't know all the signs. Picking up her iPad, she found the notes app and spoke into the microphone. "Very sad. The police are investigating what happened. And someone broke into his office at Morton yesterday."

As she spoke, the words appeared on the screen and Bryant read them. His eyebrows went up.

Cassandra nodded and tapped the microphone again. "My house, too. Andy Summers thinks it's all related, but—" She raised her palms up in a big shrug.

"What did they steal?" asked Bryant.

"From Nielson's? A laptop for sure, what else I don't know. My files were a mess and I need to go through them to see if anything was taken. They cut my couch cushions and dumped all the drawers out. But what could I have? My laptop is the most valuable thing I own, but it was in my dorm room."

His head shook back and forth slowly, like he couldn't believe her bad luck. "It's pretty obvious the thief was looking for something."

She'd hoped he might have insights about that. He'd been at Morton longer than she had. "Do you know of anyone who didn't like Dr. Nielson? I know he wasn't perfect, but his heart was in the right place."

Bryant took a long swig from his coffee. Cassandra had finished hers long ago. He typed his response on the iPad keyboard. "I don't pay attention to academic politics bull. I do my own thing." His right shoulder made a small shrug.

Maybe not, but Bryant must have worked on faculty committees. "Have you worked with Professor Zimmerman?" If she was going to use Zimmerman's research and experiences when talking to the police, she needed to make sure he was reliable.

Bryant made a so-so gesture. "I'm not a science nerd. I'm more of a history and creativity guy. I know who he is. Didn't a student complain against Zimmerman recently?"

Cassandra's lips pressed together. She typed, "Between us?" Based on their past history with the protestors and working together on the Diversity Council, she felt Bryant was a good judge of character. "Actually, you met the student last week when you came to Picotte to see me. Remember Daniel Leung?"

"The Asian kid next to the gorgeous girl on the couch?"

Cassandra laughed out loud. "Creeper."

"Hey, I treat all the female students like my sister or nieces. I'm deaf, not blind, right?" He raised his eyebrows up and down and laughed, too. "That kid seemed kind of intense."

"Anyway, the complaint didn't sound like an unethical situation to me, but I thought professors might gossip about each other."

"Interesting," he signed. "Sometimes I don't know the 'water cooler' gossip unless someone goes out of their way to tell me. I could ask my teaching assistant. The grad students talk about stuff like that."

Cassandra packed their trash together into one pile and threw it away. "I'm not looking for trouble, I just need to know who I can trust, thanks." They both had to get back to work. His winter term class started today.

She had so many things to worry about, she'd make a list in her planner before she chose which one to tackle first. Although it was another short holiday week, it already felt long.

Chapter Seventeen

Juggling a fast food bag and soda from Runza, her new favorite local Nebraska restaurant, Cassandra reached her room at Picotte Hall. She'd earned a late lunch emotional takeout meal of a Swiss mushroom burger and Frings.

Her door wasn't shut completely. Grooves in the wooden frame near the doorknob made it look like someone had forced the door open. Frowning, Cassandra took a step back and checked up and down the hall. Icy fingers of alarm traced down her back.

Empty. Voices drifted from farther down by the common room.

Although her cautious head warned her about the unidentified person or persons breaking into campus and her house, her thumping heart had had enough. She refused to let herself become a target of mischief again.

Using her elbow to avoid disturbing potential crime scene evidence—she'd had way too much experience at that lately—she slowly pushed the door open and peeked inside the darkened room. Nothing had been slashed, ripped or trashed. Her chest and stomach relaxed.

Setting the food on the desk, she flipped on the overhead light. No one had touched her overnight bag or small pile of makeup and toiletries near the mirror and dresser.

She examined the door latch more closely. Maybe the marks in the doorframe had been there before and she just hadn't noticed. But why was her door cracked open? She hadn't been so hurried this morning that she'd forgotten to pull it completely shut.

So odd. She felt like a player in a role play game where scoring points meant predicting the time and place of the next break-in.

Carrying her food to the common room, Cassandra joined Sela, another girl, and Akira chilling in front of the TV. Cassandra pulled out the warm Frings first. The Runza chefs combined onion rings and French fries into one side item that had quickly become her go-to indulgence. Savoring the crispy onion ring crunch, she sat on one of the side chairs and chewed.

Two sharp barks came from Sela's lap on the couch across the room. Murphy's mouth opened in a doggie smile of contentment. He barked once more.

For a few minutes, she'd been so distracted by the door lock she'd forgotten about him. "I know I kenneled the dog in my room..."

Akira reached out and patted Murphy's head. No growling or snarling. "He didn't like the crate. He cried."

"Kennels are inhumane," said Sela. "Responsible pet owners shouldn't lock the poor things in a cage. Look how much Murphy loves people!"

Both of Cassandra's eyebrows raised. "You folks broke into my room. To let out the dog?" Cassandra must have channeled her inner Michiko Sato because all three students shrank into the back of the couch away from her.

Murphy let out a low growl of displeasure.

"The lock wasn't very good." Akira explained, "It opened easy."

She didn't trust herself to respond in a calm, professional manner. Murphy pushed all her buttons and brought out the worst in her. Packing the Frings into the takeout bag, Cassandra carried it back to her room, shaking her head. She closed the door, but it wouldn't stay latched without using the dead bolt.

Her roof had better be fixed soon.

* * *

Later that afternoon, Cassandra met Cinda on the Nielsons' front sidewalk. "Thanks for coming, Cinda. I appreciate it."

"I wouldn't miss this for nothing." Cinda had walked down the street from her house. "Meg tagged along on your misadventures earlier this fall, and it's finally my turn."

For such a large old home, the front entry was disproportionately small with a roof barely large enough to cover the two of them. Cassandra held a bakery box containing a dozen bagels with toppings.

"I get that you have an offbeat sense of humor," Cassandra shivered in the cold. "But this is serious, Cinda. We need to be one hundred percent professional."

"I didn't mean it like that," said Cinda. "I'm just saying I live nearby. If bad guys are roaming the town, I want them caught. Pronto."

Did anyone say pronto anymore?

A forty-ish man opened the door. At first, Cassandra thought he was a family friend because his average height and stocky body resembled a fireplug more than Dr. Nielson's tall, thin frame. But the unruly eyebrows betrayed his genetics. Although they weren't gray, they were exactly like his father's, making his face a puffier, younger version of Gary Nielson.

A pang of grief snuck up on her, tightening her chest. "Hi, I'm Cassandra and this is Cinda. We're from the college. Is your mother available?"

"Yeah. Come in." He led them down a hallway to the kitchen and attached family room. Someone had cleaned up the house, replacing lamps on side tables and the couch cushions looked normal except for a few with stuffing poking through the cut edges.

Becky sat at the granite island countertop staring vacantly over a plate of half-eaten toast and a large glass of water.

"Maybe you can motivate her," said the son. "I told her we need to collect her stuff, meet with the funeral home, and get out of town again."

Mrs. Nielson blinked hard at them like she was waking up from a dream. Or, more likely, a nightmare.

"Becky, I'm so sorry about Gary." Cassandra set the cardboard box on the counter. Cinda stood off to the side a bit. "You remember Cinda Weller, the head of Counseling and Career Services?"

"I remember meeting you, but I'm having a hard time focusing right now. Forgive me."

Cinda said, "I'm sorry for your loss."

"And I'm sorry your house was broken into, Becky." Cassandra got right to the point. "The sheriff and college are doing everything possible to track down the responsible people."

"We left a lot of our stuff in Carson." Tucked inside her hand was a wadded tissue. "We'd planned to make an initial trip to check out the area in Florida and decide where we wanted to buy a townhouse. We'd planned to come back after the holidays." She blew her nose. "But instead we're planning a funeral." Tears streamed down her face. "I don't know why I'm still crying. It's been days."

"I'm sure seeing your house makes everything more real." When someone violates your personal space, it doesn't just stop when the police report is filed. Cassandra perched on the stool next to her. "I don't know what the police told you, but my house was also burglarized."

Confusion clouded Becky's lightly wrinkled forehead. "Your house, too! What a coincidence."

Cassandra and Cinda exchanged glances.

"Wait a minute." Becky wasn't as out of it as she seemed. "You think it's not a coincidence."

"The people who did this were looking for something." Cassandra said, "When they couldn't find it at your house, they tried Dr. Nielson's office at the college and my house, too."

"Our valuable jewelry and papers were in a safe deposit box at the bank. There's nothing here except furniture, costume jewelry, and a few mementos." She breathed a deep sigh. "We made donations to a consignment store and then were going to give the rest to the children, Pat and Caleb."

Cassandra waited a few moments trying to read Becky's emotional level. She wanted to ask more about their time in Florida but didn't want to upset her further. Perspiration dampened her back under her sweater and heavy coat. "When Gary stopped at my house on Saturday, he mentioned starting a job in Florida? Had he change his mind about retiring?"

"You know Gary. He couldn't go completely cold turkey. He took a part-time job at the plant repository. But after the USDA people told him about the suspicions involving his trip, he called Alan Hershey. He was just trying to do the right thing. Gary wanted to come home and clear up the college's name." Her watery blue eyes met Cassandra's. "We thought it was a misunderstanding."

"Do you remember the name of the repository?"

Becky pulled her purse off the nearby desktop and searched through it for a minute.

Several casserole dishes and bakery boxes covered one countertop and stacks of papers and folders needed sorting.

Becky handed a yellow sticky note to Cassandra. "It's called the National Repository. He planned to work part-time helping the curators manage the plant resources."

Cassandra's college roommate worked at a plant repository in Florida. "I think I know that place. Do you remember him mentioning more about the high-yield soybean seed formula?" Cassandra didn't want to pump her too hard for details, but this might be her only opportunity to talk to Becky.

"I don't know. When you've been married for forty years, half of what your spouse says goes in one ear and out the other. He probably mentioned soybean yada, yada at some point. I mean I loved Gary, but he could be naive. People took advantage of his tendency to avoid controversy."

Cinda said, "You mean like that whole episode with the cattle feed enzyme in October?"

"I knew there was nothing wrong with that beef!" Becky tapped the countertop for emphasis. "I grew up on a cattle farm, and my father mixed all kinds of ingredients to fatten the cattle. Additives make the beef taste better."

"Amen, sister! Love me some grilled burgers." Cinda said.

"Those government people worried Gary." Her face become more animated. "When we left Florida, he didn't want to stop at a hotel. Insisted on driving straight through and sleeping a few hours in the rest stops along the route. I told him that was ridiculous, but he wouldn't have it any other way."

Her son, Pat, came forward. "My father's library was filled with his research and old paperwork from Morton. He never trusted technology when everything went digital. He saved old papers in the basement, just in case." Pat seemed to warm to the treasure hunt idea. He raised a finger like a great idea had occurred to him. The gesture was an eerily exact copy of his father's. "When we were kids, we used to hide snacks in the ceiling tiles of the basement."

"I remember finding empty pudding cups stuffed up there. So did our local friendly mice. We had an infestation for months!" Becky nudged her son's arm. "Pat, you don't think he would have hidden something in the ceiling?"

Pat shrugged.

"I feel so guilty for not taking Gary seriously. When he called me Saturday afternoon, he acted funny. But I thought it wasn't a big deal. He told me he went to the graduation ceremony. I thought he was sentimental with nostalgia over Morton." Becky's lips tightened into a straight line. "I didn't want to come back, but he felt—"

The front doorbell rang, and Pat frowned slightly then went to answer it.

Cassandra said, "Maybe Dr. Nielson thought he could access his office files in order to retrieve whatever it was the government and these thieves wanted."

Voices came toward the kitchen and towering behind Pat was Deputy Tate, hat in hands. His dark brown eyes bored into Cassandra's with an intensity that raised chicken skin on the back of her neck. "Mrs. Nielson." He made a polite bow in her direction. "Ms. Weller and Dr. Sato, what are you doing?"

If Tate had cooperated with her more on the investigation, maybe he wouldn't feel threatened by her presence at her former boss's home. Cassandra's smile didn't reach her eyes. "We just stopped by to give our condolences." She tapped the bakery box. "And breakfast."

Cinda was already zipping her jacket and backing out of the kitchen. Cassandra heard her murmur, "Fixin' to leave, bud."

Cassandra didn't get to ask about the missing laptop. She raised the hand with the yellow sticky note and waved goodbye. "I really appreciate your help, Mrs. Nielson."

Becky's son walked them to the front door, leaving his mother and the deputy in the kitchen. In a lower voice Pat said, "I can't just dump my mother in Iowa at my aunt's house forever. When I go back to work, I need to know she will be safe. If someone was willing to ... to shoot my dad, and burglarize our family's house, what's their next move?"

Exactly the same concern that Cassandra felt. "Make sure your mom tells Deputy Tate everything. He has all the law enforcement resources at his disposal. I'm checking on files and people to find the extent of Morton's involvement. Let's work together and find out who did this."

When she got back to her office, first thing she'd do was find that Hangzhou Commerce College exchange trip roster and send it to Andy Summers. Then she had a good idea where she could get more information.

Chapter Eighteen

When Cassandra's phone vibrated with an unknown call from a Miami, FL area code, she grabbed it right away and slid the phone line open, a flutter of delight pulsing inside her chest so hard it surprised her. A friendly voice from home.

Five minutes later, her college friend Jocelyn Kaneshiro and she had caught up on the past few weeks since they'd last texted each other.

"Aloha! Can't believe we both mainland girls now, eh?" Her friend asked in their local Hawaiian dialect.

"Long ways from Waipahu, fo' sure," Cassandra agreed.

"Look, I know we're both busy," Cassandra switched back to her professional speaking voice. "I wanted to pick your brain. It's a really long story, but you work in Coral Gables, right?"

"Yah, the fancy long name is the Subtropical Horticultural Research Station."

Cassandra had emailed her former roommate first thing in the morning asking for a call back at a more convenient time. "Oh. I thought your job was at a plant repository. I must've gotten it wrong." Jocelyn had moved to Florida in June, two months before Cassandra left Oahu.

"You're not wrong. It's part of the National Germplasm Repositories. Like the ag research center at UH where I did an internship in Hilo." They'd been good friends since undergrad when Jocelyn had studied tropical plant and soil science. Jocelyn laughed. "I hate to be the one to tell you this, but you can't grow papaya in Nebraska. Wrong plant hardiness zone."

So funny. Not. "Cute, ya?" Cassandra would give almost anything for a fresh, juicy papaya or mango. She looked out the window at the large piles of plowed snow lining the walkways around the campus quad and shivered.

"Sounds like a really big place where you work." Cassandra asked.

"Depends what you mean by big. More like a campus of buildings all controlled by the USDA but everybody's got their own research niche."

"This is going to sound freaky, but I'm trying to confirm whether a friend of mine was telling the truth that he found a job briefly in Coral Gables. I want to find out if he spent any time working in the office there. Is that possible?"

"Depends which agency he was trying to get into. What's his research specialty?"

"Here's the thing, he's dead. He was killed last week in Nebraska. And he's not a plant scientist. He was our former college president who wanted to retire in Florida. I think the job was his way of moving south and keeping himself busy."

"I get you. The snowbirds move here and buy a house then figure out how to work as few hours as possible while enjoying the warm winters. You can't go six blocks down here without tripping over a displaced New Yorker geezer shuffling along in Velcro shoes."

Cassandra laughed. "This geezer was a few years away from the Velcro shoes, but yeah. That's the scenario."

"I'm sorry for your loss, but this town is cursed. You've already met two dead guys and a sad old lady since you got there. What the heck?"

Cassandra was getting tired of Meg, Cinda, and now Jocelyn reminding her of all she'd endured this semester. "Just help me out, Joce.'"

"There's lots of employees on campus, but we're mostly about the plants. Get over 5,000 different accessions of fruits, nuts, sugarcane, and other crops."

"He would have extensive experience with contracts and grant management." Cassandra explained what Dr. Nielson had told her about the USDA questioning a high-yield soybean plant seed, and the recent burglaries in town.

Cassandra could hear keyboard keys clacking while Jocelyn checked on her work computer. Cassandra spelled Nielson's name slowly.

"I found a Gary Nielson in the staff directory, but I don't see his full profile. When you said he had a soybean seed, you don't mean he stole an actual plant from the repository, right? 'Cause that would be especially stupid. Being a federal crime."

"I know it's unusual. The people bothering Nielson weren't looking for a plant. It's the growing process they used to make the seeds drought and disease resistant."

Jocelyn said, "There's a flag on his internal profile page, Cass. When I clicked for more info, I got a 'this is classified' error message."

"Well, shoots. So, the government really did accuse him of something that happened on his China trip. He wasn't just acting paranoid. He even asked me about the Chinese mafia."

Cassandra heard a big sigh on the other end of the phone. "Tell me you're not in the middle of more trouble. Do not piss off those people."

"I haven't done anything except make sure the college avoids a government investigation or a lawsuit." Talking to Jocelyn had confirmed her worst fears. Cassandra said, "I'd better go. I appreciate you checking for me."

"I'll talk to you again in a couple more months when you get tired of all that snow. You be careful, wahine. Don't make me come rescue you again."

"Rescue me?! Are you—"

The sound of Jocelyn laughing while she clicked off made Cassandra shake her head. All joking aside, she knew Jocelyn was right. Her house had been broken into, again. Come to think of it, her first stalker had simply faded into the wind a couple of months ago. She had no idea where he was now. Maybe he still held a grudge against Nielson. Cassandra had built relationships with people at the college, but now she began to wonder which of them were truly trustworthy.

* * *

The smell of cleaning disinfectant wafted into Cassandra's office from the outer area. As much as she liked things neat and clean, the smell was too institutional. She added buying a few plug-in air fresheners to her bullet journal's to do list. She wanted to begin the new year on the right note. A cozy apple scent or sandalwood would set a better tone than pine trees.

It felt great to be back in her office with Bridget, her student worker, out front all day to greet walk-in appointments. Winter Term three-week mini classes had begun, and a few warmly bundled up faculty and students walked from building to building. Opening the telecommunications grant proposal settled her mind. Cassandra's office was her refuge from the anxiety over her roof and the break-in.

She'd already outlined new goals and agendas for the first few meetings of the Diversity Council's reboot during the Spring semester.

Murphy was currently being pampered in the dorm by the students. They'd adopted him as their floor mascot. Overnight in his kennel, Murphy shifted position every few hours which woke her up. Then his light snores kept her awake long after he'd drifted back into doggie dreamland where he ate endless bowls of kibble and chased squirrels. Just thinking about it made her yawn and long for a nap. But no, she was going to get a full Monday's work accomplished.

Her phone buzzed again. Andy Summers. He said, "I've been thinking..."

Cassandra had his name on her to-do list also. She wanted to go over security measures for the admin building in particular.

"Yesterday's burglary at your house made me look at things differently." He sounded tired, too. "The past couple of months, there have been more break-ins than normal around campus."

Cassandra said, "uh, huh," but didn't interrupt his train of thought.

"Not exactly a crime wave or anything. Every few days, a student reported a backpack tampered with or missing items from a dorm room. Random incidents in the student center, the library, a fraternity house, someone's lock broken at the campus gym."

She'd always assumed that Andy was a good security director, but now she questioned that judgment. Shouldn't he have noticed a connection earlier and reported the increased crime to administration. "What types of things were stolen?"

Andy said, "That's the odd thing. Usually nothing. Or small things like makeup, Chapstick, USB thumb drives, phone chargers. Things that fit in your pockets. Don't get me wrong, there've been a couple of laptops, bikes, and wallets stolen this semester. That happens every year. What's not normal is the number of times I got reports that people knew someone had been there, moved things, or broken a lock but nothing of value was taken."

"Now my house and the president's suite." Cassandra said. "I haven't had a chance to go through all my files and papers, but so far I haven't noticed anything missing except my television remote control. What else is missing besides Nielson's laptop?"

"Still waiting to get the list from his wife. The sheriff's office will share it with me because the cases are linked now." Cassandra wrote notes while Andy kept talking. "I looked at the list you gave me of the people who went on the cultural exchange trip to China in October with Dr. Nielson—"

She was afraid to find out if her hunch was right. Cassandra's heart thumped before he even finished his sentence. "How many?"

"Out of the people who went on the trip, my crime statistics spreadsheet for this semester mentions crime reports from more than half of them."

The evidence supported that Nielson's death was related to the China trip. "Have you told Deputy Tate?"

"Nope. I just finished comparing my notes and called you. I can't believe how obvious this is. It was here all along. I've been taking these reports ever since October, but I never noticed the connection until now."

Cassandra jotted everything in her journal next to where she'd noted the names of everyone on the trip before she sent it to Andy. His inexplicable lapse was a problem. Granted, the semester had been unusually busy, security-wise. She paused a moment to visualize grace instead of negativity.

"Well, now that we know, the fastest way is to divide the list of names. We could start by locating where everyone who traveled with Nielson has been the past two weeks."

"This is not a *we* thing, Cassandra."

She hated hearing those words. The police weren't the only ones capable of following leads and making connections. Plus, the deputy had already made it clear he didn't want her opinion.

"I know. I know. The sheriff's office will handle it." The police did all their forensic crime fighting ninja stuff. Cassandra looked more at the big picture of relationships between the people involved. They needed her skills. "... Until they get stuck. In the meantime, I'm going to do more research." That's what academics do.

They'd hung up before Cassandra realized she'd missed her chance to fill Andy in on her telephone fishing expedition with Jocelyn in Florida. Her finger paused over the redial button.

The sheriff's office didn't want her help. She would keep her research questions quiet for now. She was perfectly capable of getting answers all by herself.

Chapter Nineteen

Cassandra surveyed the holiday limited menu choices at Picotte's dining room and sighed.

She'd planned to avail herself of the full residence hall experience by eating in the student cafeteria one night. Due to the holidays, chairs were stacked on tables and pushed to the side leaving only five tables set for meals on one side of the large dining hall.

Glancing over at a student clad in a hoodie and backwards ball cap, Cassandra realized she was standing next to Akira Higashi. "The curried chicken smells great."

Akira said, "The cook told me their rice is good, but to me Nebraska rice tastes like cardboard."

"Yeah, I think they buy it parboiled and in bulk." Cassandra made a face. "If I were you, I'd buy a rice cooker for my room. But you didn't hear that from me."

No small appliances were allowed in residence hall rooms.

Pizza was the only other option besides a plain iceberg lettuce salad. Turns out, Cassandra wasn't missing much in the way of fine culinary adventures in the dining hall.

Cassandra compromised by piling the chicken curry over the lettuce in a plastic takeout container.

Meg texted her, "We need some helpers tomorrow at our house to move furniture and paint the old office, new baby room. You're recruiting the students, so we'll buy the pizza."

On the way back to her room Cassandra stopped in the kitchen to get a drink. Lin Chow, the newly returned from vacation resident assistant, warmed her food in the microwave. "Hey Dr. Sato, who cleaned the kitchen? I've never seen the microwave look this great in the two years I've lived here! And my food doesn't smell like popcorn mixed with burnt Rubbermaid."

Cassandra smiled, "The students cleaned up Wednesday before our movie night. Didn't want everyone in the health clinic with food poisoning on my watch."

"I can't believe you convinced them to clean up." She stirred noodles in a reusable bowl. "They don't listen to anything I tell them."

"Well…" Cassandra leaned over closer to whisper, "I may have threatened them with student conduct violations."

"Good to know for the future." Lin said, "Hey, most of the students staying here are taking winter term courses. I did a head count this morning though and I didn't see Daniel Leung. Do you remember checking him in over the weekend?"

Cassandra leaned against the island countertop. "I talked to him Wednesday when I moved in."

"Well, he's not here today. No one has seen him for a while. Are you sure he didn't go home with another student for the holiday break?"

"I know I saw him Saturday for our game night." Cassandra frowned. At least, she thought he'd been part of the group who played cards.

"Okay, no worries. I just need to log where he is for the records. I don't want my boss on my butt because my forms aren't filled out right."

Knowing her boss was Marcus Fischer, Cassandra could imagine that he was a stickler for accuracy. She told Lin, "I can think of one person who might know if Daniel went out of town."

Cassandra knocked on Sela's door. She opened it and loud Billie Eilish music spilled out into the hallway. Sela's white tank top was tucked into grey joggers, her hair pulled into a low ponytail under a white trucker cap. Cassandra pressed her finger in one ear and shouted, "Hey can you turn that down a minute?"

Sela lowered the volume and came back to the door, keeping it partially closed as though she were trying not to let Cassandra see inside completely. "Hi Sela, I'm looking for Daniel Leung. Have you seen him today?"

"I told you he's not my boyfriend. We're just friends. And he's a jerk anyway. So maybe we aren't even friends."

"I just thought you might have seen him around the hallway or common room?" Cassandra strained her neck to peek around the door. "I'm not saying he's sitting on your couch right now."

"I don't remember the last time I saw him and no he's not on my couch. I know my rights, and you can't come into my room uninvited."

Sheesh. Sela went from zero to defensive very quickly. Cassandra knocked on the next couple of doors, but those students hadn't seen Daniel either. The next one she came to was Akira's door.

"Hey Akira, my friend Meg is looking for a few people to help her move some stuff in her house. I wondered if you and Daniel and maybe a couple other kids would be interested in free pizza and making a few dollars?"

"Yeah I spent all my money on Christmas gifts so I could use some cash. I don't know where Daniel is, but maybe I can ask Liam and his roommate if they want to help."

"I don't know if you know who she is, but Meg O'Brien is on staff, and she's renovating their house to make a baby room. I thought you guys might like to get out of the hall for a while and move boxes and furniture into their basement."

"Sure, the three of us can. I have class tomorrow until noon, but any time after then is good."

"When was the last time you saw Daniel?"

Akira shrugged. "I don't remember. Maybe Saturday."

"We wondered if he went home with someone and we didn't mark it down. Maybe he forgot to tell us he was leaving. We need an accurate head count."

"I saw him with Sela on Christmas, maybe. But after that I didn't pay attention."

Okay, thanks anyway. If you can get the other two friends of yours together, I'll meet you all in the common room tomorrow at 12:30 and give you a ride to Meg's house. She lives out of town about 30 minutes away."

"Sure, that's a plan."

Cassandra found Lin and held her palms up in a shrug. "I haven't found anyone who's seen Daniel since Saturday or Friday evening. I was here those nights, but I wasn't exactly taking roll. I just assumed he went out somewhere."

"I've texted and called him multiple times." Lin ate her meal sitting at one of the stools near the kitchen island. "But no one really listens to voicemail."

Daniel was a twenty-something year old adult. Expecting him to answer them every moment of his life seemed a little Big Brother. "I can look him up in the school database tomorrow and find his emergency contact information."

A girl came up to Cassandra. She'd played cards with them Saturday night, but wasn't much of a talker. "Pretty sure Daniel took off for a few days."

"Do you talk to him? Has he posted anything on social media about where he is?" Cassandra wasn't a fan of snooping around students' private lives unwarranted, but asking a few questions seemed harmless. Lin needed to complete her paperwork.

"Nah, nothing like that. He's kinda pissy though. Like he's better than everyone else. Maybe someone told him to kiss off."

"Do you mean someone in particular?" Cassandra wondered if maybe he and Sela—who weren't officially dating—had a fight. "You don't like him?"

"He complains a lot about not having any money and about the rich international students who have the nice cars and all the toys. And they don't need a job. He's kinda bitter. I don't know."

Sela had hinted at the same thing about Daniel's personality, but Cassandra didn't want to gossip about him.

Cassandra changed the subject and flashed her recruiting smile. "If you want to help us move my off-campus friend's stuff tomorrow, you're welcome to help. The more hands we have to carry their stuff to the basement the faster it will go. Free pizza?"

"Nah. I have class and then I work at the student union coffee shop."

"You're not an international student?"

The girl's long ponytail bounced as she shook her head no. "Not unless Kansas counts as international. Ha-ha. I turned in my housing papers late that's why I got assigned to this dorm. Once I was here and met all the kids from other countries, I thought it was fun. I've learned a few cuss words in other languages. My roommate is from Spain. It's pretty solid."

Cassandra thought maybe next year the administration should consider opening the dorm floors to more of a mix of local and international students. Or at least adding activities for the international students to interact informally with local staff and students.

After striking out with everyone she asked about Daniel, Cassandra decided to be proactive. One thing she'd learned her first semester at Morton was to trust her instincts.

She went back to the commons area and found Lin. Together they keyed open Daniel's door to make sure there wasn't a medical issue. The room was empty. Daniel's side of the room held an unmade bed, minimal personal belongings, and an overflowing laundry basket near his desk.

The only uncertainty was whether to wait until morning. Whipping out her phone, she called Andy Summers. "We have a situation here at Picotte. It might be nothing, but can you stop over and help me think it through?"

"I'll be there in fifteen," he said. Then the line cut out.

Fourteen minutes later, there was a knock on her dorm door. "When you say we have a situation, I get nervous." Andy was dressed more casually than usual. He'd probably come straight from his apartment. "What's going on?"

"Remember Daniel Leung? Grad student." When Summers' face still held a questioning frown, she said, "The guy from the graduation ceremony who was with the air horn girl?"

"Oh sure. The couple I walked back here after the ceremony. What about him?"

Tension coiled in her stomach. Like she'd done something wrong. He'd been her responsibility after all.

"He's sort of gone missing." The busy weekend wasn't a good enough excuse for not noticing.

"Really? How long? The police don't accept reports unless the person has been missing more than 24 hours."

"Even I watch enough TV to know that," she smiled. "Do you want to see his room?" They'd left it unlocked until Andy arrived.

Standing in Daniel's doorway, Andy said, "I don't see anything indicating a struggle. No backpack or laptop."

Cassandra poked her head in the closet. Plenty of clean shirts hung on hangers and a clothes hamper was half-filled. A large duffel bag sat on the top shelf. "I questioned the students if they'd seen Daniel. No one reported seeing him yesterday or today. I think we're over the 24-hour mark."

"He probably just went to a friend's place. Happens a lot where someone doesn't check in on campus. It's late tonight, but first thing tomorrow I'll check his key card access or if he used his cafeteria meal plan lately. We'll need a warrant to check his cell records. I'll call the sheriff's office and see if they can ping when Leung's phone was last used."

"The key card access has been bothering me ever since Sunday's break-in at the Osborne Building." Cassandra crossed her arms. "The buildings are all locked down. You should be able to pull up a list of everyone with a card. That's a fairly small group."

"Yeah, you would think so." A sickly grimace settled on Andy's face and he made a large exhale. "Key card security has been on my backlog list of things to update and improve."

Cassandra stepped aside while Lin closed and locked Daniel's dorm room door. "You mean people have keys who shouldn't?"

"Half the town has worked for Morton at one time or another." Andy held up his palms in surrender. "Until I started here, no one turned in their cards after they resigned or retired. Lots of community people had access to the building to hold meetings in the classrooms downstairs during off hours."

Even for a small town that seemed like a bad idea. "Like a de facto community center?"

"I didn't want to disable everyone's cards at once and piss off all the old guard who considered the college their own meeting space. I came up with a couple of plans to upgrade all the locks and issue new cards starting from a new date forward." Andy shook his head. "But Nielson considered it low on the priority list. And I admit I got complacent, too. Until recently, our biggest crime was underage drinking. The past few months have been complete outliers."

Cassandra said, "Well, now that we're looking at the second death in one semester, you think the board of directors might move campus security up on the priority list?"

Andy's face had turned a few shades closer to gray. His lips formed a line and he nodded slowly.

"I don't want to work in a building where anyone who has an old key card can just waltz in anytime they feel like it."

Andy's forehead glistened in the hallway's fluorescent lights. "I can probably narrow it down to whether or not it was a current student or faculty member. But other than that, if it was an old key, it's anyone's guess who used it."

They were going to need another meeting with Deputy Tate to get all this out into the open. She didn't want the police thinking Morton was purposefully covering up evidence. She had to admit they didn't look very professional right now.

"Daniel Leung was one of the students who went to China with Dr. Nielson. Do you remember from your incident spreadsheet if this room was one of the ones burglarized this semester?"

"I didn't memorize the whole spreadsheet." His voice was defensive.

It had been a long day for both of them. Cassandra softened her voice and squeezed his arm. "It will wait until tomorrow. Sorry to drag you over here after hours. Mahalo."

Tapping the side of his forehead in a brief salute, he said, "I'm always available for you. You know that."

As she and Lin watched him walk down the hallway, Cassandra felt a twinge of uncertainty.

Lin said, "Wow, must be nice to have him wrapped around your finger."

Normally, Cassandra would have been annoyed by the sexist and untrue comment. Tonight, she felt too tired to lecture Lin on proper coworker relationships. "Nah, we're just friends."

Cassandra ignored Lin's raised eyebrow and shut herself in her room with Murphy for the rest of the night.

Chapter Twenty

Cassandra needed to get her work done early on Tuesday before going to Meg's house to help with the baby's room. Allowing for the two-hour time difference in San Francisco, she waited until mid-morning to call Daniel Leung's emergency contact number. No one answered so she left a message asking for a return call.

Later at Meg's house, Tony followed Akira up and down the stairs, stacking boxes up to his chin to prove how many heavy things he could carry just like the big kids.

"I can see your muscles growing right now," Cassandra encouraged him.

Akira must have had younger siblings back home because he did a Hulk pose and growled until Tony mimicked him.

Connor scratched Burt's head. "Where's Murphy? I thought he'd play with Burt."

"I left him in his kennel at the dorms."

After Connor led the students down the hall to the home office to start on the moving, Cassandra turned to Meg. "The Picotte students seemed to enjoy petting

Murphy. This morning, I cleaned up another wet towel in his kennel. I'm thinking of letting one of the students adopt him. He's calmer at the college."

Meg poured Cassandra a glass of water and paused. Obviously, she chose her words carefully. "Murphy is sad."

Meg was biased. She was a dog person. Cassandra said, "Dogs don't get sad. People give them human characteristics and personality traits, but dogs are just animals."

Meg patted the seat next to her. "Come here for a sec and look at me. Don't play that whole cold shoulder thing with me."

What *cold shoulder* thing?

Meg said, "You refuse to see that this dog misses his mother. Murphy's like a foster child. He needs unconditional love."

Cassandra looked Meg straight in the eye. This wasn't a time to be emotional. "He's a dog. He needs food, water, and shelter. Murphy and I aren't connecting. Look, I'm okay with just saying the truth. I'm not a warm, fuzzy pet person."

"You're not some ice princess. I met Paul, remember?" Meg's smile was as warm as a sister's. "Paul believed you were a warm and fuzzy person. You don't have to open the faucet full throttle right away, but loving this poor, lonely dog would be a good start. Just pet him."

"I have tried!" Cassandra's voice raised. "He wouldn't let me. He growled at me, and he's got those little pointy teeth."

Meg closed her eyes in one of those martyred momma faces. Cassandra recognized it as the same expression Michiko Sato made when her children were being obstinate. "I'm gonna tell you a parenting tip. Sometimes children (and dogs) don't know what they want. They think they feel grouchy or sad or mad, but they really don't know why. They trust the adults and caretakers in their life (that's you, by the way) to ignore them when they're a pain in the neck or grouchy or growly."

Cassandra crossed her arms.

Meg pantomimed cradling a child. "Children and animals can sense your feelings. Hand to God, I'm telling you it's true." She raised a palm like she was swearing on a Bible. "Haven't you ever thought Murphy was cute? Even once?"

Cassandra pulled out her phone and showed Meg a photo taken when she'd been holding a piece of cinnamon donut in her hand off-camera. Murphy had sat on her kitchen floor, big brown puppy eyes looking at her lovingly. Well, actually looking at the donut lovingly.

"See? You've had a few good moments."

"If he wants to sleep in my house, he'd better figure out where to pee." Cassandra looked again at the photo. Murphy's plaid bowtie and perky white ears were full of personality. He was cute enough to be on a TV commercial. "He's cute. I'll give him that."

"He's grieving the loss of his owner," said Meg. "Imagine if you'd been ripped away from everyone you knew and plunked down in a strange house."

Cassandra raised an eyebrow at Meg. The irony didn't escape either of them.

"See!" Meg laughed. "You, of all people, should understand how strange he feels. Cut him some slack for a few more weeks and be consistent. The students love pets. It humanizes the academic machine. I think it makes you more approachable."

"Excuse me," Cassandra scoffed. "I don't need a dog to make people like me more. I'm a nice person! Even when my friends are annoying."

Moving to the baby room, she and Meg each took a roll of green painters' tape to cover the woodwork. "Is your roof fixed yet?" Meg asked.

What a relief they could change the subject. Cassandra shook her head. "A lot has happened the past few days, but no progress on the roof. You would have been so proud of my meeting with Dr. Bryant yesterday. I did ASL. I even understood some things he signed without having to write everything."

"Any more leads on Dr. Nielson?" Meg worked on the closet doorframe while Cassandra did the window.

"Remember my friend Jocelyn from Hawai'i? She works at the same plant repository where Dr. Nielson got his part time job in Florida. She told me there was a problem with him and the USDA. But I never got a chance to ask his wife about it. Also, Andy Summers said there was an unusually high number of thefts this semester, including students who went to China with Dr. Nielson in October."

"Your home burglary is related to Nielson's trip to China?"

Cassandra lowered her voice. "I'm trying not to freak out, but secretly I feel better sleeping at the dorm with more people around for protection."

"Good for you," said Meg. "What are Andy and the police doing to ensure your safety? I can't believe they hit Nielson's office and your house on the same night."

"I'm keeping it together, but it was scary to walk into my destroyed house again."

Meg said, "Please be careful."

"The neighbor guy who helped me clear the snow is the one who replaced my lock and found me a roof contractor."

"You're blushing!" Meg laughed. "I'm going to have to spy on this guy. He must be cute."

Meg had an uncanny radar for available men near Cassandra. "You want me to throw myself at Sean, too?"

"First name basis. Nice."

Cassandra laughed. "I may have babbled like a teenager the first time I met him."

Meg wiggled her eyebrows.

"Don't get the wrong idea," warned Cassandra. "He's visiting from DC and heads back after the holidays. So quit your matchmaking."

"It's not matchmaking. I'm living vicariously through your professional and dating lives."

Meg fanned out a stack of paint cards in varying shades of beige and light gray. "While you're here, which paint swatches do you like best for the nursery?"

Cassandra studied them for a few moments and pointed at one with blue undertones. "I can come over Saturday and help paint. Are you supposed to be doing stuff like that?"

"Nope. The fumes aren't good for me." Meg tapped the side of her head. "I was so smart to procrastinate until Connor had to be in charge of doing the actual painting."

"Plan on me. I saved some cute baby decorations in my online shopping cart that I want you to approve. We can make chili and celebrate New Year's together. I will miss watching football games with my dad."

"Plenty of testosterone to spare in this house. Will you promise to bring some mochi? You'll find our New Year's Eve fireworks show here a huge disappointment."

Meg looked down the empty hallway. "They must all be downstairs unpacking the office and assembling the crib."

Cassandra's phone vibrated with a call from Andy Summers. She tapped speakerphone. "Hey Andy. I'm at Meg's house and you're on speaker. What's up?"

"I followed up on Daniel Leung. The last time he used his dorm key or meal plan was Sunday morning. We've passed the 48-hour mark. I called the sheriff's office to file a missing person report."

Meg and Cassandra looked at each other. Cassandra's shoulders tightened. "I'll try his emergency contact again. Someone knows where he is. I just hope..."

Meg set the tape roll down and shoulder hugged Cassandra. "You take the students and go back to Morton. We get it. Thanks for your help. I'll send the pizza to Picotte. Daniel will be okay."

Cassandra wished she felt as confident as Meg.

Chapter Twenty-One

To say Wednesday didn't go as Cassandra had expected would be an understatement. Finally, Murphy had gone a full day and night without peeing in his kennel, and Cassandra had high hopes the day would be a good one.

Cassandra broke the remaining chunk of her cinnamon donut and popped half of it in her mouth. The other half, she casually held down to her side until Murphy greedily plucked it from her fingertips.

Andy Summers' eyes widened. "Donuts?"

"Don't judge me." Cassandra frowned. "It's the only way he'll come to me without growling."

"Next time, I'll remember to buy Murphy his own breakfast." Andy wiped his fingertips on a napkin and got down to business. "I've contacted five of the travelers from the China trip. No one mentioned trouble with authorities or Nielson doing anything wrong while he was there. But get this. All five of them had already been contacted by Gary Nielson before he died. He asked them similar questions about whether they saw anything suspicious during the trip."

"When I first moved into Picotte Hall, I spoke to Sela Roberts and Daniel Leung about their trip to China. Neither of them said anything about Dr. Nielson calling them recently. I'm going to talk to Sela again and see if she remembers anything that can help us find Daniel."

"Deputy Tate told me they checked Becky Nielson's alibi for the time of the murder. She told the truth; she was in Iowa with family."

On TV detective shows they always suspected the spouse first. Cassandra looked at her smartwatch. "Sela won't be awake for a while so I'll get a few things done before I go over."

Andy wiped crumbs from Cassandra's desk into his palm, balled the trash together, and hit a banked shot into her trash basket. "See you later."

Less than an hour later, Jocelyn from Florida called Cassandra. Her voice was quiet, "Howzit. You didn't hear this from me, but your guy Gary. Nielson worked for the Germplasm Repository for like 48 hours. That's probably a record."

"I can hardly hear you."

"This is a federal facility and I don't want to be recorded. I'm sitting outside at the employee picnic table."

Cassandra frowned and opened her journal to a new page. On second thought, she closed the journal. If Jocelyn thought it was important to keep their conversation a secret, Cassandra would respect her wish. She didn't want to get her friend in trouble.

"Tell me what happened."

"I talked to the repository office manager. They know everything, right? She told me they found Nielson through our headhunter agency we use to recruit former executives."

"He never mentioned a headhunter to me, but I guess it was just a part time job."

"He passed the interview. First day on the job, the assistant met him and helped him do the onboarding processes. He met the team. Second day, a couple of official looking guys showed up and holed up in his office with him."

"How bizarre!" Cassandra said.

"Yeah. That happens to me, I'm going to spill everything I know in the first ten minutes just to make them go away." Jocelyn continued, "The guys leave. Nielson packs everything on his desk into the brown file box that he'd brought in the day before. Tells my friend he wouldn't be able to stay after all. Apologized all politely and left the building. End of story."

So, Nielson had learned about the accusations against Morton and himself and immediately quit his job. Cassandra waited several beats of silence. She could hear the motor of someone trimming weeds in the background behind Jocelyn. "I can't wrap my head around what Dr. Nielson could have done wrong. He told me they suspected him of having a soybean seed formula."

Professor Zimmerman had said the research outlines the process the company used to create the genetic breeding of the seeds. Even if no one had carried actual bean seeds on the plane into the country, they could still get in trouble for stealing corporate proprietary information.

Cassandra said, "He found a job at your repository where you preserve the world's collection of genetic plant materials. What if the government is right and Nielson stole plants or seeds from China and planned to breed them with other plants from the repository?"

Jocelyn gasped. "That would be espionage. From what you've told me about him . . ."

"I just can't imagine mind-mannered, No-Nonsense Nielson doing something so secretive. He's kind of a flake."

"Maybe that's part of his cover."

Not the Dr. Nielson Cassandra had known. And liked. "That's just it, Nielson was an open book. He didn't have a cover. Mahalo, Jocelyn."

"Watch your back. Tell Auntie Michiko hello for me next time you talk to her. Aloha."

Cassandra closed her eyes and took a deep cleansing breath. Which reminded her that she had forgotten to do her yoga earlier this morning. Living away from home had thrown off her routine in so many ways. The slamming doors, loud voices, and sharing a bathroom were stressful, yet at the same time comforting to know she was surrounded by people.

She had texted Sean Gill earlier in the morning and got no reply. She tried him again. All she wanted was to check on the house repairs, but strangely he had ignored her all morning. A simple short answer wouldn't take him long. It felt like everyone around her was acting weird, but maybe she was the problem.

Deciding they both could use fresh air and Murphy needed a shishi break, Cassandra bundled herself up and walked him over to Picotte Hall to grab a quick lunch.

She opted for the cafeteria salad bar and a banana to save for an afternoon snack. Murphy napped on the common room floor while she ate and read articles on her iPad. Few students were around. She assumed most of them were in class or studying. The winter term tended to have homework due nightly to get through the material.

After cleaning up, Cassandra led Murphy down the hall and knocked on Sela's door. She wasn't taking any attitude this time.

Today, Sela's outfit was a black jumpsuit paired with a long leopard print cardigan that reached past her knees giving her the stature of an elegant giraffe. Black eyeliner and mascara, her only makeup, hair falling in natural ringlets down her back. The girl was stunning without even trying.

White earbuds buzzed in her ears and her head nodded in time to the beat. She was not expecting Cassandra. Her expression turned to caution, and she pulled out one earbud.

"Hi Sela. I have some questions for you. Do you want me to come inside or we can talk in the commons?"

Her lips opened as though she'd give a smart aleck reply, but instead she grabbed her key card from the nearby countertop and closed the door behind her.

They sat in gray accent chairs in the corner, away from the kitchen where a few students were eating and talking.

"I'm getting in touch with the students who went on the trip to China in October. I know we've already talked some..." Cassandra held up a palm to head off whatever she was going to say. "... but I'm not asking about you and Daniel, together. I want to know more about what happened on the trip."

Sela looked less resistant and nodded.

"The last time you told me what you thought about Dr. Nielson. You seemed to have him figured out pretty well."

Her eyes warmed at the compliment.

"You said the older gentleman on the trip didn't treat Nielson well. What do you remember?"

Sela nodded. "We were at a reception. My music ensemble finished playing—"

Cassandra raised her eyebrows.

"—I play violin. I'm posh like that. Anyway, after we finished playing, I went to the buffet table and got a small plate of fruits and mooncakes. I was halfway through my glass of wine when I look up. Dr. Nielson and another old white dude were nose to nose, and the other guy..."

"Mr. Soukup—"

"—Soukup has Dr. Nielson's tuxedo jacket lapels in his two fists. His face is dark red like he was about to have an aneurism. Nielson's arms flailed out to the sides. Another professor stepped between them and pushed them apart."

Becky Nielson hadn't mentioned any arguments. "I wish you had told me about this earlier."

Sela shrugged. "I thought about it more after you asked. It wasn't that big a deal at the time. Now he's dead though."

And Cassandra needed to understand this situation better before it was too late. "Did you see how it started?"

"Nah. Afterward, everyone kind of buzzed around while Nielson left the room."

"Well, it helps me understand a bit more." Cassandra tucked one booted leg under her and shifted on the edge of the chair.

Sela leaned forward like she was getting up to leave.

"Hang on. I need your help. No one has seen Daniel since Sunday. We've contacted his family. I'm worried about him. Are you sure you haven't talked to him at all?"

Sela's expression seemed purposefully bland. She looked off to the side. "I don't know where he is."

Cassandra had learned how to spot a liar from years of imposing student discipline at many levels. She decided not to call her on it, yet. "Well, I hope he hasn't been kidnapped or hurt in a car accident."

"Daniel has nothing worth getting kidnapped over. His family is poor. Daniel has a huge chip on his shoulder. He thinks anytime you buy something nice or go out to eat it's showing off your money. Like it's a crime. Excuse me, I'm sorry life's not fair. Should my family give up everything we have so we're broke like him?"

As tempting as it was to go down that road, Cassandra didn't have time to get into an argument about income inequality and social classes. "Please let me know if you hear from Daniel. We need to talk to him."

They both stood.

"Just curious," said Cassandra. "Was your dorm room broken into this semester?"

Sela stopped in the middle of the hallway and frowned. "How did you know? Jerks stole my lanyard with my room key card."

"That's all that was missing?"

"I had to pay five bucks for a replacement, but I couldn't replace the commemorative keychain though. I know it was only touristy Chinese junk, but it was special and now it's gone."

"I've seen a few extra of those Leifeng Pagoda keychains floating around." There was probably a box of leftovers in the main office. "I'll see if I can find you one."

Sela smiled. "Thanks."

"Please keep your door locked and yourself safe."

Sela's eyes narrowed and her head tilted like she might say more, but her mouth remained closed. Cassandra's instincts said Sela hadn't told the whole truth. She didn't want to scare Sela but if someone was targeting people from the trip, she could be in danger too.

Once she got her coat, hat, and gloves back on, Cassandra and Murphy walked back toward the admin building. When her phone chirped, she squinted at the display on her watch. Fischer! She wanted to talk to him, but what would she say? Digging her phone out of her coat pocket, she answered before it disconnected.

"Hey, we were out in a boat all afternoon, and I didn't have my phone on me. We went parasailing and paddle boarding. The water is so clear here!" Fischer's voice was happy and relaxed. "Is everything good there?"

She didn't want to drag down his day, but everything was far from good here.

"It's nice to hear from you. I'm doing well," Cassandra fibbed. "Thanks for checking in... you didn't have to do that."

"You're a bad liar. I heard about Gary Nielson. Everyone must be pretty upset."

"You must have gotten Mr. Hershey's email. I don't think many people in town knew Nielson was back, but yeah it's been tough."

"How are the Picotte students?"

She decided not to mention the part about living with them. "Well, another problem there. Daniel Leung has been gone a few days."

"Like... he went out of town for the weekend, gone?"

"No,... like it's been 48 hours and Andy Summers had to call the sheriff, gone. I'm sure we'll find him." She grimaced at her attempt to make it sound like they had it covered.

Children's laughter in the background distracted Fischer and there was a long moment of silence. "Oh, that's good. Daniel's probably visiting a friend and forgot to check in. I'm sure he will turn up soon with a good story."

College students all got lumped together with a reputation for partying and irresponsible behavior, but Cassandra knew plenty of mature, responsible young adults who worked hard to earn their degrees. Daniel seemed more like the latter and Cassandra was convinced something bad had happened to him.

More commotion on the line. Fischer was having way more fun than she wanted to know about right now.

She said, "See you Sunday after you get back."

"Thanks—" the connection cut out abruptly, but she got the idea.

Later that afternoon, Bridget, the work study student, appeared in front of Cassandra's desk leaning closer than normal and stage whispered, "Dr. Sato. There are some... men outside to see you."

She'd been entering calendar details for spring semester events and hadn't heard anyone come into the Student Affairs suite. Cassandra frowned. "Send them in, Bridget."

Bridget's eyes opened wide like she was trying to communicate something to Cassandra, but she didn't know how to interpret the signal.

Two men in plaid shirts with dress pants and matching winter coats with a logo on the chest stepped into her office.

Murphy stood up and sniffed the black loafers on the closest guy. Not a growl or bark. Absolutely no attempt to protect Cassandra.

The loafer guy set his mouth in a pleasant smile, while the other was more stoic.

Several steps back stood Sean Gill, looking awkward.

What the heck?

The stoic one said, "I'm Phil Jones and this is Randy Thomas. I understand you've already met Sean Gill. We're looking into a complaint concerning missing soybean seed research."

Gill's normal jeans and casual sweatshirt had been replaced by dress pants and a coat identical to his colleagues. For several moments Cassandra just stared at him slack jawed, holding her breath while she processed the scene in front of her.

"We're following up on several leads but haven't located the actual computer files yet."

Were these the same guys who had talked to Dr. Nielson in Florida?

Cassandra coughed to stall until she was sure her voice wouldn't squeak. Closing her door, she resolved to make this information sharing conversation go both ways.

She held up a finger. "Before you ask me anything, why are you at Morton College in *my* office?" So much for keeping Morton's reputation out of this mess. Her stomach cramped into a knot.

She had invited the men to sit on the small sofa around the low coffee table on one side of her office. She had turned around an armchair to face them and Gill had opted to stand and lean against the door.

Sean cleared his throat. "Ah... that's on me, Dr. Sato, and I apologize for any inconvenience. When you told me about Gary Nielson's death, I thought it seemed odd that a man who'd been here for only a few days had been killed. It's probably been ten years since anyone was killed in Carson. I looked into him more and talked to the sheriff."

Wait, Deputy Tate had barely given Cassandra the time of day, yet he shared details about the robbery with *him*. One eyebrow raised.

"Technically, the agency I work for is part of Homeland Security. I may have emphasized that part."

Why, because Homeland Security sounded more impressive than the USDA? Men.

Phil, the friendlier guy, said, "Sean works with us under the USDA. Together we realized that the likelihood of

Gary Nielson's sudden death and our investigation into the complaint about the illegal importation of proprietary plant products might be connected."

For the next hour, Cassandra answered their questions with what she knew about Dr. Nielson, the goodwill exchange trip to Hangzhou, and Morton's plant research.

After their conversation, she concluded two important things. Dr. Zimmerman had been right all along: high-yield soybean seed research was a much bigger deal than she'd ever considered. Secondly, the next time Cassandra saw Sean Gill, she was going to kill him.

* * *

Cassandra had time to refill her coffee mug and answer a few emails before her phone buzzed with another call. Derek Swanson. Seeing his name on the display no longer made her back clench in an involuntary shudder, but she couldn't help the natural defensiveness against journalists she'd developed after years of being misquoted and misunderstood.

Derek Swanson was an eager reporter for the *Omaha Daily News*. With the recent spate of incidents on Morton's campus, he'd written several in-depth articles about the college.

"Hello, Dr. Sato. This is Derek Swanson."

Less than three hours since the homeland security guys showed up on her doorstep and already, he'd found out.

"Hi, Derek. Now's not the best time." She added an extra pleasantness to her voice hoping to hide the tension she felt.

"I'll get right to it. I heard you could use help finding a missing student. I called to offer the full investigative manpower of the state's largest newspaper." Although his journalism instincts were good, his people skills needed some work.

"We have quite a bit of help already." A sharp pain tweaked her right temple in warning of an oncoming headache. The last thing she needed right now was a thirsty reporter stirring up gossip. His last article about the student protests and recent presidential meltdown had been published less than a month ago.

"Heh. I bet you do have help. Those three wise strangers from the East appearing by surprise are only a good thing if your door's in Bethlehem and your name is Mary."

Swanson seemed to have informants all over town keeping him updated with the latest gossip.

Cassandra could really do without the Magi jokes right now. "We can't talk about specific students due to FERPA laws, and I'd appreciate it if you'd respect their privacy."

"No worries. My main story I'm writing is about Gary Nielson's death. Kind of an extended obituary talking about his service to the college and Carson community."

"Okay, that will be nice. Dr. Nielson was involved in a lot of good work during his time." A sigh of relief slowly ebbed from her lungs. "Again, I've only been at Morton for one semester. I could give you a list of key people to interview who worked with him longer. Maybe once the police investigation is complete, there will be a memorial service and you could cover that."

"About that police investigation..."

Cassandra dropped her head. "Morton College has no comment. The sheriff's office is doing the investigation."

She couldn't tell him about the soybean seed research, the missing student, and the part about how she might have been one of the last people to talk to Nielson before he was shot. She clamped her lips together.

"Don't you find his retirement situation odd? I mean Nielson goes to China one month. He sets up an expensive agreement with a sister college to promote international student and faculty exchanges. His food service contract and cancer research project escapes unscathed after the situation with that deaf student's death in October. Those were both big wins for him. Why was his next move retirement?"

Cassandra had asked herself that exact question many times since the beginning of November. Nielson could've saved them all a lot of heartache if he'd stayed and continued his work. And maybe saved his own life, too.

Swanson had a way of connecting dots together faster than anyone Cassandra had met. He really had a nose for conspiracies and hidden motivations. Only she didn't want to become the subject of one of his stories.

"It's too soon to answer any of those questions. And with the holiday shutdown, our campus offices have a skeleton crew. I can't help you today."

When the called ended, Cassandra patted herself on the back for not revealing anything confidential to Swanson. Her temple throbbed again. She opened the top right desk drawer and rummaged in the tray for the bottle of Excedrin. Swanson had helped her a little in the past, but she didn't trust him. Once he smelled a story, he was a bulldog. A controversial exposé would be a horrible way to start off the New Year.

Hours later the news notification on her phone announced the headline she had been most dreading, "Local College Trouble Comes in Threes."

Chapter Twenty-Two

As soon as Cassandra had finished work for the day and dropped Murphy off at Picotte, she drove to her house. Running the spiral steps two at a time, she shoved the door open into the spare room. Sean Gill had changed out of his fancy workwear into old jeans and a paint splattered t-shirt. The ceiling had been repaired and drywalled, and he stood on a stepladder edging the ceiling using a wooden paint brush. Trans-Siberian Orchestra played on his portable speaker.

Her balled hands rested on her hips. "You're an ass!" Her hand itched to smack him.

"Hey! I'm sorry you're mad, but I'm just doing my job. Illegal importation of plants or foreign confidential and trade secret information is a federal crime."

"What do you mean *doing your job*? I'm not your job." She was so gullible! She had completely trusted this guy. "You told me you were home visiting your parents on winter break!"

She'd even planned to join his whole family for game night. Which most likely would never happen because he probably made that up, too.

"I *am* visiting them! And if you haven't noticed, I've spent quite a few hours fixing my neighbor's house while I was supposed to be on vacation."

She didn't know if she was madder about him calling in their school or that he wasn't really her new friend. Cassandra's eyes narrowed. "Did the USDA send you here to check into Morton all along?"

"It's Christmas break! I had this trip planned months ago. My buddy Craig and I fixed your roof! We chopped the tree and stacked wood against your house." He held out a palm toward her. "I still have the splinters, see?"

"You could have told me you worked for the USDA. I would've understood if you had told me you knew more about Dr. Nielson."

"I'm sorr—

Wait, Andy knew Sean Gill from high school. He must have known Sean worked for Homeland Security. Why hadn't Andy said anything? Maybe Cassandra should be mad at several people for keeping her in the dark.

"Go ahead. I'm listening." She crossed her arms over her chest.

Sean Gill stepped off the ladder, rested the paintbrush on the lid of the can, and sat on the floor leaning against the wall with his feet out in front.

"I just had a hunch that something was off, so I asked around. I didn't know those guys were coming to town until this morning."

So that's why he'd avoided her messages earlier.

He ran his hand through his hair. "I understand you're mad. But I really do want to be friends. And I felt bad about your roof. By the way, Craig's going to send you a bill after I finish up painting."

Cassandra took off her puffy coat and draped it over the wooden railing atop the staircase. She pulled a folded drop cloth out of a pile and shook it out before sitting near him on the floor. Her black work pants were going to be covered in construction dust, but she resolved to wash them later.

Gill said, "I tried telling them that you didn't know about imported soybean seeds, but someone did an online search. Multiple odd events have occurred since you first arrived on campus in August."

"Not because of my presence. I've worked my booty off this whole semester." Cassandra stretched her arms around her bent knees and hugged them closer to her body. "Not to sound callous, but the USDA should maybe stop trying to ruin Morton College's reputation and instead start working with the local law enforcement to locate our missing student."

"A student is missing?"

"Daniel Leung. No one has seen him for a few days. I'm worried that whoever threatened Nielson might hurt him or someone else from the delegation to China."

Gill looked at the ceiling for several moments and Cassandra could see him running scenarios in his head. "Because of the campus thefts? Summers told me about them."

"Get out, you talked to Andy Summers about Dr. Nielson?"

"I told you I checked around. I know you told the police about the threatening texts Nielson received and his denial that he did anything wrong. Andy told me you both suspected a connection between the increase in petty thefts and the folks who went to China."

Real friends shouldn't keep secrets. She'd deal with Andy later.

Cassandra rested her forehead on her knees trying to fit what they knew into a coherent picture. "Professor Zimmerman worked with Daniel Leung on his thesis advisory committee. There was tension between them. If Nielson really stole a proprietary soybean formula—and you have not convinced me that is true—wouldn't he have talked to Dr. Zimmerman about it?"

Gill pulled his phone out of his coat pocket and tapped the screen. "The guys in my office looked at Zimmerman, too. He does similar research, but we didn't see any evidence that he'd begun a project soon after the China trip using the new information."

"Unless he was having a student begin the preliminary work for him." The hard floor was making Cassandra's backside sore. She pushed herself up to standing. "In order to do *my* job, I need to know which team everyone is on. I thought Nielson was one of the good guys. Daniel Leung is missing and right now my priority is finding him. If Zimmerman is involved somehow, he has a motive to derail your investigation. I've seen and heard so many negative stories about Bob Soukup who was on the China trip too."

Sean stood too and brushed off his pants. "Yeah, you mentioned Soukup earlier. He's a first-class racist jerk, but I don't think espionage is his style."

"Why not? His daughter told me he used to manage the ethanol plant outside of town. He sounds like a big-time capitalist."

"Soukup likes being a bigwig involved in every aspect of town," said Gill. " A businessman, a philanthropist, a councilman. He wants local power, not international deals."

In hindsight, she should have asked Dr. Nielson more questions when he'd been at her house. Cassandra said, "But if Nielson was responsible for stealing the plant research, you're saying he planned the whole goodwill trip to China as a cover for a larger crime?"

"Here, I have some notes from when the investigators met with Nielson in Florida. He was initially flagged because of the complaint from the Chinese consulate."

Gill tapped a few times on his phone and read from an electronic notes file. "He told us he received some threatening messages. The first message he thought was a wrong number, so he ignored the text. After the second text, Nielson called his phone carrier to block the number, but since the text was sent from a burner phone, the carrier couldn't trace it. The third message was more direct. Nielson said he called the board chairman of Morton College—"

"—Alan Hershey." Cassandra was getting a little excited that she finally knew enough facts to string them into a hypothesis. "Who told me that he asked Nielson to come back and clear up the accusation against Morton."

"Nielson was in charge of the China trip. For nearly ten days, he spoke to a variety of Chinese representatives."

The idea of No-Nonsense Nielson as a suave James Bond spy made her roll her eyes. "He was doing his job, leading the campus group!"

Sean said, "Chinese companies have been involved in corporate espionage for years. They've stolen windmill plans, corn seeds... who knows what they're stealing next."

Picking up his paintbrush he said, "Once I finish inside and we get the new shingles on the roof, we'll be done with your repairs. I'm just, kind of... concerned about your house getting broken into. I've been keeping an eye out. With Dr. Nielson and the college and everything, I think it's safer for you to stay at the dorms through the weekend and give the police more time to work their case."

Sleep deprivation made her sound less confident than she wanted. "I'm sharing a bathroom with 15 twenty-year-olds. I want to sleep in my own bed again."

The sincerity in his eyes was hard to ignore. Still, he had omitted some very important facts and she didn't completely trust him. Cassandra pictured Nielson's postcard where he posed on the fishing boat with his catch of the day. He had looked so happy in the photo. "Dr. Nielson told me he returned to Morton to set things right. Your investigators scared him off and then you failed him. He's dead because of them."

Sean Gill's chin lowered to his chest. He looked tired, too.

Cassandra took a long, slow breath. "You seem to be on Deputy Tate's good side. We're all coming at this from different angles. Maybe it's time we worked together to find Daniel before it's too late."

Chapter Twenty-Three

Cassandra fast-walked across campus in the predawn darkness, thinking about how drastically foreign this New Year's Eve would be without fireworks or outdoor parties.

Falling asleep hadn't come easy the night before, even safely tucked into the residence hall surrounded by students. She'd fluffed the flat pillow and pulled the institutional beige bedspread provided with the dorm room up to her ears. Murphy's rhythmic breaths came from the corner of the darkened room while Cassandra mentally replayed everything that had happened during the day.

Anticipation for another long weekend was the only thing keeping her hustling, her breath forming a cloud ahead of her while she moved. Arriving in the Student Affairs suite long before her student worker, she flipped the lights on and headed directly to the coffeemaker to start a pot. The college was scheduled to close at three, and between attending Dr. Bryant's Deaf Culture class, editing the grant proposal, and taking walk-in students, the day would be full.

Once the comforting gurgle of water dripping into the pot began, Cassandra unzipped her coat and approached her inner office door.

It was ajar.

Heart pounding, Cassandra knew she should leave the office and call security. Ignoring that urge, she pulled her coat sleeve over her hand, pushed the office door open, and gasped.

All of the dark wood bookshelves were emptied, their contents in two mounds of books and knick knacks beside the student chairs facing her desk. Using the same covered hand, Cassandra turned on the lights and walked behind her desk. The drawers were pulled out. A small empty shipping box and a stack of file folders sat on the desktop. A few had slid to the floor, their papers blanketing the carpet. Even the center drawer that contained mostly pens, sticky notes, and extra junk had been handled.

Taking a step back, her boot crunched on glass. The small storage credenza beneath the window was mostly untouched. Her eyes counted each treasured family photo, until she realized one was missing. Bending over, Cassandra poked through the papers on the floor until she felt the frame. Raising the photo, tears formed in her eyes. She remembered the day she'd received her doctoral hood, posing between her parents holding a green diploma cover, and wearing her commencement gown piled high with colorful fragrant leis.

The degree was significant not only for marking years of difficult coursework and completing her dissertation.

Taken less than two years after Paul's death, it had been her first life milestone without him.

Splintered glass covered the photo in a kaleidoscope of color, and when she wiped away the tears running down her cheeks, blood dripped onto the frame. Dropping the frame onto her chair seat, she found a small cut on the edge of her hand, blood dribbling under the wristband of her coat.

Pulling one tissue from the box on her desk, Cassandra applied pressure to the cut. The granola bar she'd eaten for breakfast turned into a leaden lump in her stomach. Returning to the main reception room, Cassandra sat hard on an upholstered accent chair and tapped her smartwatch with a finger. "Call Andy Summers."

The female voice confirmed, "Calling Andy Summers..."

Twenty minutes later, Deputy Tate and an older deputy arrived. Andy was inside her office with another officer taking photos and talking on his phone. Cassandra remained in the chair, dazed, her booted feet spread apart, still wearing her coat and holding a ceramic mug of coffee that Andy had given her a few minutes earlier.

Tate pulled up a rolling desk chair and sat facing Cassandra, their knees nearly touching. His light brown curly hair was still damp from a shower and his smooth face smelled of a musky after shave. She realized she didn't even know where in the county Tate lived. All she knew was that he was built like a linebacker but impressed her with his intelligence and calm.

"Dr. Sato, how're you doing?"

Inside her head, the voice that sounded remarkably like her mother's told her to sit up straight and pull herself together. She was no wilting flower.

She told her mother to zip it.

She smiled at him. "Not the best way to end the year, Deputy." Taking a long drink of the coffee, she felt the heat slide down her throat and into her chest, warming her from the inside out.

"Yeah, I'm ready for this year to be done, too. Even with all the break-ins, this guy hasn't left any prints but eventually, he will mess up. He seems pretty desperate to find what he's lost. We will catch up to him, I promise you."

The fingerprint tech was still doing his thing when Cassandra's work study student, Bridget, arrived. "What's going on, Dr. Sato?"

She hung up her coat on the rack by the door and peered into Cassandra's office at the men and mess inside.

"Are you okay?"

Cassandra nodded, but didn't budge. Maybe another cup of coffee would help. She raised the cup toward Bridget who frowned at her and went to refill it.

Sitting in the same desk chair that Deputy Tate had used, Bridget handed her more coffee and sipped from another mug. "What should I do? Is there someone you want me to call?"

Something in the girl's concerned face made Cassandra snap out of it. Or maybe it was the extra caffeine kicking in. "They're almost done. Then you can help me clean up. Thanks."

Within an hour, Tate and his coworker had packed up their equipment and left. Andy stood in her office apparently waiting for Cassandra to join him.

Cassandra narrowed her eyes and quietly told Bridget, "Why don't you take a break for about fifteen minutes. I'm going to talk to him." She flicked her head toward the office.

Bridget whispered, "He's the nice one."

Bridget could be funny, sassy, and sometimes impatient. The tension coming off Cassandra while she stood and removed her coat must have been enough body language that Bridget nodded, grabbed her cup, and scooted out of the suite.

Slowly Cassandra faced Andy and crossed her arms, feet shoulder width apart. "Any fingerprints?"

"Lots of them. He will run them all, and let us know if anyone other than Morton staff or students were in there."

Cassandra opened her mouth to chew him out for not telling her that Sean Gill had been poking around behind her back.

He held up one hand. "Before we do this, could I get a cup of coffee?" Without waiting, he beelined for the snack corner and doctored one up for himself.

Cassandra entered her office and turned toward the couch. She hadn't noticed earlier, but her large framed Wyland oil painting was propped backwards against the wall. The brown paper backing had been cut open and a large corner peeled away revealing the empty space between the painting and the back. Quickly she looked at the front, checking whether the undersea scene was still intact.

"Why would someone think I hid something behind my artwork? That only happens in Hollywood heist movies." First her photo frame and now this. Upset before, now she was seriously angry.

"Cassandra, can we sit for a second?" Andy walked around her and turned one of the armchairs so it faced her small couch. "I need to tell you something."

A little steam in her head eased out while she settled into the couch, wrapped her hands around the lukewarm mug of coffee, and fixed an expectant expression on her face.

"Look, I know we're just friends. I do." Andy looked into his cup. "But friends care about each other, right?" Lifting his eyes, they pleaded with her to agree.

What the heck was he going to tell her? She was upset about Sean Gill and the USDA, and Andy was babbling on about feelings?

"Yes..." she agreed hesitantly.

"When Dr. Nielson was shot, I got worried about you. Most all the other administrators and students had left town and you alone were left in charge." Setting his coffee on the table in front of him, he raised his palms defensively. "I know you can take care of yourself. I know you're tough and adventurous. I mean, you moved four thousand miles away from home to the middle of Nebraska. This isn't a place for wimps."

His long-winded rationalization had better wrap up soon.

"Look, like I said, I worried when Nielson was shot that you might be next. I saw Sean Gill at church. Our families go to the same one, and he was there with his parents. I knew he was home for the holidays, and I asked him to keep an eye on your house."

He sat back and waited.

Cassandra nodded. "So, you're the one who suggested he offer to be my new best friend and neighborhood watch dude? You know his office is investigating a case against Morton for illegal importation of plant... yada, yada." She waved a shaky hand in the air. "...whatever. It's too early in the morning for this crap."

His eyes widened. "Yes—I mean, no! I mean—yes, I knew he works in Maryland for Homeland Security. He was the valedictorian of his graduating class. Couldn't wait to leave Carson and make it big far away. He's the kid everyone's mother uses as an example for how to become successful. Not everyone wants to become a federal investigator or leave their hometown, but he's still held up as the model."

Cassandra raised an eyebrow. There must be a long story behind all that emotion, but she wasn't going to let him change the subject to big city vs. small town life.

"Andy, why didn't you just tell me right away that you'd asked him to watch my house? Why keep it a secret?"

"I know you value your independence, and I thought you'd be mad. I swear, I had no idea that he'd call his coworkers and check on Nielson's role in the Chinese accusation."

His phone rang. He shot her an apologetic look before answering. "Summers...yes..."

Two minutes later, he hung up. "That was one of my officers. He ran the records for who accessed this building in the past twenty-four hours. One of the key cards belonged to Dr. Gary Nielson."

"Whoever shot him stole his key card?" Cassandra had always thought Andy Summers ran a competent department, but she was beginning to question that assumption. "You mean no one disabled it after Nielson retired? Wouldn't that be a standard outboarding process?"

Eyes closed, he nodded his head. "There's more. My officer ran a history on that card alone. Turns out, it was used last week to get into the library. I ordered a complete search of every corner of the library."

"I'd like to know why he accessed my office." Cassandra's eyes darted from wall to wall, stopping at the empty shelves and piles of debris. This felt personal.

Andy said, "I think we were wrong, Cass. We thought Nielson's shooting was about his trip to China. But if the killer is searching your office and the library, there's more we aren't considering."

Andy stood and zipped his coat. "I'm heading back to my office. Need me to send maintenance over to clean up?"

"No, my student and I can do it." She'd had enough of other people touching her stuff. Besides her cleaning standards were higher than ninety percent of the population.

She didn't return his conciliatory smile. She wouldn't break their friendship over this whole thing, but she'd make him squirm a little until she forgave him.

Chapter Twenty-Four

A couple of hours later, Cassandra sat cross-legged on her recently vacuumed office floor surrounded by file folders and stacked paperwork. Luckily, she'd worn pants instead of her normal pencil skirt. She and Bridget had repaired and hung her Wyland painting, shelved the books, and cleaned up the rest of the debris from her latest invasion. Reorganizing papers was the last thing necessary before her appointment at Cinda's office.

Twenty minutes later, Cassandra stepped into Cinda's spacious office overlooking the opposite corner of the snow-covered quad.

Cinda moaned around a bite of food in her mouth. "Oh gawd. Before I die, I have to learn how to make kolaches from my husband's granny. It would be a crying shame if this lard-filled goodness disappeared from the earth when she passes, bless her heart."

Seeing Cinda never failed to inject a boost of cheeriness into the day, no matter how badly it had begun. A ceramic plate on her desk held small pastries that looked like they'd been baked in a rectangle pan and cut into squares. Cassandra would call them Danishes, with each treat containing a different filling the consistency of apple pie. "I'll try this blueberry one. Although I'm going to need an elliptical machine for my basement the way I'm going."

Working out in the winter months had slipped Cassandra's radar of frozen tundra winter considerations. Normally, her daily yoga regimen and walking to work every day was plenty of exercise to keep her feeling healthy and strong. Being cooped up in the house all winter would make it harder to avoid gaining weight. Lard-filled sugar bombs wouldn't help.

Tallied in the weight maintenance good column was the strenuous snow shoveling. She prayed Nebraska wouldn't get blizzards every week. If that happened, she'd pay the neighbor kid to use his snowblower on her driveway.

Cinda pushed the last bite into her mouth and brushed crumbs from her hands into the napkin spread across her lap. Neatly she gathered the edges and folded them around the crumbs, tossing the ball into her trash can. "Okay, General, what's our plan?" Her voice changed to sound like a professional radio announcer. "We merely have to avoid allowing Morton's century-long tradition of an excellent, affordable liberal arts education being shredded before a court or the media."

Then, Cinda wiggled her eyebrows. "Maybe that hunky neighbor of yours can run interference for us at the USDA?"

Cassandra laughed in spite of her anxiety. Cinda was always trying to set her up with the best-looking guys in town. Now she'd set her sights on someone who lived in a different state.

Cassandra frowned. "He's still on my naughty list for poking around behind my back. He could have just straight-up asked instead of calling in his work buddies."

Cinda waved away his misjudgment with one lazy hand gesture. "Whatever. Tell me, who do they think is behind the whole Chinese espionage conspiracy? I think Bob Soukup finally lost his mind and decided to become a full-on gangster. There's been rumors about him since before I moved here. He knows where all the bodies are buried."

"Seriously, why do people joke about that kind of thing? Dr. Nielson is dead. Not the pretend kind of dead on an NCIS episode." Cassandra grimaced. "This is such a pretty town. I thought there weren't any secret bodies buried. Can't we just live in a quaint little place without conflict?"

"Okay fine, if it's not Old Man Soukup, who is it?"

"I love that you're trying to cheer me up. But just stop. We need to focus on finding Daniel and answering these concerns from the investigators. Someone trashed my house and my office. Let's focus!" Cassandra snapped her finger as if that could draw Cinda's attention to her point.

Cassandra said, "I told the USDA guys that the first person they should check is Professor Zimmerman. I thought he was a good guy, but he's the campus expert about soybeans. He's on Daniel's thesis committee. He had a long-time working relationship with Dr. Nielson. Maybe something went wrong with the research and Zimmerman worried Nielson would report it." Cassandra shrugged. "Who knows what skeletons Nielson knew about."

Cinda sipped her coffee. "You could be onto something. Starting with Professor Zimmerman is a good idea."

As Cassandra and Cinda made the blessedly short walk from the Osborne building to the science building, Cinda asked, "How close are you to moving back home?"

"The house is almost ready, but I'm not sure I am yet." Arctic wind whipped between buildings and cut into exposed skin on Cassandra's cheeks. Cassandra pulled up her coat's hood and yanked the zipper as high as it went. "When I arrived in Carson in July, I had a well-designed plan. I knew who I was, what I wanted from life, and why. I've spent most of this semester triaging messes created by other people. Now my house is a fixer upper, and I'm afraid to stay home alone. For the life of me, I can't remember why I thought moving here was a good idea."

"I'm sorry, sweetie. We're sure glad you moved. Even if you're going through a trying time. I'll add you to my church's list for prayer intentions."

Cinda was in a prayer group?

The science building's classrooms were mostly dark. Before they entered the faculty office area, Cinda said, "I've watched every episode of *The Blacklist*. One thing I've learned is that those federal officers can't be trusted. You never know whose side they're on. Like Sean says he's helping you, but how do we know they aren't working an angle benefitting a greater good? Morton College could be sacrificed on the altar of soybean millions."

Maybe all that sugar had given Cinda delusions. Cassandra rolled her eyes. "*The Blacklist*, really? Those are FBI agents, not USDA plant inspection people. C'mon, be serious just this once."

Doors were closed and no students waited in the reception area. Most faculty were on break except the ones teaching the three-week winter term classes.

Cinda approached the receptionist desk. "We'd like to speak to Professor Zimmerman please." She used her most exaggerated drawl.

The thirty-something year old man with a tattoo peeking out the top of his turtleneck sweater pulled out small earbuds and smiled at them. "Zimmerman?" He confirmed and pointed over his shoulder to the corner office. "Sure, go on inside."

Cassandra followed Cinda and knocked on the open door.

Professor Zimmerman's face lit with friendly recognition. Cassandra sincerely didn't want him to be the bad guy. Surely her instincts couldn't be that wrong. "Hello ladies! To what do I owe this pleasure?"

"Hello. We're helping the campus security follow up on a missing student. When we spoke last week, I asked about your research with Daniel Leung?"

Zimmerman nodded and looked to his left and right around his office. To say he squirmed uncomfortably would be pretty accurate. "Right, I remember. How can I help you today?"

"Daniel is missing. We're wondering if he'd checked in with you at all?"

Zimmerman frowned at a nearby wall calendar whose December photo was a winter plains landscape with a falling down barn in the center. Not exactly advertising tourist destinations. "I haven't seen him since before Christmas."

Cassandra asked, "Does he still have access to all of the lab's plants and equipment? There's an inventory of those plants, right?"

"Grad assistants have twenty-four-hour access to the labs. During the semester, they work at odd hours."

"You'd know if any plants were missing?"

"I don't understand. You said he's missing. There's not enough space to sleep in the lab, if that's what you mean."

"Just brainstorming ideas, Dr. Zimmerman," said Cinda. "Keeping the students safe. We're afraid Daniel might be in trouble."

When Zimmerman raised his head, the glasses magnified his eyes to disproportionate saucers in his narrow face. "Well, er . . . are you sure he's not just on vacation?"

He was acting twitchier than the previous times she'd talked to him. Cassandra formed her lips into an insincere smile. "We've checked, but as far as we can tell, he's not on vacation."

Cinda stepped closer to his desk. He shrank back. "When was the last time you saw Dr. Nielson?"

Zimmerman gulped and stammered, "I don't think that's any of your business."

Cinda shrugged. "Maybe not, but the police will be here pretty soon, and they'll ask you the same questions."

He crossed his arms and his lips closed tight enough to make lines form at the corners.

Cassandra shook her head and glared at Cinda. "I think we've gotten what we needed to know."

Hustling back to her office, she kept her head down, trying to avoid notice. In the Osborne Admin Building, she walked down the narrow top floor hallway, passing the large picture windows. In her pocket, her phone vibrated with a call.

Sean Gill and his two plant inspector co-workers walked three abreast down the main sidewalk toward the science building. If Zimmerman and Soukup were good guys—that was a big if—who were the bad guys? More importantly, where was Daniel?

Andy Summers' name appeared on the phone display. She hesitated a moment. Although tempting, ignoring him would be petty and unprofessional. She answered the call.

While she observed the men out the picture window, Sean Gill's head turned. A fresh chill shivered up her back when their eyes met across the quad.

Chapter Twenty-Five

"Hey Cassandra, it's Andy." Um, yeah. Caller ID. "Are you busy? Could you come to the library, please? I think there's something you'll want to see."

The voice was the same old Andy, but his tone was more tentative. Instead of treating her like a sister he could boss around, he seemed unsure whether she'd hang up on him.

When she met Andy in the library's lobby, she noticed only two students sitting at help desks but no one else milling around.

"Wow this place is dead—" Cassandra's eyes widened as she regretted her unfortunate word choice.

"You have no idea." Andy said. "This way." He led her to the stairwell and down to the basement.

She'd been on this level only once before during her first campus tour. Basement stacks were creepy, long aisles of musty smelling books and boxes of microfilm and old files. One half had been upgraded in recent years to new automated sliding bookshelves. Summers turned toward the far corner in the older section tucked into a cool, darkened area farthest away from the stairs and elevators.

A small encampment had been set up with a rumpled sleeping bag and pillow, two wooden chairs propped up with a blanket like a tent. Her nephews built tents like that using couch cushions and their bed blankets. "Daniel?" Cassandra guessed.

An unzipped duffle bag spilled out t-shirts and socks. The decaying smell of old takeout food came from a small trash can nearby full of Styrofoam containers. Wrinkling her nose, Cassandra wondered if mice were active in freezing temperatures.

"I'm waiting for the sheriff and the crime scene guys again. I've seen the fingerprint guy so much the last few weeks, I'm going to owe him a New Year's beer."

Cassandra made a slow 360-degree turn, taking in the distance to the nearest place where people would be walking by. In the ceiling, she didn't see any small domes indicating security cameras. "You haven't found Daniel yet? Just this stuff." He had strategically selected his position.

Andy crouched down and pointed at a small stack of lined notebooks. Using his pen, he poked the top cover open to show her the first page of notes. Mathematical notes and pencil drawings.

"Once we fingerprint it, we'll know for sure, but yeah. I sent a couple of officers to search this building and the student center. When Daniel comes back, we'll take him in for questioning."

"I just hope he's okay."

The corners of Andy's eyes crinkled in a half smile. "Cassandra, I like how you always look for the best in people. But this time I think you're being naive. Just because

Daniel's a student doesn't make him an innocent victim. He's involved in this thing with Nielson. He could even be responsible for the burglaries too."

Cassandra stayed an arm's length away but peered into the open gym bag. "Extra Chapstick, a box of granola bars. Do you see those Leifeng Pagoda keychains? Maybe you can match the missing items from your security reports this semester to the stuff in Daniel's bag and dorm room. Sela said she was missing her keychain. He must have grabbed those from the box on my desk. I found one underneath some papers on my office floor. I thought I'd give it to her. It looks like you were right about Daniel."

Summers was already heading back toward the stairs. "Innocent students who have paid room and board fees don't usually hide in the library with a box of granola bars."

Back in the lobby, Cassandra checked her watch. "Okay Andy, I only have an hour until we shut down for the long weekend. I'll go back to my office. I hope you find Daniel soon."

Summers' lips tightened. "Me, too. This is not how I planned to spend New Year's Eve."

Cassandra's hand rested on the door to leave, but now she was curious about how a single guy in rural Nebraska spent New Year's Eve. "Big party tonight?"

"My brother, his wife, and I go to The Home Team's New Year's Eve bash. Meet up with some high school friends and play darts and keno." He shrugged. "Nothing big, but it's our tradition."

She waited a heartbeat for an invitation that didn't come. Apparently, she'd made her position very clear where she and Andy stood and that didn't include New Year's Eve traditions. She was completely fine with spending the evening alone. It wasn't the first time, and likely wouldn't be the last.

Walking back to her office, Cassandra tried to imagine ringing in the new year playing darts. Much different than the huge house or beach parties she usually attended on New Year's Eve, binging on rich foods and pooling her money with family and friends to set off more fireworks than on July 4th.

Fischer was due back in town Saturday, and she hoped to see him over the weekend. She also hoped to get her stuff moved back to her house. Could she find time to clean and organize, too?

First, she needed to end the workplace year on a tidy note. She cleaned up the outer office, watered the plants, and finalized the rough draft of the telecommunications grant and texted Dr. Bryant to confirm their next meeting on Monday. Closing the office with a feeling of satisfaction, she returned to her dorm room with Murphy.

In her comfy clothes, she padded down the hall to find a soda in the kitchen. Cassandra was determined to enjoy her last evening or two with the students. Rounding the corner, she recognized Sela standing in front of the open refrigerator looking inside. Her pants were brightly colored leggings topped off with an oversized hoodie that had been pulled halfway up her head, leaving a high ponytail of curls spilling out over the top.

"Hey Sela—" Cassandra's cheery greeting cut off halfway when Sela turned around sharply, surprised. "—sorry I didn't mean to... are you okay?"

Sela's face held no makeup except a thumb sized smudge of mascara under one eye. Definitely not ready for a rowdy night out on the town anywhere.

Closing the refrigerator door with one hand, she tugged the side of her sweatshirt's hood higher up her face. Saying nothing, Sela shook her head and brushed past Cassandra, around the corner and walked toward her room.

Cassandra followed close behind and when Sela opened her door, popped a foot out in the opening so Sela couldn't slam it in her face. "Look, we found Daniel's stuff in the library." She pleaded, "Do you need my help?"

"I'll tell you what I told him. Leave me out of it. If my name gets connected to this, my mother will yank me out of school and back home."

"Tell me what happened. Did he hurt you?"

Sela removed her hand from the door and stepped into her room leaving it open for Cassandra to enter.

Cassandra stood just inside and spoke quietly. "I'm not trying to get you in trouble if you weren't involved."

"I saw him earlier and he's a disgusting mess. He begged me to run away with him like this was some romantic movie. No freaking way I'm giving up my life." Her eyebrows raised into perfect arches while her head tilted left and right in a defiant negative.

"If you know where he is, please tell me."

"He's scared of his cousin, Jason. Daniel said he only wanted to feed poor people in the Global South. We both wanted to get more involved and talked about during our trip. I believed him, but it's too late now. He says he's not going to jail." Her arms crossed in front of her.

Cassandra waited several moments to see if Sela added anything or showed any indication she'd be willing to help find him.

Finally, Cassandra thanked her softly and left the room.

So, Daniel had asked Sela to go away with him, and thought he could avoid the police. Cassandra didn't understand the comment about feeding the poor, but her main concern was convincing him to turn himself in before anything awful happened in a confrontation with police.

No way could she have a relaxing night in with the students knowing he was in serious trouble. Cassandra went back to her room and texted Andy. "I think Sela knows where Daniel is, but she won't tell me."

Ten minutes later, the reply said, "We have Daniel. Meet us at the sheriff's office on Main Street."

"Is he hurt?" Cassandra replied.

"Not hardly. He resisted arrest."

Although she'd seen the duffle bag evidence herself, she still felt disappointed that Daniel had been the campus thief.

Pulling on her warm suede boots, Cassandra took Murphy outside to do his business. She was on her way to put Murphy in his kennel in her room when she saw a small group in the common room. "Hey guys. Are you folks going out tonight?"

"Nah, we're ordering pizza and binge-watching Parks and Rec." Akira's enthusiasm was endearing.

"Would you guys mind if Murphy hung out with you? I can give you his food bowl and leash. I shouldn't be gone long. Take him outside if he starts sniffing the rug." She did not want to be on the hook for cleaning the common room's carpets.

Grabbing her coat and bag, Cassandra walked to the parking lot. Murphy would be happier tonight with the students. The dog kennel was pretty small, and it did seem kind of cruel to lock him away in there for hours at a time.

She worked very long hours during the semester, often into the evenings. Another reason why she wasn't dog owner material.

Five minutes later, Cassandra entered the nondescript storefront on Main Street where the sheriff and his deputies conducted business while in Carson.

The conference room door was open.

Inside, Daniel Leung sat sullenly in handcuffs at the nice wooden table, a bottle of water in front of him. His hair was dirty, his cheek scratched near his jaw, his zippered hoodie stained, and without getting close she could already smell him from the doorway. Deputy Tate and another officer in a brown uniform arranged video camera equipment on a rolling metal cart, separating cords and plugging them in on the other side of the room.

She swallowed hard and stood against the wall next to Andy Summers. In a low voice near her ear Andy said, "We already read him his rights. He asked to talk to you instead of a lawyer."

Cassandra crooked her finger and went back to the hallway. Andy followed her. Deputy Tate remained inside with Daniel. "*Now* Tate's okay with me talking to Daniel. Why the change of heart?"

Andy shrugged, "He won't talk to us. Just keeps asking for you."

For days they'd been worried she'd mess up their investigation. "What if I say the wrong thing?"

"How about we both go in there?" Summers tilted his head both ways until his neck cracked. "I'll make sure he doesn't touch you, and I'll shake my head if you ask him something off limits. Just get him to talk. Whoever he's working with is probably waiting to hear from him. The faster we move, the less chance for anyone to get away."

Obviously, time was important, but presenting a calming energy would help everyone in this tense situation. For a brief moment, she paused to center her intentions. When she didn't move right away, Andy squeezed her elbow. "You got this. And I'll have your back."

Cassandra unzipped her coat. Setting her hat and gloves on the table, she sat across from Daniel. Tate removed Daniel's handcuffs and left the room, but the door remained open. "Hey Daniel. We've been really worried about you. You've been gone for almost four days."

Daniel said, "I have to get out of here. This was all a mistake." Grabbing the water bottle, he opened the lid and took long swig.

Everyone else saw a tough guy, at best a petty thief, at worst a criminal somehow involved in killing Dr. Nielson and stealing a foreign country's property. Cassandra saw a twenty-three-year-old scared kid whose cerebral cortex was obviously not fully developed.

Cassandra folded her hands in front of her on the table and stared into his dark brown eyes. "Campus police have evidence that items stolen this semester were found in your duffle bag. The best thing you can do is answer their questions."

The bottle crinkled when he set it down hard on the table. "I can't tell them anything."

"Look around you," said Cassandra. "You've been sleeping in the library instead of the dorm. You're under arrest."

His eyes filled briefly, and he rubbed his wrists where the handcuffs had been.

"Are you in danger from the same people who killed Dr. Nielson? Sela said your cousin scared you."

Out of the corner of her eye she saw Andy frown, but she ignored him.

"I never said I was scared. If I get kicked out of school, my family will hate me. I'm sorry I took the stuff. It was just a bunch of junk. I'll return everything, just let me go."

Cassandra said, "Sela said you asked her to run away with you. Today."

"She told you!" Daniel's voice was barely above a whisper but gained strength as he became angry. "You'd take that witch's word over mine. I've got seven years' worth of student loans to pay off. I don't have a rich mother to buy me a BMW and Spring Break trips every year. What else did she say?"

Whoa. Apparently, his friendship with Sela was more complicated than Cassandra had guessed. "Something about feeding poor people in the Global South..."

"I went hungry growing up." Daniel let out a sigh so big his shoulders slumped. "I swore that someday I'd help people in developing countries. I'm concerned about the future of the planet."

Stealing their stuff was a strange way of helping people. Including breaking into Cassandra's house! She swallowed her anger. "Okay, let's tell the officers how you were trying to help people. I'll sit here with you."

She nodded at Andy, who went into the hallway and came back in the room with Deputy Tate and the video tech. Tate nodded to the tech then sat next to Cassandra. Placing a yellow legal pad on the table and opening a file folder, he spoke to the camera on a tall tripod. "Statement from person of interest, Daniel Leung. Do we have your permission to record this?"

"Yes." Daniel's voice was barely above a whisper.

Cassandra felt a person move quietly into the conference room and stand against the wall near Andy. Glancing to her left she saw it was Sean Gill. He didn't speak.

Tate said, "Before we started taping, you said you meant to feed poor people. Can you explain that?"

"For my master's thesis, I study soybean plants. I've been working on a high-yield seed that is drought resistant. Farmers in newly industrialized countries would have access to an important food source."

"I don't think you meant it to go this far," Tate said. "You took something from China and now it's gotten bigger than you realized. "

That explained why Sean Gill was present.

"I didn't *take* anything from China." For what was probably thirty seconds but felt like several minutes, they stared at a silent Daniel. Tate acted like time didn't matter.

Gill stepped up to the table and put his palm down in front of Daniel. "Enough."

Daniel's head jerked back a little in surprise. He'd been completely focused on Cassandra and Tate and hadn't acknowledged everyone else in the conference room.

"I'm Officer Sean Gill from the USDA. We didn't say you took seeds or plants from China. What about the computer file?"

Daniel clamped his mouth shut.

"For weeks we've been investigating proprietary soybean seed research reported missing from a Chinese seed corporation." Sean turned to Cassandra. "If he doesn't help us soon, we're just going to throw him in a cage."

Daniel raised his head. "You don't know what you're talking about. I don't have the computer file. If I knew where it was, I wouldn't still be here."

Now she was totally lost. Cassandra looked over at Andy Summers, then at Tate and Gill. Sean Gill seemed to be the only person who understood, but he didn't jump in with more specific questions.

Daniel said, "I've racked my brain for weeks to find the answers and..." He locked eyes with Cassandra. For the first time she saw real fear in them. "It must have happened at the final reception before we left China."

"Was this the party your cousin Jason attended?" asked Cassandra. She remembered Sela had mentioned meeting him in China.

Daniel nodded. "He works for the seed corporation that hosted the party. Jason and me, we shared our research. Combining traits from his Chinese soybean seed together with mine would make a completely new version and I could patent it myself when I finish my thesis."

Cassandra remembered her conversation with Dr. Zimmerman. "If you sell the soybean seeds you would stand to make a lot of money. Even if you charge a discounted price to countries with emerging economies, right?"

His head nodded absently. "At the reception before we left China, the host representatives gave all of us swag bags. Very nice stuff. Much better than the little plastic trinkets in the souvenir shops. When Jason handed me my swag bag, he also gave me a special USB drive. I dropped it in my bag without thinking."

He stared at the table in front of Cassandra, as though reliving the memory of that night. "When I looked around the room, Sela and others in our group just held their little bags because that is more polite. A few students opened the bags to look at the swag. So, I didn't think it would hurt if I did the same. I sat on a couch and picked though my bag. On top was a nice blue t-shirt from the Hangzhou College of Commerce."

Cassandra raised an eyebrow encouragingly.

"Dr. Nielson was sitting right next to me. I didn't know him very well, but he was friendly in a grandfatherly kind of way. I wasn't paying close attention, but when I held up my blue t-shirt to check the size, he did the same. Mine was way too large for me, but I didn't want to act impolite, so I tucked it back inside the bag. Nielson's shirt was dark gray and at least two sizes smaller than mine."

Cassandra started to see where Daniel's story was headed.

"Nielson says, hey my shirt looks like it would fit you better, huh? Wanna trade? And... I said, sure. Instead of switching t-shirts, Nielson just gave me his whole bag. And I gave him mine. We flew home. Later, when I opened my USB drive, it was empty. No soybean seed file. I've been looking for it ever since."

Tate said, "We have a witness who says you lied about your alibi on Sunday, December 27th."

That was a big change of topic. Tate must be trying to trip Daniel up or catch him off guard.

"I don't know what you're talking about."

Tate opened his small notebook and flipped back several pages. "You told investigators that you were with Sela Roberts overnight Saturday and Sunday morning. Ms. Roberts said you left her room by 10:00 p.m. on Saturday. That fits within Gary Nielson's estimated time of death Sunday morning. Can no one else confirm your whereabouts on Sunday?"

Daniel's normally handsome face contorted into hard stone. "She's lying because she doesn't want her mother to know I spent the night. I don't care. I used her like she used me." Bringing both hands up to his face, he used the heels of his palms to rub his eyes.

Tate leaned closer to him. "Used her?"

"No one would suspect Miss Perfect Sela of being involved," Daniel sneered. "Plus, her mother could pull strings anytime Sela broke the rules."

Tate closed his notebook and folded his hands on the legal pad.

Tate's voice was calm and professional. "Lying or not, your alibi is no good now. When we check the gun from your duffle bag, we'll be able to prove you shot Dr. Nielson."

Cassandra let out a small gasp. The accusation was so direct and sure.

"Dr. Nielson left me a voicemail message asking if I'd seen anything suspicious on our China trip. He left one with Sela too, and neither of us called him back."

Daniel squirmed in his chair and drank some water. "When I saw Dr. Nielson at the graduation ceremony, I remembered the night with the T-shirts. I left him a message saying, 'I need that USB drive.' But he didn't follow my directions."

Cassandra's eyes closed.

"I know he had mine because we switched bags. That morning at his house we were looking for the USB drive when he found us. Nielson said he talked to the USDA while he was in Florida and would clear his name."

Daniel's cheeks reddened and it seemed to sink in that he was in a lot of trouble.

"Why didn't he just give me the keychain? I couldn't let everything I've worked for be ruined. I pulled out my gun." Tears formed in Daniel's eyes. "Nielson told me he didn't have a USB drive from China. I showed him mine and said, 'like this. Where's yours?' He said, 'I don't know what I did with it.'"

Again, Daniel looked straight at Cassandra. "It was an accident. I didn't mean to shoot him. The gun just went off."

"A warning shot?"

"Exactly!" Daniel said. His head fell forward into his hands. "But the gun moved, and the bullet hit him. It wasn't my fault. It was an accident."

Cassandra's soft heart hardened.

Daniel pleaded, "After he fell on the kitchen floor, I panicked. I knew he'd call 9-1-1 right away. I grabbed his laptop off the counter and ran."

Cassandra looked to her side at Andy.

"Then why are you still running?" Andy asked.

"At first, it seemed like no one realized it was me. I couldn't find what I needed on his laptop, so I kept looking. I wanted to forget the whole thing. But now my life is ruined no matter what."

Maybe. But he ran away without giving Nielson first aid or calling an ambulance. Cassandra didn't feel empathetic.

Andy said, "You broke into dorm rooms, offices, and two houses looking for a storage drive keychain?"

And walked away from a dying man. The fog of disbelief at the depth of Daniel's self-centeredness lifted long enough for Cassandra to flash on a memory.

She knew what Nielson had done with his Leifeng Pagoda keychain.

"Look, I'm past my deadline." Daniel fidgeted with his water bottle. "If I don't find that keychain, I'm dead."

Sean Gill said, "Who are you working for?"

Daniel didn't answer.

"We can't protect you if you won't tell us why you're hiding."

Another long pause while Daniel finished his water and stared at the table.

Deputy Tate said, "Okay, let's go back to the beginning. I want to make sure I understand everything."

Cassandra's stomach was in knots. She'd been gone from Murphy too long already. If she listened to Daniel's whole story again, she'd be sick. It was time to let the officers finish their jobs.

"I need to go." Cassandra grabbed her belongings and said hurried goodbyes. She refused to make eye contact again with Daniel. She had believed he was a victim, only to find out he was a murderer.

Andy touched her elbow when she made it to the hallway. "Cass! Are you okay?"

"I'll be fine. I'm going back to Picotte." She saw the concern in his eyes.

Outside in front of her car, Cassandra gulped frigid air into her lungs to quell the urge to be sick in the snow pile.

Time seemed to stand still while she marveled at snow clinging magically to overhead tree branches. Down the block, the only business lights came from the windows of The Home Team bar. Large piles of plowed snow framed parking lots, blanketed the central public park, and muffled sounds of arriving partygoers. She wouldn't have been surprised if George Bailey himself ran down the Main Street shouting that he'd just seen an angel.

Knowing how Gary Nielson had died was a relief, although she felt sorry that he'd exited this world helpless and alone. Wishing Morton was a wet campus, she really wanted to bring a bottle of wine back to her room. In the other direction a couple of blocks away, bright lights lit up the parking lot of the Gas and Sweets store.

She could make a quick stop before going back.

Chapter Twenty-Six

From her vantage point in the liquor aisle at the gas station, Cassandra peeked up to the round mirror in the corner of the ceiling. She was thirty-four years old and if she wanted to drink a whole bottle of cheap Chardonnay on New Year's Eve, she wasn't going to feel guilty about it. At the same time, she wasn't in the mood to bump into any students or judgy small town gossips.

Cassandra's gloved hand closed around the top of the wine bottle and she turned toward the refrigerator section to find a snack pack of cheese and crackers. Dr. Shannon Bryant walked past the end of the aisle and briefly looked her way. When he realized who she was, he stopped and waved hello. "Ready to party?" He signed.

She didn't want to get into the details of her horrible evening, so she half-smiled and nodded.

"Oh, I got your text," Bryant signed. "Sorry I didn't respond. Meeting on Monday at 9:00 a.m. works for me, too."

She gave him a thumbs up. Couldn't she just sneak out of here without a long conversation?

He said, "I'm driving to Kansas City to meet some friends. Study your ASL this weekend!"

He laughed. She nodded some more and waved goodbye, her fake smile turning sincere. "Prepare to be impressed."

He waved bye, and she headed for the cash register where Mr. Soukup himself rang her up. Overhead fluorescent lights made his thick, wavy gray hair glow like a halo. He eyed her while she completed her credit card transaction without any small talk, for which she was grateful.

As she pushed open the glass door, she glanced back into the store in case Shannon Bryant was close behind her. Seeing no one she recognized, Cassandra went around the side of the building to her car and unlocked it using the key fob.

The keychain Dr. Nielson had given her when he retired dangled from her car key ring. She'd seen it often during the past six weeks without really examining it. A short breath caught in her throat. Anticipation mixed with dread. Why was a keychain worth killing a man?

She rested her phone in the console drink holder and placed the wine and snacks on the passenger seat. Flipping on the dome light in her car, she examined the keychain more closely.

Made of a high-quality metal die cast four-sided Pagoda shape, she noticed a rough spot near the ring. When she pulled gently on the ring end, a USB plug pulled free of the keychain. Clever marketing idea.

Daniel had wanted *his* keychain and risked his entire college career and future freedom to find it. Tempted to turn around and return to the sheriff's office, Cassandra wanted to check the USB first before she involved anyone else. Everyone on the trip had received identical keychains, plus the extras that Daniel had stolen. If this USB was blank, Cassandra didn't want to make a big scene for no reason.

She pulled her laptop out of the tote bag, onto her lap, and fired it up. Sticking the USB drive into the adapter, she waited for it to open. By the time she navigated to the USB file and opened the document, she was completely engrossed.

Her phone's home screen flashed a text. Her eyes glanced down to the console. Andy Summers wrote, "Daniel's gone. He asked to use the bathroom, then escaped."

Wait, *what*? Frowning, Cassandra reached for her phone. Before she could unlock it, she heard a metallic click.

Her driver side door opened, and cold air rushed into the car. Startled into a scream, she turned toward the door. The computer slid off her lap and onto the passenger seat.

An arm snaked around her neck, and one gloved hand clamped over her mouth while another grabbed her around the torso. Her head smacked the doorframe as she was yanked out of the car. Kicking out wide, she fought to grab the seat, the steering wheel, anything stable.

A sharp pain stung her neck. Stars flashed in her peripheral vision, then everything went dark.

Chapter Twenty-Seven

Slowly Cassandra felt a throbbing pain in her shoulder, and the fuzziness in her head cleared. The acrid smell of gasoline and dirt reacted like smelling salts to her foggy brain.

Heart pounding, her eyes flew open and darted around the space surrounding her. Curled into an unnatural fetal position, she lay with her wrists awkwardly bound behind her back. Her jaw moved but tape across her mouth tugged her skin. Underneath her cheek, the floor was cold concrete covered in a decaying muck Cassandra didn't want to inspect too closely. She heard faint whimpering for several seconds before realizing the noises came from herself.

Closing her eyes, she called up the last memory she'd had before awakening here. Gazing at the laptop screen in her car, she'd seen an official looking research memo about the soybean seeds. Her chest tightened as she relived the startling moment of the car door opening and being grabbed from the side in one fast movement. Had she even screamed? She couldn't remember.

Her nose uncovered, her breaths came in short gasps. Cassandra forced herself to inhale one big breath in and hold it. She couldn't even hyperventilate properly with the tape over her mouth anyway.

Several deep breaths later, the tightness in her chest had subsided and the panicked feeling dissipated leaving behind frustration. Tears slid down her cheeks.

She'd never been physically hurt before on purpose. Never been in a schoolyard fistfight. Never spanked by her parents. Even the Halloween stalker creep had been terrifying without physically laying a hand on her.

She listened for footsteps or nearby traffic noises. She had to get out before the people came back.

Her shoulders ached. She needed a clear plan. One more big breath. She implored spiritual help from Paul, her dead grandparents, and ancestors. Their positive energy would help her focus.

Daniel Leung and whoever he'd been working for must have taken her. Meaning they either needed to keep her alive for later, or they didn't really want to kill her at all. When her captors came back, she could find out what they wanted and give it to them or pay whatever ransom they requested.

Cassandra guessed that Nielson had known the soybean seed research was on the keychain he'd given her. When he'd been confronted by Daniel, had Nielson forfeited his own life to protect Cassandra and the college's reputation?

Cassandra couldn't wipe the tears away. What little vision she had clouded over with the wetness. She had to get herself together.

Now that her eyes had adjusted to the gloom, she could see an engine, shelving, cobwebbed hoses and electrical cords hung on the walls, and large shapes covered in tarps. Filtered light streamed in from two dirty windows high up on the wall. She was in a barn or shed and although the floor was cold, it wasn't like lying in a restaurant freezer.

Voices and vehicles in the distance made her breath catch. Pulling her wrists apart, she felt thin plastic bite into her skin.

Her lower arms and shoulders were numb. Straightening her legs, she moved her ankles in small circles to restore the circulation, grateful she'd changed into warm sweatpants before getting Andy's call. Rolling toward her front, she tried to sit up but with her numb arms behind her back, she had no way to balance. When she scooted to a seated position, a wave of dizziness forced her to stay put for several more minutes.

Insecurities magnified in the stillness. Did anyone appreciate all of her hard work and passion for serving students? This level of sacrifice was not what she'd envisioned on the path to becoming a university president. She was a fool to move from paradise to this stupid, frozen tundra anyway.

She'd watched enough TV crime thrillers to know that getting her hands free would be huge. Sitting up felt much better on her shoulders and arms. As blood flowed back to her fingers, her arms and hands burned with painful pins and needles. Now that she moved her legs around more, some of the tape near her ankles loosened, and she could slide her feet beneath her. If she balanced slowly like a careful yoga pose, she could stand. Maybe she could inch along, one foot in front of the other like a gymnast walking a balance beam. A sigh of relief went through her while she concentrated on keeping her balance and letting her limbs come alive again through the slow, painful process.

She needed something sharp to get the ties off her wrists but didn't see any cutting tools among the junk hanging on the walls. Each time she shuffled a few steps, puffs of dust stirred up around her legs, making her cough.

She had no idea how long she'd been there, although judging by the amount of sunshine coming through the windows, it had to be morning.

Finally thinking more clearly, she knew she had to hurry. Shuffling a little at a time, she moved from shadow to shape, looking for a tool or sharp edge. It took her five minutes to move three feet in any direction. And it was disheartening to realize the room had no cutting tools. One wall contained an 8-foot-tall double wide metal shelving unit containing old gallon paint cans, bags of fertilizer and dog food, and engine oil containers. When she tried rubbing her hands back and forth on a corner of the shelves, she cut her wrist. Blood slowly dripped down her fingers.

She ignored the pain and kept rubbing the shelf, going slowly. If she moved too much, the shelf rocked precariously, and she didn't want to knock the whole thing over. She moved around the shelf feeling lower and higher edges and corners, searching for a nick or exposed lip that would be the sharpest point. As she worked, she closed her eyes and thought about her family.

It would be early morning in Waipahu. Dad had probably already drunk his two cups of hot black coffee and gone out back to his garden to work. He tended orchids and herbs with the patience and precision that only an older Japanese man could bring to the task. Watching him garden was like watching Mr. Miyagi teach the Karate Kid how to do it properly. Cassandra's brother Keoni had never possessed the required level of attention for detail, so Cassandra had tagged along with her father.

You would have thought after all that time hauling wood chips, digging in the soil, pulling weeds and picking vegetables for their dinner that Cassandra would be an excellent gardener. What a joke. While she knew what tasks needed to be done and how to do them, on her own she managed to forget to water every week or she'd overwater and drown her plants.

Once she'd moved out, her mother had taken over the care of Cassandra's poor houseplants and her father now taught his gardening tasks to the grandchildren. Hopefully they'd learn better than Cassandra had.

Her mind wandered between the past and present while she worked on the ties. She couldn't even be sure she was rubbing on the same spot of the plastic. The TV shows never showed how long it took to do this! If only she could cut to commercial and the next scene began in 90 seconds, she'd be free. Ha. Her many preconceived ideas of how things should happen were all thrown out the window.

Finally, she noticed her hands had more movement, more freedom. This was working! The ties loosened. Within a few more minutes, her hands were free.

Ripping off the duct tape wrapped around her ankles, she ran to the metal wall and searched for a light switch. Past a riding lawn mower, an old car under a tarp, and a couple of other covered machines, she came upon a large overhead garage door and next to it a smaller regular door. Holding her ear up to the door first, she tried the knob. It turned, but the deadbolt was locked.

Leaning against the door, she wanted to cry, or laugh again. She wasn't sticking around to find out why they hadn't already killed her.

She studied the smaller door with a standard knob and keyed deadbolt. It didn't seem super fancy. Reaching behind her ear, she pulled out two bobby pins that held what was left of her hair's bun in place. "Well, this worked for Jason Bourne. Let's try it in real life."

She flattened one pin into an angle and stuck it into the keyhole, added the second bobby pin, and jiggled the top one gently up and down. She felt resistance, but nothing clicked or turned. Ten, maybe fifteen minutes later, her forehead was sweaty with the exertion and the frustration of wasting valuable time.

How else could she break out? The windows were too high. She turned her attention to the overhead garage door and noticed a red button high on the wall between the regular door and the garage door. Could it really be that simple?

Her eyes shut for a moment to pray for divine intervention. Jumping as though going up for a layup, she tapped the round button and held her breath. It clicked and the opener made a brief noise then stopped. Cassandra froze. If anyone nearby had heard that noise, they'd come after her now.

Waiting thirty seconds until her heart slowed to a more normal pace, Cassandra studied the overhead door. There was a long metal bar stretching the whole width of the door.

When she stepped closer, she realized the bar was wedged into a notch on the side rail. Walking to the other end of the door, she realized the bar was also locked in a similar notch.

Backing up, she noticed the center had a handle and maybe a couple of springs. What if she... grasping the handle, she twisted. Nothing gave way. She'd been sure that would do the trick. One last time she twisted and pulled at the same time, feeling the bars move toward the center, unlocking from the side rails. She ran to the button and slammed it hard. A loud clanking noise echoed throughout the bay.

Chapter Twenty-Eight

The garage door took forever to slide open. As soon as there was two feet of clearance at the bottom, Cassandra ducked underneath and popped out into the blinding sunshine made worse from the snow reflection. Blinking fast, she was hit with a gust of wind so cold the inside of her lungs filled with icy air. Her breath was suspended in her chest in shock.

Instinctively she crouched down against the shed's wall, making herself as small as possible until her eyes adjusted. To her left was a three-foot-tall stack of wooden landscaping ties. To the right, partially covered by the snow, was a rusted wheelbarrow, old tires and rotting 2x4s. Tire tracks grooved in the unshoveled snow leading to the garage door. Side stepping her way to huddle close to the junk pile, she shivered.

A chain link fence defined the boundaries of this shed from a field to the left. Farther to the right another fenced in lot stored off-season boats and RVs. Maybe one baseball field length away was a parking lot behind a one-story building. She could run to that building in less than a minute.

Thank God she'd pulled on her suede boots at the last minute before heading over to the college. Her puffy winter coat blocked the worst of the chill, but she'd lost her gloves. The bulk of the wheelbarrow cut the wind as she looked down the driveway.

Squinting at the sign extending above the roof, she read backwards. It said Gas and Sweets! Several cars were parked in the lot behind and alongside the store.

Except hers. The Honda she'd parked on the side of the store was gone.

Snow had drifted along the metal fence as high as three feet in some spots where the wind piled it up. The seconds ticked by while she considered her options. She didn't know who or what was parked around the sides or back of the shed. If she sat here too long deliberating, she'd freeze to death before she even made a decision.

Slowly standing on shaky legs, Cassandra snapped the hood under her chin and stepped toward the drive.

Before she'd gotten more than three steps, the muffled sound of footsteps in the snow made her heart jump. Turning her head, a scream erupted from her mouth as a man wearing a thick hooded jacket ran at her full speed.

She looked again at the parking lot, so close and yet too far. Why had she taken so long to decide which way to run? By the time Cassandra's head came around and her hands came up to confront the man, he was nearly on top of her. At least six inches taller and fifty pounds heavier, she knew she wouldn't be able to fight him.

His face and neck were covered by a fleece mask which muffled his angry yell. "No, go back!"

But she recognized his voice. "Daniel?" she shouted. "Just let me go! Don't do this!"

"I can't let you go." He grabbed her from behind and around her neck and chest.

Cassandra squirmed and wriggled, but he was stronger than his wiry build made him appear. She yelled "Help! Help me!" But between the wind and the distance, she didn't think anyone heard her being dragged back inside the building.

Once inside, he shoved her and hit the garage door button to close it again. Tripping over hoses and junk on the floor, she landed hard on her shoulder.

His hands rested on his hips while his chest huffed with the exertion.

"Stay there. We're leaving soon." Daniel pulled his phone out of a jacket pocket and frowned at the screen while he tapped and scrolled.

Cassandra sat up, rubbed her throbbing shoulder, and readjusted her messy hair into a ponytail. "Why did you run away from the police, Daniel? And why take me?"

"I saw your keychain at the dorm. I watched you, but I could never get it away from you. I thought it you had Nielson's USB, you'd report me." He removed tarps creating dust clouds that rose and settled around her, and revealed two snowmobiles nearest the garage door. "Taking you will make sure I get out of here in one piece!"

Cassandra sneezed twice, wiping tears, and dust from her face. "Don't do this. It's not too late to change your mind." When she looked down, her hand was scraped raw where she'd slid on the floor and blood seeped from her previous cut. She squeezed the side of her hand to apply pressure.

"Just be quiet!" He grabbed a red gas can and filled the tank on the nearest snowmobile with jerky, agitated movements, sloshing a little over the sides of the hole and filling the air with the smell. Then he moved to the next one and did the same thing. Cassandra quietly moved to a crouch and inched away from him, scanning the wall for a weapon heavier than a broom handle.

Three sharp knocks sounded on the smaller door and a male voice said, "Let me in. Quick!"

Daniel keyed open the deadbolt that Cassandra had unsuccessfully tried to pick earlier. An average sized guy rushed inside and closed the door behind him. "Everything's set up. But there's a statewide hunt on for you. And her."

He tossed a food bag at Daniel who caught it neatly and a similar one at Cassandra. She watched it arc in the air toward her and land on the dusty floor with a small thud.

"Someone reported seeing you on the highway going toward Lincoln. No one thinks you're hiding out right behind Main Street."

She hadn't even realized she was hungry, but she had missed a couple of meals.

The new guy turned, and his brown eyes glared at her with a coldness that made sweat dampen the back of her neck.

A lump formed in her throat. She'd been ready to either talk Daniel into letting her go or fight him to escape. The odds of overpowering both of them were nonexistent.

Cassandra had no intention of dying in a cold barn in Nebraska.

The guys stood near the garage door, phones together, pointing and making a plan in voices too low for Cassandra to overhear all the words. While minutes ticked by Cassandra sat on the floor, watching them while she ate, recalling all the action movies she'd seen where the victim fights back. Hermione would have pulled off the perfect stunning spell. Katniss had her trusty arrows. Cassandra had a PhD in Higher Education Administration. She could vision and leadership them into comas.

While they were talking, she reached out for a long metal pipe wrench wedged under an old engine.

After what seemed like hours, Daniel's partner—she assumed it was his cousin, Jason—zipped his coat and pulled up his hood. "It's time."

Cassandra didn't move. If she played difficult, maybe they'd give up and leave her there to make their getaway.

Daniel lifted a leg over the nearest snowmobile and settled onto the seat. He turned and held out a helmet toward her. "C'mon. Get in front."

Cassandra chose the frosty tone of voice she used when scolding unruly undergrads. "I will not get on that thing."

Daniel pulled a black neck gator up past his cheeks and snapped the chinstrap of his helmet. Reaching into his coat pocket, he tugged out a small handgun, leveling it at Cassandra. "I said, get in front."

Before she'd even thought of a retort or moved, the other guy appeared at her side. He grabbed her by the upper arm and yanked her to standing while the wrench clanged on the ground behind her. For a second, everything froze while she stared at Daniel and felt solid metal poke into her left ribs.

He pushed her closer to Daniel. "Get on or die now."

The fear in Daniel's eyes echoed her own. This person would not be manipulated or tricked. "They're looking for us, Jason! We need her until we get out of town."

Lifting her leg over the long double seat, Cassandra climbed onto the snowmobile. Daniel handed her the helmet. Her arm throbbed where Jason had grabbed her.

Cassandra felt a hard object poking in her back and assumed it was the gun barrel. Fear and annoyance sharpened her words. "Aim that thing somewhere else. I don't trust you to not fire it by mistake."

"Neither of us have a choice anymore." His warm breath was so close to her ear, a shiver went down her back.

Jason pulled his helmet over his head and hit the red garage door button.

"Maybe you should drive," said Cassandra over the noise of the opening door. She needed an escape plan. "Where are we going?"

Reaching in front of her with his right hand, Daniel turned a key in the ignition and started the engine. Jason's ride roared to life several seconds later and after a few adjustments he zoomed outside.

"Right side is the throttle. Squeeze the lever to go. Left is the brake. Let's move."

She felt paralyzed.

"Follow Jason!" he yelled.

Cassandra grasped the right grip and thumbed the throttle lever until she felt the machine lurch forward a few feet. She let go of the throttle, her chin snapped into her chest, and she slid forward on the seat from the change in momentum. She could feel his arms around her sides holding her steady.

Cassandra pressed the lever more slowly until they moved more smoothly. She had no idea what she'd do when it was time to take a corner. She'd always imagined it would be fun to try winter sports while she was living in Nebraska, but this was not the way she'd hoped to learn.

At the end of the driveway, she expected Jason to head through the parking lot to the right and down a side road. Jason had said the police were looking for Daniel and knew she was missing, too. She willed a passing car to stop them.

Instead, Jason rounded the fence and rode into the wide-open cornfield two blocks off of Main Street. Frozen stalks rose several feet higher than the snow. Some areas had been blown bare, and in other parts the wind had formed tall snow drifts.

There wasn't a clear road or path to follow. For the next several seconds she practiced using the throttle until she heard Daniel yell, "Go faster!"

Pressing harder on the lever, she peeked down at the speedometer. The gauge moved up to 50 mph. Her knuckles were white from hanging on tight, but the rest of her hand was bright pink from the cold.

Jason got to the end of the first field and came to a road. He slowed slightly and shot across the opening into the next field. When Cassandra rode down the small ditch and up to the road, the rough sound of the bottom riding on bare gravel startled her and she slowed again. To their left, a tall embankment lined with trees followed parallel to the direction they rode.

For ten minutes they continued riding through fields covered in at least eight inches of pristine snow, skirting around farm buildings, small ponds, and crossing a couple of frozen creeks. She tried following Jason's tracks as much as possible over the larger snow drifts to minimize the bumps and roughness. The sun lowered directly behind them, underlighting each layer of fluffy clouds with an orangey pink glow as it sank. It would have been breathtakingly beautiful if she hadn't been frozen in every sense of the word.

Chapter Twenty-Nine

When she crested the top of a large drift, blowing snow whipped against her cheeks through the face opening of the helmet and she closed her eyes for a second. Riding felt like surfing atop a huge wave. Flying effortlessly until the free fall moment and the rag doll jerking of her crashing body underwater.

Trying to keep up with Jason was hard work. She kept him in her sight but couldn't force herself to go the same reckless speed. That last landing had been as violent as slamming against the hard ocean floor during a wipe-out. For the few seconds they'd been airborne, Cassandra wondered if she could throw Daniel off the snowmobile and ride to the nearest farmhouse for help. Unfortunately, there was no guarantee she wouldn't crash and hurt herself in the process.

"Where are we going?" Cassandra yelled when they made it to a level straightaway. Driving gave her some power and she considered ways she could use it to her advantage.

DEAD OF *Winter Break*

She didn't really expect him to tell her the truth, but it was worth a shot. They'd traveled at least eight miles east. Maybe Jason had a car waiting on a side road nearby.

"Wahoo. The airport."

Yikes.

"It's getting dark out. I can't see." Cassandra had slowed down so much they could barely see Jason ahead of them. Daniel told her to stop.

The first time she squeezed the brakes it was too hard, and she lurched ahead smacking her helmet on the windshield. His body slammed into the back of hers. She waited for the pain that would come when he shot her, whether by accident or on purpose.

Her thumping heart told her she was still alive. Without the loud engine, she attempted one last time to talk to him. "I know you never meant to hurt anyone, Daniel. I bet if you stop this right now and take me back to Carson before anything else happens, they will go easier on you. We can show up at the sheriff's office and turn ourselves in. I'll sit with you and make sure they listen to your side of the story."

He stood on the running board and leaned over to flip the switch that turned on the headlights. "It's not that simple. My uncle owns the company where Jason works. He found out what we did. My uncle has been paying for my schooling. If I go to jail for murder, I will have disgraced my mother and her whole family. This is the only option left. I have to leave the country."

He sat again and nudged her back. "Let's go."

On the right side handle she noticed another switch. When she touched it nothing happened right away, but as they started again the grips heated up. Finally, her fingers thawed a bit, although her thumb ached from pressing the throttle lever so tightly.

She increased their speed to catch up to Jason. The last thing she wanted was him turning around and riding alongside them.

Over the next hill, a farm appeared on the right side. A one-story house with several large sheds clustered near fenced in pens for animals. Tall pine trees lined one side of the farm as a windbreak. Gradually she caught up to within several hundred yards of Jason but stayed to his right and drifted closer to the farm.

They had to be nearing the Wahoo airport. If she didn't make a move soon, she'd be on a plane with two desperate guys and even fewer options. Remembering the last time Daniel had told her to stop, she waited for the next big snowdrift.

Tensing, she gripped the handlebar and squeezed the brakes hard. Just like before, she slid forward and her helmet knocked the windshield.

She heard Daniel yell, "Wha—" at the same moment she felt him push against her back and lean to the left to keep his balance.

Letting go of the brake, she thumbed the throttle all the way to the handlebar, and they shot forward over the drift. Already unstable, Cassandra felt the snowmobile lift as Daniel jerked backwards. He grabbed her coat with his hand as he tumbled off the end, but she was going 40 mph by then and he hadn't been prepared. Glancing over her shoulder she saw a puff of snow where he'd landed.

She turned a hard right and raced toward the farm praying someone was home. Unless he was hurt, she knew Daniel would call Jason and they'd follow her. She probably had less than a few minutes to find help or she'd have to get to the road and hope to see cars or another house.

Roaring into the area between the house and barn, Cassandra parked by the back door of the house and ran up to the back patio doors. She banged on the glass. "Hello! Help! Is anyone there? Hello!"

Inside the spacious kitchen a middle-aged woman with shoulder length hair wearing an apron came to the door holding a long chef's knife. Standing on the other side of the glass she frowned, and her mouth opened into a big "oh."

Cassandra caught sight of her reflection in the door and removed the helmet so the woman could see her face. She put her palms together, "Please, call the police! They're chasing me!"

For several seconds they looked at each other, neither of them moving until the sound of a snowmobile engine grew louder. Cassandra desperately cried, "Open the door! Please! They'll kill me!"

Finally, the woman reached out and unlatched the door. Cassandra ducked inside and the woman dropped the knife on the counter and grabbed a metal pole. Cassandra backed into the kitchen afraid she'd picked the wrong farmhouse, but the woman quickly bent over and wedged the metal piece into the base of the door frame so it couldn't be forced open. She turned off the kitchen lights and pulled the blinds shut on the back door.

"Downstairs!" she yelled and ran to a doorway with steps leading to the basement. At the same time, she pulled a cell phone out of her pocket and punched in a number. "This is Shary Miller out on Highway 92. Hurry! That missing woman is here, and the bad guys are after us. We'll be in the safe room in the basement."

For a woman who looked at least fifty years old, she moved quickly. They reached the corner of the basement where a sturdy smaller room with white walls and a door with several locks stood open. The woman scooted inside, and Cassandra followed right behind her. Ms. Miller grabbed the door, locked the deadbolt, and slid two heavy steel pins into place.

Cassandra had picked exactly the right farmhouse!

Inside, the 8x10 foot room was outfitted like an efficiency apartment with extra shelves for canned goods and extra supplies plus a tiny toilet with a fold-down sink. Ms. Miller touched several buttons on a remote control and the room's TV showed a channel broadcasting the local news.

After several minutes, Cassandra's official Morton College portrait appeared on the TV with the banner, "Search continues for college staff member and student last seen in Carson on Friday night."

Cassandra unzipped her coat as her hands and body came to room temperature.

Another screen near the door showed two views of security cameras set up on the front and back entrances to the house. Her breath caught when she saw two figures trying the doors on both sides of the house. After several minutes they weren't on camera anymore. Maybe they'd given up. Cassandra wished she'd thought to grab the key before getting off her snowmobile.

"Can I borrow your phone Ms. Miller?"

She nodded, handed it to Cassandra, and sat on a bench. Cassandra hadn't memorized anyone's phone numbers. In the browser, she looked up the Morton Campus security number and called Andy. It forwarded directly to his cell. "Summers," he answered.

"Andy! It's Cassandra. I escaped from Daniel and his cousin." In the small room her voice was too loud, but she was so hyped up she couldn't contain herself. She still couldn't believe the maneuver had worked and she'd thrown him off the snowmobile.

"Thank God you're alright!" Andy said. "We got the dispatch call, too. We're not far away."

"I'm fine. Look, you guys need to get to the Wahoo Airport. They're meeting a plane." She didn't actually know the time or what kind of plane, but she hoped that the police would be able to figure it out. She gave him what few details she could and hung up.

Unable to sit down, she marveled at how much storage was tucked away under the benches which doubled as twin beds, or on the pantry shelves that rimmed the room a foot from the ceiling. Cassandra said, "Thank you so much. This room is amazing. You have everything a few people would need for days."

"My husband insisted on building a safe room," Ms. Miller said. "'Keep out the crazies,' he said. I just wanted a strong tornado shelter, but this is state of the art. Our first house got hit fifteen years ago and blew the whole first floor off the foundation. If I hadn't been in the laundry room under a mattress, I might have blown away with it." She opened a small door on the wall and pulled out a pistol. "If those guys get inside the house and come down here, I'll take care of them." Pointing the gun toward the ceiling, she opened a latch in the wall next to the door revealing a hole small enough for her to stick out her gun and fire at any incoming crazies.

If Daniel and Jason were smart, they were already back on their way to the airport.

"Where is your husband now?" Cassandra asked.

Ms. Miller shrugged a bit and smiled, "He went into town to meet his buddies for a beer and watch football at the bar. He'll be upset he missed out on all the fun!"

Not ten minutes later, another dark figure appeared on the front entrance security camera and Cassandra held her breath. Were they back to finish her off? Frowning, she watched the person ring the doorbell several times. He wore a heavy coat and stocking hat like everyone else this time of year, but something was familiar about him. He stepped back and looked around the door and frame. Finally, the light showed his face.

Cassandra whirled around, "Can you open this room now? I think the bad guys are gone, and I need to answer the front door."

Chapter Thirty

Within minutes, Cassandra and Shannon Bryant were hurtling down the highway in his four-wheel drive SUV. The sun had set completely, and the interior console lights showed his broad smile. When she'd answered the door at Ms. Miller's house, he'd wrapped her in a quick hug and signed that it was his responsibility to take her to the hospital in Wahoo to get checked out.

As happy as she was to see a friendly face, she was more interested in meeting Andy and the others at the Wahoo Airport. She didn't know how to talk to Bryant while he was driving. The lights of town approached, and she wanted to ask him to make a stop before the hospital.

She tapped Bryant on the shoulder. He flipped the overhead light on and looked over. "Five minutes," he signed.

Cassandra shook her head. "No. Please. The airport." Only she didn't know the sign for airport, so she just signed airplane and mouthed the word airport.

In one way, she felt embarrassed that their conversations were as short and simple as cavemen. At the same time, it was pretty cool she'd learned enough ASL to chat with him.

He kept the car aimed straight ahead and his eyes shifted from her to the road every couple of seconds. Bryant's brows met. "Other guys to airport. You, to hospital."

Her shoulder ached, her hand was scraped, and she probably had a big bruise on her knee. Nothing a long soak in the bathtub wouldn't cure. She understood it was wise to see a doctor to be sure whatever drug they'd given her hadn't done any damage, but there were more important considerations now. "First the airport. We have to stop them!"

Whether she'd appealed to his sense of adventure or he was just humoring her, he nodded and turned after the big lake on the side of the highway. A driveway approached near a small blue sign with an airplane on it. Bryant turned in, but they were stopped by a Saunders County sheriff's car.

Bryant rolled down the window and typed into his phone. He showed the screen to the deputy and waited while the deputy spoke into the handset clipped onto his jacket. Cassandra held her breath. She'd been involved this far, she wanted to make sure Daniel and Jason were caught.

The man stepped back and waved them through, pointing straight ahead to a cluster of cars at the end of the gravel drive. To their left was a store, and to their right a couple of small businesses. Past them, on the right it looked like a cluster of storage warehouses. Pulling near the parking lot in front of a large industrial building, she saw Andy Summers talking to Deputy Tate and Sean Gill. Behind them were more deputies.

Cassandra craned her neck to the left and saw three small planes with propellers parked between the large hangar and a smaller hangar to the left. Past that everything was dark except the runway lights glowing along the cleared airstrip.

Before Bryant had even unbuckled his seatbelt, Cassandra was out her door and running up to Andy, Gill, and Tate. "They're coming on snowmobiles. Jason arranged for a plane to pick them up here. They both have guns. You have to stop them!"

The words came rushing out so fast they all just stared at her for several moments. Her normal calm collected self had been replaced by the alter ego who had outsmarted her captors. And she kind of liked her more aggressive side.

Tate said, "We have a drone in the air following them. We're moving our vehicles to the storage area, so they aren't visible from the field or the road."

She turned to Andy, "Daniel and Jason hid me in the little barn on the property behind the Gas and Sweets. You need to check how they got the keys from Mr. Soukup and if he knew about them using the barn. I wonder if the snowmobiles are his." She had disregarded all the rumors about him being some kind of mob boss, but now she was glad she wasn't a body buried under a random parking lot.

Andy's eyebrows raised. "That's good to know. I'll tell Tate to trace the records. Maybe the rumors about Soukup aren't all myth. Look, we need to move our cars. You can wait in that parking lot." He pointed to the left where an aviation repair shop had a small parking area near the field.

She and Bryant hopped into his SUV and parked near a tall light which made the inside of his car bright enough that they could see each other. His dashboard clock displayed 6:08 p.m. Less than twenty-four hours earlier this entire drama had begun. She couldn't imagine how it would end.

She signed, "I thought you were going to Kansas City for a New Year's Eve party?"

He laughed. "I was. But when I left the gas station, I saw many police cars on the street. I waited for a few minutes but couldn't see what had happened."

He adjusted the interior temperature setting on the dashboard and pointed to the heated seat feature on her side. He signed, "Then I went to my car and saw yours sitting in the parking lot. But you weren't inside the car. I knew you had left the store. When I looked in your window, I saw your purse and the wine you had just bought."

For several minutes he explained how he'd walked back to the sheriff's office and found Andy, Tate and the others inside. They told him about Daniel Leung's escape, and he told them about Cassandra's abandoned car. Soon they had begun searching for both of them. "Yeah, I saved your life and missed my party." Bryant folded his arms across his chest and smiled.

Signing "thank you," didn't seem enough for all he'd done. She tried to radiate gratitude in her smile and eyes. Allowing people to help her didn't come naturally, but she could see Bryant was pleased to be her friend.

While they talked, the law enforcement cars disappeared around the other side of the large hangar. Several minutes later, two sets of headlights came through the snow-covered fields to the southeast and paused on the opposite edge of the runway.

Cassandra leaned forward in her seat. No planes had taken off or landed. Bryant said the airport normally closed at sundown. The drivers pulled out onto the runway and rode toward the larger hangar. The snowmobiles stopped, but their headlights stayed on and Cassandra guessed they kept the engines running.

After another couple of minutes, lights from a small plane emerged from the cloudy evening sky as it glided down to the runway. When the plane touched down, it quickly disappeared out of sight. Daniel and Jason waited on their snowmobiles until the plane taxied back and stopped between the large hangar and where Bryant had parked.

Everything seemed to move in slow motion while the jet's door opened, and a stairway smoothly unfolded. Daniel and Jason turned off the snowmobiles and stepped toward the plane. If they ran, they'd be on board within ten seconds and could fold up the stairs behind them.

Where were the sheriff and his deputies? Cassandra put her hands on the dashboard. She signed to Bryant, "Where are the police? What if they E-S-C-A-P-E?"

Bryant shrugged then pointed. Coming around the corner of the hanger two sheriff's cars with lights flashing were followed by Andy's work cruiser and another car. One car stopped in front of the plane's nose, the other two parked behind it. Andy's car went all the way around and stopped near the hangar wall blocking off that path.

Cassandra heard shouts as officers surrounded Daniel and Jason with guns drawn. They both stopped, Daniel dropped his gun and raised his hands above his head. He turned and said something to Jason who still held his gun. For heart-stopping seconds, Cassandra thought his cousin might choose to shoot Daniel. He must know that would be the last move of his life. Her breath held, she whispered, "Drop it, Jason. Please."

Jason crouched down and placed it on the ground then slowly came up with his hands over his head too. Tate rushed up and shoved him to the ground. While the others and Andy held their guns on Jason, another figure stepped between the officers with guns and approached Daniel.

Bryant tapped her shoulder, "Who is that?" he asked.

Cassandra spelled out, "Sean Gill. He's from the USDA."

While they watched, Gill reached out and patted Daniel's jacket around the chest area, unzipped the top and stuck his hand inside. He came out with a small object, gave it a little toss in the air and walked away. A deputy moved in, handcuffed Daniel, and led him to the car.

Cassandra told Bryant, "Morton doesn't want S-P-I-E-S." She spelled 0-0-7 and signed none.

Bryant flipped on his headlights and put the car in drive. "Time to go to the hospital. You need your head tested. You got hit hard?" He laughed as he pulled away from the airport.

Chapter Thirty-One

Anticipation fluttered in Cassandra's stomach as they rounded the bend in the road that revealed the cheery, wooden "Welcome to Carson!" sign on the highway. Bright sunshine in a clear blue sky matched her mood. Even though it was January second, she felt the clean slate of a new year in a way she'd never experienced before.

A vase rested on the floor between her feet filled with purple orchids and covered with protective cellophane. Meg and Connor had shown up with the flowers after the emergency room doctor had decided to keep Cassandra overnight for observation. The overzealous medical attention aside, she truly appreciated the appearance of friendly faces after her ordeal. Re-reading the little card where Meg had written, "Love to our brave wahine! You gathered some righteous mana this week," made Cassandra smile again with gratitude for such caring friends.

She did feel more powerful.

Smiling at Marcus Fischer who had met her at the hospital to give her a ride home, she felt older and wiser than when he'd left on vacation little more than a week ago.

His sun-kissed cheeks and nose looked out of place in this winter landscape.

She'd spent most of the car ride from Wahoo telling him everything: from Dr. Nielson's burglary and death, to the tree falling on her house, ending with the kidnapping, and capture of Daniel Leung and his cousin Jason.

Fischer said, "I missed all the holiday fun. Who knew the Mexican beach would be safer than Carson?"

"Next year, I'll skip the chaos," Cassandra chuckled a bit. "I'd prefer a Mexican beach, too."

Andy had brought her cell phone, tote bag, and a change of clothes sent from Cinda to the hospital as soon as the sheriff had brought the men to the Wahoo jail. "Two farmers called in to the police complaining about snowmobilers trespassing on their property before we got the report from Mrs. Miller that you were safe. Tate and the others mobilized quickly since we'd already been out looking for you on the county roads and ditches."

"Thank you," Cassandra had told him. "I hope you get some sleep tonight, too. It sounds like you need rest as much as I do."

Sean Gill had called Cassandra after Andy left and told her that he would turn over the USB thumb drive to the local Homeland Security office in Omaha first thing Monday morning. "Your home repairs are completely finished, and you can move back in immediately," he'd told her. "My mother would still love to have you over for dinner and game night before I leave later this week."

She owed him a batch of thank you cookies for everything he'd done on her house. "You went above and beyond the normal neighbor duties. I appreciate your help."

"Had to keep up my boy-next-door image."

Both her eyebrows had raised, but she was glad he couldn't see. Good thing he didn't live here full time.

Right before she'd fallen asleep, Fischer had arrived home and called her. The only way she'd convinced him to not drive immediately to the hospital was by promising that he could drive her home the next morning.

Again, Cassandra focused on the present as they rolled past the Methodist church, the Gas and Sweets, and Main Street.

Fischer gently squeezed her arm, "We're all glad you're safe."

He signaled to turn onto Cassandra's street, but she stopped him, "I need to pick up my things from Picotte."

Thirty seconds later, Cassandra gasped, "Oh, ... and Murphy!"

Fischer pulled into the staff parking behind the dorm and Cassandra hurried out of his Audi. Together they walked down the empty hallway toward her room. Granted it was mid-morning on a Saturday, but Cassandra thought at least a few students would be conscious. Luckily, she still had her room key to get inside. Fischer gathered the dog food and supplies while Cassandra hoisted the overnight bag on her shoulder.

She wanted to get home and call her parents in the privacy of her own living room, although she still hadn't decided how much to tell them about her weekend.

Feeling guilty for leaving Murphy with the students for several days instead of hours, she wondered where he was. They kept walking toward the common room and sure enough, his kennel sat right in the corner near the stone fireplace. Someone had taped a paper sign to the top. "Murphy goes outside to pee every three hours. He likes pizza and chicken, but not salad. Do not feed him chocolate. If you have to leave him alone, put him in the crate." It was signed with a hand drawn pawprint.

When she turned around, Cassandra noticed Sela Roberts sleeping on the couch with Murphy curled up into a white little ball against her torso.

A lump formed in the back of her throat at the level of responsibility they'd taken on in her absence. She'd met a whole new group of students and loved the chance to form more lasting bonds that only came from spending time together.

In that moment, she resolved to leave her office more often and hang out with students doing non-academic things. It was something Dr. Nielson had advised her to do earlier in the semester and now she acknowledged he'd been right. If the campus was going to become more welcoming and inclusive, it had to start with the relationships built by administrators willing to meet students in their everyday lives.

Cassandra set the bag on the floor and sank onto the soft ottoman in front of the couch. Murphy's head popped up at the disturbance. Slowly, she reached out a hand to let him smell her, ready to pull her fingers out of harm's way if he lunged. He sniffed a couple of times then stood and hopped into Cassandra's lap. When she scratched under his pointed ear, he nuzzled in closer to her hand.

Stunned, she looked up at Fischer to make sure this wasn't a dream.

Sela woke up with a yawn and a stretch, her cropped top revealing a vast expanse of toned stomach. "Dr. Sato!" She sat up. "He cried for you, but we took turns keeping him company."

"Thanks, Sela. I appreciate you all looking after Murphy while I was gone." Cassandra made a mental note to send a bunch of pizzas to the floor later in the week as a thank you gesture.

Fischer brought them home, carrying her stuff into the entryway. Luckily Sean Gill had installed the new keypad touch lock so she could get inside without her keychain and house key.

They arranged a time to pick up her car from the police lot on Monday, then Fischer left so Cassandra could rest.

Appreciating luxuries like heat and electricity she normally took for granted, Cassandra changed into thick socks, pulled on a long sweater, and nestled into the couch with a soft fleece blanket and her laptop.

Seconds later her father's face popped onto the FaceTime screen. "Aloha! Hau'oli Makahiki Hou."

"Happy New Year to you too, Daddy. Did you and mom stay awake until midnight?"

"I admit that your old man fell asleep before 9:00 p.m. but that probably doesn't surprise you. Hold on, I'll get your mom."

Soon her mother's thin face appeared on 2/3 of the screen, close enough that Cassandra could see faint lines around her mother's mouth.

"It's late there, eh. Why you didn't call yesterday? Too much New Year's partying?" Her mom's voice scolded teasingly, but her eagle eyes searched Cassandra's face. Looking away from her mother's scrutiny, she cringed. So much for covering up the truth.

Cassandra's nose wrinkled while she fibbed. "Actually, no partying this year, Mom. I sort of helped the police catch the people responsible for my boss's death."

A lump formed in her throat as reality hit. Her parents would have been devastated if she had been seriously hurt.

"Everything's fine though now," Cassandra whispered.

Her father's mouth made a straight line, and her mother frowned. Her father looked straight into her eyes to her soul. "You'd betta be more careful."

"Sorry you were worried." He knew her too well.

Her mom said, "Good thing we're visiting you over Spring Break. I read an article on the internet about the Nebraska Cornhuskies. What kind of strangers you live around, eh?"

Cassandra closed her eyes and prayed for patience. A few minutes later, she signed off and set her laptop on the side table.

Murphy edged to the couch, nose at seat level, watching her intently. Bushy eyebrows over liquid brown eyes seemed to raise, human-like. He barked once.

"Truce?" she offered.

She still couldn't interpret his moods, but tentatively she patted the empty space by her side.

When Murphy scrambled up onto her lap, it felt like a new beginning for both of them. Hugging him lightly to her chest, his soft fur tickled her chin. He moaned softly, and a fragment slid into place over the hole in her heart. After all these years proving her independence, Cassandra was ready to make space in her life for a sidekick.

Epilogue

Sunday before Spring Semester

During the final minutes of the string quartet's two song performance, Cassandra Sato glanced down at the Opening Convocation program in her lap and smoothed the front of her academic gown. Seated left of the stage, the musicians' skills were impressive, and Cassandra understood why they'd been chosen to travel to China earlier in the semester. Sela Roberts played the violin with graceful movements, her black outfit matching the other members of the ensemble.

Normally colleges did not begin spring semesters with such formal events. However, Mr. Hershey had insisted that Morton needed to turn a new page on the academic yearbook.

And Cassandra could get behind any occasion that allowed her to wear her robe again.

Gathered in the Performing Arts Center were most of the freshman class, faculty, and staff. To the right in the front row, Cassandra saw her neighbor Mrs. Gill, a former long-time Morton employee, and her husband. Cassandra smiled at them warmly, remembering with satisfaction that she'd won the Scrabble game at their house by playing "maximize" on a double word score spot. Beating Sean and the trash talk that had followed reminded Cassandra of her family's holiday nights together.

As Cassandra surveyed the standing room only crowd, she saw Bob Soukup, board members, and even Margie Gallagher, owner of the Home Team Bar in the audience. Only a month ago they'd all gathered for fall commencement, oblivious to the difficult times that lay ahead.

Cinda Weller stood to the side of the stage—part of her usher duties—and finger-waved at Cassandra. They had chatted briefly with Meg in the lobby before the convocation. Cinda had said, "I still can't believe you had the whole snowmobile-ride-to-the-airport-kidnapper-capture adventure without me."

"Cinda!" Meg cried. "She was tied up and held at gunpoint. You have children to think about."

"Next time I'm kidnapped, we'll stop and pick you up, too." Cassandra patted her arm. "I promise."

Cinda had made a kissy lips pucker and Meg rolled her eyes. After they'd gone off to find their seats, Andy Summers had come up to her next.

"I signed Buckley up for a therapy dog class at the Wahoo hospital this spring. Do you want to register Murphy, too? If we're bringing them to campus often, we should train the dogs to interact with students."

Cassandra started to say no but took a moment to check herself. Joining a new group might be good for her to meet people and bond more with Murphy. "Yeah. I'd like that. Send me the link and I'll sign us up."

Andy had moved to the secure area behind the musicians, a beaming smile on his face.

Back on stage, Hershey stood at the antique wooden lectern reading from his script. "Today marks an epiphany and a new beginning. Students, know that you have the full support of the board, administrators, and faculty to help you reach your collegiate goals. As we leave the fall semester behind, we look forward to better days ahead. We also come together today as a community to honor the memory of Gary Nielson. Now I'd like to introduce my esteemed colleague, former Morton College president, philosophy professor emeritus Dr. Mike Bergstrom to say a few words."

From Cassandra's spot on the stage, she smiled at Bergstrom's Einstein-esque hair, trim beard, and round spectacles. He wore the same cardigan sweater with leather elbow patches she'd seen on him several times a week before he'd retired at the end of fall semester.

He cleared his throat. "We are gathered here today to remember Gary Nielson. Friend, mentor, and all-around pain in the neck."

The crowd politely chuckled.

"Oh, don't act like you didn't think so, too." Bergstrom peered over the top of his reading glasses. "There were times when the best thing about Gary was his wife, Becky."

More chuckles. This seemed more like a roast than a memorial service.

Bergstrom removed his glasses, the skin around his blue eyes crinkling, and gestured to Becky Nielson and her family also seated on stage. Her son's hand rested on Becky's shoulder. "But seriously, allow me to express our deepest sympathies from all of the faculty and staff who worked with your husband and father for many, many years."

While the stage party had waited in line to be seated before the program, Cassandra had chatted for a few minutes with Becky Nielson. Becky said she was anxious to return to her sister's place in Iowa and stay there for a few months while the Carson house sold and closed.

Cassandra had asked what her next step was. "Gary always promised me we'd go on one of those European river cruises. But we never got around to it. Maybe I'll take my daughters-in-law or go with my girlfriends."

Bergstrom continued, "Not only did Gary serve the Morton community for more than forty years, he returned to Carson to preserve Morton's reputation and ensure the college's research would continue, even to his own detriment. For that we are all grateful."

Bergstrom tidied his papers. "The great philosopher Fred Rogers wrote, 'In times of stress, the best thing we can do for each other is to listen with our ears and our hearts and to be assured that our questions are just as important as our answers.' In many ways, Gary was similar in temperament to Fred, and I think he'd understand that his passing has left us with unanswered questions. He would advise us to listen with our hearts."

While the audience applauded, Cassandra noticed Becky wiping her eyes with a tissue.

"We invite another former president, Dr. Deborah Winters to come forward and share a memory at this time." Stepping off to the side, Bergstrom waited expectantly.

Rising from the back row on stage, Dr. Winters, tall and thin with light gray hair wearing stylish low heels, strode forward. Mr. Hershey met her at the end of the aisle and took her elbow to assist her to the lectern. She shook him off with a feisty grin and adjusted the microphone. "I didn't think they'd ever let me speak at one of these shindigs again." She laughed, and the audience joined her. She pointed toward the left side of the crowd at Bob Soukup. "They let you in here still, huh Bob." She chuckled. "Declining standards in higher education..."

Mr. Hershey's face slowly turned a shade of purple and he seemed unsure whether to hop up and stop her before she said anything inconvenient, or to let her go out of respect for her previous service.

"I have a confession."

Hershey sprang up and stood behind Winters, ready to sweep her away from the podium if she went off on one of her unpredictable early Alzheimer moments.

Cassandra frowned. Inviting Winters to attend was gracious. Allowing her to speak in front of a large audience was an especially bad idea.

"Gary took our secret to his grave. For that I'm grateful, but it's time to tell the truth." She winked at Dr. Bergstrom. "It was Alec Kovar, me, and this clown," she hooked a thumb to her left at Bergstrom, "who took my housemother—the old bat—Mrs. Williams' VW Bug apart and put it back together on the library's roof. Nielson was our professor at the time and overheard us gloating about it during his biology class. We could have been expelled, but Gary never tattled. He was a good man." She sniffed loudly and returned to her seat leaving Hershey awkwardly staring after her.

The audience looked at each other, bewildered. Bergstrom rested his hands on his large belly, tilted his head back and laughed heartily. The ice broken, everyone else shared in the laughter.

Hershey collected himself and returned to the podium. "Thank you, Dr. Winters. Now it's time for an important announcement. As you know, Morton College has begun a national search for a new president. The board of directors has decided to name Dr. Robert Gregory as the Interim President until such time as a permanent successor can begin in the fall."

A smattering of applause came from the floor.

Cassandra met Cinda's wide eyed stare. Bob Gregory, the Business Office Director, as the Interim President? The millennial-hater who thinks two-ply toilet paper in the rest rooms is a luxury expense. That geezer would be her new boss.

Cinda mouthed, okay Boomer.

Cassandra had to agree. It would be a long semester with the penny-pinching president at the helm. Luckily it was only for one semester. How much damage could he do?

While you're waiting on the next story, if you would be so kind as to leave a review on Goodreads, Amazon, or BookBub.

Reviews are like chocolate frosting on a Rice Krispie treat. They might not be necessary, but they sure make a good day even better!

Get extra scenes, book reviews, and more by joining Kelly's mailing list at

https://mailchi.mp/78c3aaa46ef3/kellybrakenhoffnews

Acknowledgments

Dear Reader,

Writing a book during a pandemic is hard. Let's face it, doing anything during a pandemic is hard whether you're working from home, in person, homeschooling, isolating, medical front lines, sick or well. Introverting was so hard. What carried me through the dark days was escaping with my fictional friends into fictional Carson, Nebraska. I realized after 5 months "working from home" that stories really do matter, both for me as a writer and you as a reader. Thanks for walking with me during this one.

Special thanks to my topic experts for sharing their time and expertise. Craig Franzen for making soybeans understandable to a city girl. Emira Ibrahimpasic, global studies professor, who opened my eyes to the root causes of issues that even affect residents in small Midwestern towns. Matt Herrman for his piloting and airport experiences. Sue Nelson for her endless supply of Southern phrases. Lori Ideta for your stories, photos, and cheery bitmojis.

Thanks to Michelle Argyle for her beautiful cover design. Sione Aeschliman, your editing voice still echoes in my head during revisions. I'm so grateful for the path we carved together for this series. Thank you, Steve Parolini for your editing wizardry, and for making me chuckle in every chapter. Thanks to Mickey Mikkelson for publicity help.

Special shout outs to Chris Timm, Jean Hinton, Pete Seiler, Sherri Brakenhoff, and Dad for your proofreading superpowers and reminding me when I was lost in the weeds. Those pesky typos don't stand a chance against you.

My Mom, Jean Decker, is my first reader, late night brainstormer, cheerleader, and relentless book flogger who doesn't work on commission, but accepts payment in hugs, dinners, and wine. I'm blessed to have you along for the ride.

Thank you PPH friends, Sisters in Crime Guppies, Elizabeth Cooper, and so many others online or in person who have lent support or a brainstorm along the way. I'm sorry if I missed adding your name. RIP Sadie our 15-year-old cockapoo who I still miss every day.

I love you Dave, Joe, Claire, Jon, Kate, Colton, James, Oliver, and Ellie. Lyla, we can't wait to meet you soon!

About the Author

Kelly Brakenhoff is an American Sign Language Interpreter whose motivation for learning ASL began in high school when she wanted to converse with her deaf friends. Her first novel, Death by Dissertation, kicked off the Cassandra Sato Mystery Series. She also wrote *Never Mind*, first in a children's picture book series featuring Duke the Deaf Dog. She serves on the Board of Editors for the Registry of Interpreters for the Deaf publication, *VIEWs*. The mother of four young adults and two dogs, Kelly and her husband call Nebraska home.

Made in the USA
Monee, IL
04 March 2022